Deceptio

Part Two of the Ayto

A Novel

By

James Lynch

2022

This book is a work of fiction. Any similarity to persons living or dead or to organisations or places existing or previous, is purely coincidental.

ISBN 978-1-3999-3157-1

Table of Contents

Prologue: Recall to Ayton

Andrea Goral's father, Ondrej Goral, had been born into abject poverty on a small litter-strewn and insanitary campsite not far from the town of Prerov in the Czech Republic. His mother, who died in childbirth, and her relatives were members of a discriminated and despised minority community, the Czech Cikán or Rom community. They had been subject to genocide during the Second World War, because of which, roughly half the population had perished.

Ondrej had always felt the discrimination made him out-of-place in his birth home, and in the early days after the Czech Republic joined the European Union, his opportunity came to choose a new life. He finally decided that the time and opportunity had come to leave his homeland once and for all and seek a brighter future elsewhere. As a first step in that departure, he had moved to Prague, where he had found employment in the tourist industry with an organisation owned by another member of the Czech Roma community.

It was in Prague, while conducting his newfound profession of tourist guide, that he had first met his future partner, Isabel. She and her close relatives were in the café near the statue of Sir Nicholas Winton in the ornate Habsburg-era central railway station in Prague. Symbolically for Ondrej as it turned out, Winton a British diplomat, had rescued many discriminated Jewish children from the country on the eve of the Second World War. Isabel and her kinfolk were from a town called Ayton in the Midlands of the United Kingdom, and they were visiting Prague as part of a tourist holiday.

It so happened that Ondrej often took a coffee in that place as there were so many potential client tourists for him there. He habitually approached tourists inquiring if they would like a guide in the city. In this case, responsive to his offer of tourist services, he was invited by the group to an informal chat in the café and a free coffee! From their conversation he learned that Isabel's mother was the politically high profile Mrs Emily Burnley Crowder OBE, a very active local councillor and long-term resident of the ancient town and chairman of the refugee reception committee of the local city Council.

Isabel's dapper father, Jack, owned a very successful financial advice business in the town centre and he was politically active as a local councillor but from a different party to her mother. Ondrej's future partner, Isabel, was ending her final year at school at the time and the only other sibling was her brother, Doug. He had served as an officer in the Balkans during Operation Resolute and on return had been killed in the London 7/7 bombings in 2005.

Ondrej had been profoundly impressed by the group's description of their lives in their age-old hometown of Ayton-on-the-Wold. He was thoroughly enchanted by their lively conversation and openness, which he had never encountered before in his rather restricted life. He was especially delighted by the conversational skill and knowledge of the young daughter of the family, Isabel, who was addressed as Izzy by her folks.

As a direct consequence of that meeting, and encouraged by a smiling business card invitation from the father of the family, Jack, Ondrej had decided there and then, to move from Prague to the UK. He would settle in the small, historic town in the English Midlands called Ayton-on-the-Wold. It would be there that he would make the town his home. His future life would be there and on arrival he would seek employment there and meet a future life-partner like Isabel. That was the new and most ardent aspiration of his life.

It was soon after he arrived in the town of Ayton-on the-Wold that he had once again met the daughter of the people he had met in Prague, Isabel Burnley Crowder. She was a precocious young woman, on the point of completing her final year at school and with an open offer already to attend Imperial College in London for a degree in engineering the following autumn. Well known and liked by students and staff at her college, she was a talented athlete as well as an academic success story. She played the clarinet in the school orchestra too. She had been elected head girl for the final year at a time when many of her contemporaries were cutting or starving themselves or becoming hooked on drugs. She was affectionately known as Izzy by her friends at school and her kinfolk at home.

It was through the work of her mother, Emily, and her mother's efforts, as a local councillor, for the town's reception strategy for new migrants to Ayton, that he had fortuitously met Izzy again. By this time, Ondrej had changed his first name to Andy in order to help him with his search for employment in the town. Sadly, as part of that search for employment he had, by chance, become involved with what turned out to be, not a tourist information agency as he had thought, but the powerful and violent local Albanian mafia crime syndicate. It was peddling drugs and prostitution in the town and had begun trading in and using weapons. Only after accepting their initial friendly offers of employment and later 'donations' of drugs and becoming indebted to the mobsters did he realise the gravity of his mistake.

His relationship with Izzy blossomed and as he was her first serious boyfriend. After only a short while during the summer holidays after she had left school, Ondrej and Izzy had fallen in love and had subsequently planned to get married and set up home together. Their plan was to stay with her mother and grandparents at first before finding and being able to afford a place of their own. In advance of their intended marriage, however, Ondrej had become a debtor to the local Mafia crime syndicate, whom he could not repay and he was murdered by one of local criminal mobsters in a dispute about his debts. By that time he and Izzy had been seeing each other every day and sometimes at night-time in the flat of a school friend, when both the girl's parents were absent. Izzy became pregnant. With the untimely death of Ondrej, the issue with her mother and father was whether she should keep the baby or have an abortion.

Against pressure from both her father and her mother, she was adamant that she wanted to keep the child. Additionally, she still wanted to pursue her now one-year deferred studies at Imperial College with the help and support of her relatives, for which she appealed and which was willingly accorded. Thus, Izzy's daughter was born when her mother was just eighteen years of age. In the absence of a father, she was brought up on her own but very ably supported and assisted by her mother and grandparents for almost two decades. In spite of the preceding contretemps about an abortion, they were now proud at the arrival so soon of their first granddaughter, whom they adored and named Andrea in fond affection for her deceased father, Ondrej.

Over the years, Andrea had followed in the footsteps of her mother, Isabel, who in the meantime had qualified as an engineer and taken up a junior position with a local building construction firm. By dint of her mother's studies and later career aspirations and the business commitments of her grandparents, Andrea had had a fairly free and easy upbringing. She was loved, cared for and supported in every way by her family but neither over-indulged nor too closely supervised nor indeed subject to over-expectancy of achievement. She was encouraged to make her own decisions, subject to a gentle interactive requirement for accountability.

Her light-touch upbringing had contributed to her personality as a determined and independent-minded young woman. She was not swayed by peer-group or social media pressures, but rather made her own mind up about her decisions and how she lived. She was now on the threshold of her second sixth-form year and like her mother she had been elected head girl. With the strong but sensitive support of her nearest and dearest, she was bidding fair like her mother to take up her offer of a place to study engineering at Imperial College in London after the summer break.

Meanwhile the criminal mafia syndicate in Ayton that had led to the downfall of her father, Ondrej Goral, had fundamentally changed in its personnel and business model. It was no longer a group of petty criminals based on a particular region in Albania, and led by a godfather-like local character. The newly organised criminal syndicate had become an international business corporation. The new model had thrived rapidly, becoming richer and more powerful, as more and more middle class residents and youngsters turned to drugs. The immediate past leadership of the Ayton business had been a disaster. They had been replaced by the Tirana executives of the criminal syndicate for inadequate performance. A new younger and more diverse and pushy generation was taking over and the older Tirana grandees were gradually being ousted.

After the crime syndicate had refocused its business model and internationalised its business approach, helped in part by the population displacement of the wars in the Balkans and the Kosovo war above all, it had grown in power, influence, expanse and profits. But it had at the same time retained traditional values reinforced by a vow of silence and fidelity to one's own agreements and those of fellow workers in the clan. The new more business-like approach had resulted in the snowballing of economic resources, ruthlessness in business and negotiation, corrupt recruitment of local collaborators in social, political, administrative and law-enforcement, and where and when and if necessary, extreme violence to achieve their desired goals.

Through bribery and venality with a large allocation of business acumen, the local criminal syndicate in Ayton had commenced a well-funded campaign to recruit more collaborators in the key sectors, including the local community organisations. This led to the recruitment of dozens of traffickers for trade across county lines. Under the direction of two new lieutenants, chosen by the bosses in Tirana, Albania on the recommendation of the boss of bosses in Barking, East London, Tristen Rexhepi, a brand new team, led by Samir Pecic and the much younger Xhoel Gegaj, were seen as turning a new page in the economic business in Ayton. They were sent and went into the Ayton fiefdom for one major purpose, namely to make ever upward growing profits for the organisation.

New ways of working were also evolved as part of a more co-operative approach with other similar organisations, which together took over the national market for cocaine. They were adopting an altogether different model of business from their godfather-led predecessor organisations, more like a big business corporation in structure, organisation and approach. These new co-operative groups had gradually taken over the market for cocaine in the region and the organisation of prostitution in the town, sometimes against the fierce opposition of other ethnically based criminal gangs from Turkey, Italy, Kurdistan and Nigeria and more local intended incursions by criminal gangs from some of the major cities such as Liverpool, London and Manchester. On other occasions they had cast aside their rivalry with rivals in exchange for increased profit, achieved by working co-operatively with their former enemies and rivals in a strongly networked alliance with financial advantage to all members.

At the insistence of the Tirana bosses, there was now a much closer and regular evaluation and monitoring mounted by the Barking, East London boss, Tristen Rexhepi, at the behest of the Tirana overlords on the development and progress of the Ayton business with a wise eye to the bottom line. A steady and healthy growth of the balance sheets and increases in remittances to Tirana was a *sine qua non* for the new managers.

With similar arrangements in other parts of the UK, the Albanian mafia was in a favourable position to impose its new strategy of business on its subordinate peripheral organisations. Included in that approach was the expansion of the so-called county lines operation of networks and corridors for the export of drugs beyond one jurisdiction to others. Thus they progressed from larger to smaller towns and thence into rural, coastal and other inland provinces and the surrounding countryside. By the early 2020s the value of this trade was estimated at approximately thirty billion pounds a year and it was growing very fast.

Gradually Samir and Xhoel had increased the county lining of the cocaine and other drugs allocated to them by London and sometimes sent directly from one of the ports, airports, stations and other goods transit centres. The office in Ayton had unsuccessfully tried to follow the national policy on county lining by extending sales to the whole geographical area and incipiently further afield. At first, sometimes against the fierce opposition of other illicit, local indigent gangs from London, Manchester and Liverpool.

More recently the Ayton managers had begun to realise the dividends of working more cooperatively with those with some of the other criminal drug enterprises. But the increase in sales had been too sluggish to satisfy their masters. A large stock of drugs had consequently built up over the months in the gang's headquarters building and in several of the gang's other properties in Ayton awaiting further recruitment of young county liners. At the request of the boss in London, that recruitment was currently supposed to be the major priority for them.

The pattern for the transfer of the profits of this trade to other centres in London, Tirana and elsewhere abroad had been altered massively. Many vicarious channels had always been used to export their earnings, including back to the clan in Tirana. The many channels included illicit bank accounts, insurance companies, the money transfer services of such organisations as Eastern Union, MoneyGrammatic, car washes, etc. The use of valuable objects such as precious stones and even vintage postage stamps is on the rise used to channel their ever-larger ill-gotten gains back to the gang bosses on the continent and thence to Tirana or in some cases as payment to Chinese middlemen for the facilitation of drug purchases and transportation from South America. In the honeypot of Ayton-on-the-Wold, the Albanian mafia market their goods, especially amongst the young middle classes and the young, who were often hooked on drugs prior to their enticement into county lines engagements as couriers.

In addition to the alleged financial under-performance of the business, it presently faced new challenges as part of the new business model of the whole corporate structure. This involved the periodic scrutiny of their books by officials from the Barking headquarters of the criminal enterprise in the UK and the prospective sudden and unexpected arrival of the Chief Executive in the UK as part of unannounced visitations. Unhappily for them, his arrival coincided with the first steps by a new Chief Constable in Ayton to destroy the local business of the clan, based on drugs, prostitution and human trafficking, and to clean up the town once and for all.

In the almost two decades since the murder of Ondrej Goral by a mafia gang mobster, the complexion and civic values of the City of Ayton-on-the-Wold had undergone a radical change. There were many more people of colour, more members of minority groups and more citizens of different credal backgrounds. This new cultural pluralism was manifest not just in those residing in the town but those employed in the town in every retail, business and state sector of employment as well, some of whom were holding senior positions in the community. It was no longer unusual to see people of different cultural backgrounds wearing different clothes on the street or in community recreational gatherings and schools and in businesses.

When the Ukraine war broke out, the local council rapidly set up a co-ordination unit to organise the reception of refugees into the community. It assisted and supported them in their settlement to find accommodation and in some cases employment for them. A local appeal was made across the town for accommodation and homes for both families and single persons. The response was almost overwhelming and dozens of offers of clothing, food and accommodation were received, including some offers of houses for families. Special language tuition sessions were arranged so that children of refugees could begin to function in a new language and cultural environment. Some of the offers were received from now longstanding minority communities, whose parents had themselves been refugee in the town at the end of the Second World War. The Polish community, for example, offered their church hall for the initial reception of the Ukrainian refugees and emergency feeding for newly arriving families with children and babies and for single persons.

In the centre of the town, there was now full-time staffing of a renovated and larger police station. The station was even staffed at night-time and during the day the station's staffing complement had been substantially reinforced at a time of national cutbacks. A new reforming Chief Constable, by the name of Horace Lashley, who was of West Indian background, had been appointed from a senior position in the London Met. He therefore already had a successful career tackling the younger generation mafia criminals in Barking East London. He had a reputation as a no-nonsense police officer and a vigorous campaigner against crime in his domain. For the first time a woman had been appointed as Deputy Chief Constable. Heather Compton-Jones came from the Met, where she had established herself as a successful officer. She was appointed to lead a new special unit set up by the newly arrived Chief Constable to tackle budding criminality in the wider conurbation and the emergent ever greater power of the criminal syndicates in the community. In addition, she was given the task of developing the capacity and efficacy of the newly established drugs and prostitution unit in the force. Rajiv Gundara was appointed as an Assistant Chief constable after several years serving in the force already with a direct commission to clean up the mafia drug and prostitution rackets in the town.

The city's movement to greater pluralism included the health and social care sector too. Indeed these were sectors, which were increasingly staffed at least in part by ethnic minority members as were some of the new retail businesses in general stores and greengrocers in the area and in the local cottage hospital and health centres. In the cottage hospital the most senior nurse was Liliana Oliveira, a woman of Portuguese heritage. The most senior physician was Hamid Khan, a second-generation man from Punjabi Pakistani kinfolk, who had been trained at the Nottingham Medical School. Even the previously very selective Ayton Ladies Association had members from minorities in the city as full and active participants and in some cases occupying senior positions on the committee.

So Ayton in 2022 was much more comfortable with pluralism than it had been two decades previously when the first batch of migrants had arrived. It had changed and was continuing to do so, but it still faced major challenges. Some of these challenges emanated from the increased presence of criminal syndicates in the city and especially the Albanian mafia criminal gang. Some of the members of this criminal fraternity were recruited from the small otherwise law-abiding Albanian-speaking satellite communities in the UK, similar to those set up after the Kosovo war in other European countries. Increasingly, however, the syndicate's growing demands for additional 'soldiers' and workers was being satisfied by the recruitment of men from hostels established to accommodate asylum seekers, including one such hostel in Ayton, of whom some twenty five percent approximately were Albanian. Indeed some poverty-stricken communities in Albania are being denuded of their populations and attracted by the mafia gangs to the UK and in many cases an uncertain future.

Of course there were other criminal transnational gangs active in the town. This often led to violent and sometimes lethal competition and conflict at first with knives and more recently and frequently with guns. This diversity of criminality had accentuated the endemic spread of drugs in the middle class community and especially amongst the youth of the city.

The drugs problem and the increasing spread of prostitution provision in brothels in different parts of the city were two of the major challenges, which the newly reinforced police force in the city and its new Chief Constable faced. A third challenge, which the police faced, was that since the arrival of two new 'chief executives' for the local 'business', Samir Pecic and Xhoel Gegaj, the town was becoming a major hub for the county lining of cannabis, powdered cocaine, crack and heroin.

This growth in drug dependency had a severely detrimental impact on the community's young people in the city and in the surrounding more rural areas and the growth of substance use across generations and consequent drug addiction. The aim of all the criminal gangs was to escalate the involvement of children, some as young as ten, to assist in the county lining of the drugs. For this recruitment the primary schools and colleges were in the gang's sights. Some children taken into care in the city, miles away from their homes, relations, and friends were residing now in privatised care accommodation and they were especially vulnerable targets for the recruitment by the criminal gangs.

For the new Chief Constable, Horace Lashley and his team in Ayton, the task was not only to frustrate the aims of the dominant drug barons and their cartels but also to bring them down one by one. The aim was to prevent them continuing to criminalise a whole generation of the city's youngsters. How to convert those worthy intentions into concrete plans against opponents with little or no resource constraints such as those faced by the police was the major task.

This is the story of that conflict between the forces of law and order and the criminal syndicates, which were corrupting a whole generation of the city's s population and the main personalities involved in that struggle.

Chapter One: The Plan

Samir Pecic and the much younger and still handsome Xhoel Gegaj had arrived in the UK from Albania some twenty years previously. They had initially identified themselves as Kosovar refugees in order to achieve preferential immigration consideration. As Xhoel's widowed and impoverished mother had implored Samir to take her sole son with him to give him a better opportunity in life, they posed as father and son. Xhoel was a mere lad at the time of their entry in a small boat across the Channel to the UK. They had both worked for the mob for a short while before being sent by the mafia bosses in Tirana, Albania, to Barking to toughen the mob's expansion of its income-producing network in the UK.

It was no coincidence that an older man and a youngster had been sent, to take account of the intergenerational tension beginning to arise in the Clan's Barking, East London enterprise. At that time it was increasingly acute in the large estate in the East End of London where the younger members of the criminal gang were based. They comported themselves in a totally different more bombastic and public way from the older generation.

On arrival both Samir and to a lesser extent Xhoel had been employed in the capital for some time, during which they both melded well into the organisation and its culture, learning the ropes through experience so to speak. As Xhoel grew up he had successfully learned the drug and prostitution trades quickly and well in the company of his mentor, Samir. On the basis of that experience, with Xhoel having grown up in the organisation into a handsome young man in his very early twenties, they had just been redeployed by the supreme British boss of bosses in London, Tristen Rexhepi, to the Midlands, to a small, quiet town called Ayton-on-the-Wold.

They arrived in Ayton after a disastrous financial period for the gang in the UK, during which the office in Ayton, a predicted rich picking ground for drugs, prostitution and weapons, had more or less collapsed. At the same time, in a co-ordinated national police campaign over a thousand of the mafia's mobsters nationwide had been detained for questioning and most of them had been swiftly and successfully charged and jailed for lengthy periods.

As a consequence of those events, the Clan had lost millions of pounds in cash, stock of workers, drugs, especially cannabis, powder cocaine, crack and opiates, guns and precious objects such as gems and vintage collectable postage stamps. Worst of all, the gang had lost face *vis-à-vis* the other criminal groups involved in the same trades, such as the Turks, Italians and Kurds. These criminal gangs were now increasingly bold and successful in poaching the trade of their former partner in trade, which was now seen, as seriously weakened and exposed. This irked the bosses in the UK and on the Continent, especially at a time when the market was on an exponential rise, with at least three million people using drugs in the UK and a quarter of a million addicted to opiates and crack. The syndicate bosses were determined to bounce back and retaliate swiftly and commercially by cutting their prices and, if that was not successful, through naked violence against their competitors.

Like their predecessors both Samir Pecic and Xhoel Gegaj originated from Albania. They hailed from one of the small villages similar to Thethe in the Dukagjin highlands, a mountainous region in the north of the country, east of the town of Shkodra and north of the river Drin. The region was an area where the anciently derived values of 'family' and tribe were traditionally the sole determinants of attitudes, social and moral standards and loyalty to the 'Clan' and its leaders and members. These tenets were the guarantors of the impermeability of the Clan and its business enterprises and it was their successful record nationally, based on these austere and constant principles that the man and now grown-up boy had brought with them to Ayton.

Samir and Xhoel had a good record for working together in the higher interests of the criminal enterprise after their arrival in the UK as asylum seekers from Kosovo. They had worked together in Barking in East London as part of the mafia control group for the whole of the UK, before being transferred a short time ago to Ayton to take over the business previously so unsuccessfully run by two previous Albanian crime syndicate mobsters, Albin Haxhiu and Bakri Rexhaji. The former, Albin, was now in prison serving a very long sentence for murder, drug pushing and people trafficking for prostitution. If he ever got out, he would surely be a target for the mob as he had tried to abscond with the mob's money and the mob had lost thousands of pounds and quite a bit of stock through what the bosses considered to be his appalling misjudgements and betrayal.

The latter, Bakri, had narrowly survived a murder attempt by his colleague in the market square in Ayton. He recovered after many weeks in a local hospital. Spared a more drastic fate by his close relationship with one of the Clan bosses in Tirana, Albania, he had been recalled to Albania for a more mundane livelihood as caretaker of a group of the mob's houses in the more rural Dukagjin highlands.

Immediately after their arrival in Ayton, Samir and Xhoel had quickly assembled a team of staff, recruited largely from the small satellite Albanian community in the UK or of late enticed from among the one in four asylum seekers, who were of Albanian extraction, and entered the UK illegally via the Channel route at that time. A later estimate put the proportion somewhat higher at six of ten in one year over a short period. These latter were poached from the asylum seeker hotels, one of which is situated in Ayton, by so-called shepherds, already engaged mafia soldiers, predominantly to man the indoor cannabis farms. Some of the more experienced new recruits, however, worked for the two men as enforcers and guards for their various premises and prostitution houses in the city. The two men considered that they had been relatively successful, taking into account the mess that the previous management team had left behind. But that was not how the boss of bosses in Barking, East London saw it and his financial guru, even less, as the two men would soon discover to their cost.

On this occasion, they were seated comfortably in what was termed the snug of one of those buildings used as one of their brothels in Ayton. They were informally discussing the next steps in expanding their successful business for the Clan. Samir, the more senior partner spoke first and he put forward his proposals tentatively intending them for discussion.

"To my mind there are two major objectives that still need to be addressed in order to help us meet the bosses' target of doubling the income of this patch in the next year. One is to establish some further women's houses, which are a constant and developing source of readily launderable cash. The other, it seems to me, is to improve our system and capacity for recruiting more runners to carry the cocaine and other drugs that we get from Barking out into the wider Midlands region. It's clear to me that we need to establish a better system for recruiting couriers outside of the immediate area. We have already recruited some runners in the local college and we need several more to cope with the ever increasing load of drugs being sent to us by the bosses in London as well as the dramatically expanding market for our very competitively priced products."

There was normally no conflict between them at this stage and his close colleague, the much younger Xhoel Gegaj, responded positively. He expressed his agreement and pointed out that they had to expedite these measures as the boss of bosses, actually the lieutenant of the mafia bosses in Europe, was due to pay them a visit in the near future.

"I agree and we must not forget that the big boss from London, Tristen Rexhepi, will be descending on us within the next couple of weeks, demanding an account of the actions we have undertaken so far and requesting to see an expanding return on the balance sheet. Going by past performance, he or one of his colleagues, will want to give the books a detailed examination and we shall face a mountain of queries. Are our books in a good condition, Xhoel? That is your responsibility."

Xhoel reacted positively to the inquiry about the books and then posed a question with a note of anxiety in his voice.

"What do you think he will be looking for in particular, Samir?"

In replying Samir made several suggestions.

"Well I'm pretty sure he will want to see a substantial growth in cocaine and crack sales and cash from prostitution, even perhaps the opening of a further brothel here in Ayton. Above all, he will want to see a hefty upturn in overall income and remittances to Tirana and via a variety of channels to other overseas destinations."

He paused to ponder it further.

"He might likewise want an account of any gun dealings and the source, price and destination of the weapons. I suppose he will have additional more general inquiries such as whether we have had any trouble with the other syndicates in the area and if so which ones. Additionally, of course, where are we getting our soldiers from to defend our patch and our dominance of the market and how much we are paying them?"

Xhoel agreed with the proposed establishment of one more house of prostitution, which would increase their earning by at least fifty per cent, but it would in addition require recruitment and training of further soldiers, most probably from the local asylum seeker hotel. But he followed with a suggestion, which failed to take into account one of the main tenets of the innovatory and successful Mafia new business model: low but sustainable prices and good quality, delivered on time.

But Samir was more cautious and was not convinced.

"A third house at this time might prove a house too far, with the intensification of police surveillance in the town and the establishment of a special unit within the local force covering drugs and prostitution. It might potentially damage our other pot of business in trading powder cocaine, crack and a much smaller market in heroin. They say that the new Chief Constable of Ayton is committed to breaking our hold on both those areas."

Xhoel added an amended suggestion to Samir's list.

"Would it then not be better to stay with what we have and make it more profitable, possibly in some cases by raising the price slightly?"

Samir responded clearly showing his greater experience of newer mafia business practice than the younger Xhoel. “It’s a possibility, but we would have to discuss any such measure with the boss when he comes up from London, as it is the Clan’s normal business policy to reduce prices or at least keep them low, in order to cripple any alternative sellers. Besides, we have other serious problems as well. We have lost out ‘ears’ in the local police. Harry Hamble, one of the assistant Chief Constables, has been arrested and put on a number of charges related to his friendly information gathering for us. That means that for the moment, until we find someone else, we are working blind. The boss will surely want the gen about that.”

“Yes, that’s right. I think it was at the behest of the new Chief Constable and his fanatical anti-corruption stance that Harry’s activities were uncovered. And of course, due as well to Harry’s careless and imprudent management of the money, which he has been taking from us.” Xhoel added his stricture.

“Yes, you’re right. But whatever the reason, it blindsides us for the moment.” Samir added.

“Yes, but we still have Jack Burnley Crowder, who supplies us with info in return for drugs and money. He’s very useful isn’t he? And furthermore he’s an influential and knowledgeable participant in the towns' business activities, a member of the local golf club and a member too, of the same private club in the town as some of the other senior officers of the local police force. He might be able to help us to recruit a suitable replacement police officer." Xhoel suggested.

"Maybe." Was Samir's unconvinced and non-committal reply. "But that reminds me that one of our sources has reported that Jack's grand-daughter, Andrea, was appointed at the beginning of this school year as head student in the college. There may be a pathway there to recruit more kids, as couriers for county lining and they are relatively easy to enlist … and fairly cheap too."

"So shall we arrange an early meeting with Jack Burnley Crowder and see what he says and in any case how do we tackle that meeting?"

"We have to think whether to invite Jack to bring his grand-daughter to meet us. But that might just frighten him and her too. Or it could be that we should be thinking of offering him a little bit more of a fee. Or should we be considering whether we have any pressure we can exert on Jack to introduce us to his granddaughter? Get in like that perhaps? What are the weak spots of the two of them? One option we have would be to threaten to expose Jack's relationship with us perhaps. But that may not be in our own best interest. In any case, we need to think of a fairly early approach to precede the visit of the London boss. On further deliberation, I am convinced that the issue of a collaborator in the local police will be one of the first issues that he will raise with us, when he arrives."

Samir speculated more thinking aloud than as a firm proposal.

At this juncture in their discussion, the telephone in the bar of the snug rang. Xhoel immediately went across the room to answer it. On picking up the telephone, his only words, were, "OK, I understand."

"Samir, it's someone from Albania, called Dritan Prenga. He insists that he only wants to speak to you."

He handed the phone to Samir.

The conversation was quite brief and responsive on Samir's part.

"Yes, I understand perfectly. We shall expect them next week."

With that brief reaction, the conversation ended.

"What was that all about?" Xhoel demanded inquisitively.

"It was a message from the bosses in Tirana that they are not satisfied with the progress of the Ayton account and they are sending the London boss, Tristen Rexhepi, and one of his finance colleagues, he didn't give his name, to have a closer look at the books. They want to understand what headway is being made, and ominously, how the London delegation might help with any improvements. They'll be here next week."

"Wow!" Exclaimed Xhoel in utter astonishment. "Then we shall need to get a move on and start the preparations immediately."

"Yes, you're right and as a first step, I'm going to ring Jack Burnley Crowder to call for some action. It's about time that he started to fully earn the money we are giving him each month. What are the main things, do you think, that we need from him?"

"Well, I think we should call him in soonest for a discussion of how he can help us increase the county lines distribution network by recruiting more youngsters. Furthermore we need to know if there are any serving police officers in his club, who for one reason or another may be subject to helping us in return for a modest financial assistance. Ring him now. He should still be at the office." Xhoel suggested helpfully and concerned.

Samir picked up the phone and called Jack Burnley Crowder at his office in the centre of town and got straight through.

"Hello, Jack. It's Sam here. Hope I'm not interrupting anything important. We have just had notification of one of the regular supervision and inspection visits that we have from the London set from time to time."

There was a short pause probably for a question from Jack and then Samir responded.

"Next week. You know. We've had them before and I believe that you may have been involved as an interviewee during a previous one. We would like to meet with you urgently."

The reply was inaudible to Xhoel.

"Yes, well, Xhoel and I thought that you might be able to help us prepare for the visit next week, as they tell us that there will be a finance whiz as part of the visiting team. In view of the urgency could we meet at the weekend, Saturday or Sunday are fine for us. But really. Whatever is convenient for you Jack?"

Again Jack's reply on the telephone did not enter the room. But its positive content became immediately clear as Samir replied.

"OK, then Jack. We look forward to seeing you after your golf at 14.00 hours on Sunday afternoon. Kind of you to fit us in at such short notice. At your office then on Sunday. Bye!"

"Well. That's the set up for Sunday afternoon. We need to have a firm agenda for what we are looking for from him and carefully weigh how he reacts to our requests. You know what a slippery customer he is." Samir explained deprecatingly.

"You did well to manage to get him so early. He is mad on golf and weather permitting, he always plays two or three rounds across the weekend. I do believe he does some of his business on the courses as well." Xhoel noted.

"Yes, we shall just have to see if his golf puts him in a receptive frame of mind towards our demands." Samir responded humorously.

"It would be good if we could get a couple of names of local business men, from him who might be susceptible to a small financial encouragement. Men in the Law or finance or better still some policemen or even judges is what we want from him. People who might be susceptible to a further earning opportunity or are in straitened financial circumstances. And we also need to get some word from him about his granddaughter and county lines couriers. She could be very useful in obtaining more youngsters for our county lines work."

"Yes, if she will cooperate! We shall have to raise it with Jack at our meeting on Sunday afternoon."

Chapter Two: The Response

The room was packed. The Chief Constable, Horace Lashley, led the large police representation at the meeting attended by the head of the freshly established drugs and prostitution wing. Deputy Chief Constable Heather Compton-Jones accompanied by her assistant, Superintendent Rajiv Gundara, Detective Inspector Maria Clarke, in charge of the major investigation into a lucrative drug and prostitution set-up in Ayton and Assistant Chief Constable Mark Brownlow from the National Crime Squad together with approximately twenty officers including some who worked on a beat. Additionally there were several representatives from the local authority, including Senior Officer June Browning, as well as local authority officers responsible for children's and women's affairs and equality. Similarly, John Casey from the National Financial Fraud Squad had been invited as an observer.

The Chief Constable chaired and opened the fairly large meeting with all due seriousness.

"To open this meeting, may I express a very warm word of thanks and appreciation to all of you attending this gathering. Your attendance is expressive of the widespread concern about the criminalisation of this town and the corruption of a large part of the youth of this city, as well as the need for urgent action to tackle and erase this scourge on our society. Above all, the gathering is an initial reaction from many quarters about the veritable tsunami of cannabis, powder cocaine, crack, heroin and some other opiates, which is increasingly engulfing this community of ours and seriously blighting the lives of many of our young people. Sadly this growth is encouraged by an apparently ever growing public demand and enabled by the criminal gangs, who inhabit our fair city. I must emphasise that your police force shares your concern about this public menace and is planning to deal with it immediately as a matter of top priority."

The Chief Officer stopped and met the approving gazes of his audience for his statement of intent. Satisfied with the mute but obviously supportive reaction, he proceeded with his delivery.

"Firstly I should like to add that the problem is exacerbated by the arrival of stronger strains such as crack, which are beginning to arrive, together with different opiates. Both of these drugs can cause psychosis, even death to all users but especially in our young people. Consumption of cheaply available cannabis is fed more and more by the proliferation of indoor cannabis farms, staffed by the recent arrival via the cross-channel route of a stream of young male migrants from Albania, who are often lured into a life little better than slavery. Secondly just to set the context, this mornings' meeting is one small part of an overall national strategy to address these issues. The overall aim is to substantially reduce the level of serious and organised drug and prostitution crime affecting the UK. At the same time, we have to take cognisance of newer developments leading to criminal drug cartels working in unison on the production, distribution and sale of drugs. This has substantially reduced the price of drugs on the market and in turn that has markedly increased the number of consumers."

The Chief Constable halted for a short while to consult his papers. As he was about to continue with his prepared script, Senior Officer June Browning from the local authority social services, interrupted him.

"Chief Constable, I am sorry to interrupt you but consequent on your comment about stronger drugs, this seems the right place to raise the issue of the large number of deaths lately involving fentanyl and over-prescription too."

"Not at all, June, and thank you for the question. To reply briefly, the problem of over-prescription has been recognised nationally by government and by the medical profession. Here in Ayton, we have had consultations with medical colleagues locally about this issue and its consequences. There have been national initiatives by medical and law enforcement bodies. Likewise National Health

Service has I understand reminded doctors not long ago about the dangers of over-prescription and recommended a radical reduction, especially of drugs such as fentanyl, which you mentioned. Nationally prosecutions for trafficking in fentanyl have been successfully completed and a short time ago one man was sentenced to three years imprisonment for the import of the drug directly from China. The main source for the drug at the moment, however, remains the dark web. To summarise, over-prescription has been substantially reduced but, although still minute in comparison with the total quantity of drugs being trafficked on illegal markets, it is still a worryingly too frequent occurrence. Fentanyl is a newish threat. But is has been recognised and is being tackled most vigorously at both national and local levels. Thank you again for your very pertinent query."

The Chief Constable responded cordially and then continued.

"Can I just say how grateful I am for the assistance of the other agencies including the national crime agency and the Social Services Department from the local authority for their support, assistance and attendance? Locally, there is literally a mountain to climb. Nationally there are estimated to be some seventeen hundred drug cartels often co-operatively active. Similar estimates seem to point to the existence of several crime syndicates active in our town plying drugs and prostitution as well as people trafficking. The main target in this town today, however, is for the moment, the largest, richest and most powerful of the several transnational syndicates, which is moreover one of the most powerful locally resident criminal organisations, the Albanian Mafia. That is where we shall start. But it is important to note that even in a quiet, small-town like Ayton, there are several criminal gangs at work at the same time, not just one in the same field of drugs and prostitution. Some of these have established local headquarters here in addition to one or two brothels by some of the gangs. Sometimes these criminal gangs work alone, sometimes they co-operate and sometimes they resort to violent conflict between and among them with knives and/or ever more guns used to settle disputes. As I have said, some of these gangs are international, some are overflows from the big cities here in the UK like London, Liverpool and Manchester. But all profit wealthily from illegal activities and merchandise that are always in great public demand in the UK and in this locality and which cost the exchequer and services such as the National Health Service millions every year. Indeed, some of their products and some of these activities are in rapidly rising public demand. For example, as first and foremost cannabis, sometimes called by other names such as coke, rock, snow, blow, white, toot, nose candy, base, flake, powder and smack, but including other drugs as well, such as powdered cocaine, crack, heroin and other opiates. Prostitution, people trafficking and some incipient gun running are a steadily growing problem. Some few of the largest transnational syndicates are implicated in the full chain of the illicit drugs trade, starting with the cultivation and followed by the cutting process, distribution and sale of substances, all of which are subject to drug prohibition. Just in case anyone has a request for further information or clarification, I'll stop there after that brief, slightly complex start intended as a general overview before moving on to our specific target today."

Mark Brownlow put a question about the approximate number and wealth of such gangs.

"How many such criminal gangs are typically active in the UK and locally here in Ayton? What is their current size and what is their income per annum through their illicit activities?"

"We do not have very up-to-date figures, but a decade ago, one estimate put the number of such criminal fraternities in the UK at 7,500 with a membership of some 37,000 members and the approximate cost to the country of £100 million a day in crime and lost revenues. Those figures will almost certainly have increased since that estimate. The illegal drugs market in the country as a whole is very big business, with approximately seventeen hundred active cartels working in the sector, with an overall profit variously estimated at over nine billion pounds annually. Locally we do not have exact figures yet but we estimate a total of half a dozen gangs, dozens if not scores of members and an annual earning capacity of up to one hundred million pounds and slowly but surely increasing all the time."

Sergeant David Berger wanted to know about the illegal sale, possession and use of weapons locally.

"Do we know the level of commerce in illegal weapons here in Ayton at the moment and which criminal gangs are involved?"

The answer was stark.

"We do not know the extent of local commerce in illegal weapons, but we know that it is growing and the sophistication of the weapons is being increased as is the date of their manufacture. The main supplier tends to be the Albanian criminal syndicate, which is to be our focus today. But there is no doubt that the involvement in the arms trade, in their procurement and in their use by other criminal gangs is on an upward trend too."

"But I'd like to continue now with the focus of my contribution to this meeting being on the currently proposed operations to eradicate this plague from our streets. The issue for us is to devise a strategy that will begin the process of demolishing the stranglehold of one of those groups on this town, through their drugs and prostitution activities and their incipient involvement in people trafficking and weapons. As a first step and more specifically, the local counter terrorism force is currently planning to take out one of the two brothels, owned by the Albanian syndicate, during this week. The other one, which is additionally one of the gang's major drug storage sites, will be closed down later next week. That is not just a police action but one requiring sensitive care and support for the innocent, cruelly abused victims, who will be released by the police action and will need care and protection for a long, long time to come. I am obliged to the heads of those other agencies, which have already been involved in the detailed planning of this evening's action in a supportive role. So, just for the moment I think I have said enough to get the meeting moving, focussed on action here in Ayton, this criminal gang and the first step in the proposed action. The time for talking shop is long gone! Over to you!"

Mark Brownlow from the National Crime Squad responded.

"Chief constable, thank you for the summary and for the invitation to the National Fraud Squad to participate in these planning meetings as observers. The main thing that keeps these criminal gangs going is the lure of the huge profits to be earned. As the Chief Constable has emphasised, this is fuelled by dramatically increasing availability and ever-growing public demand for what they are selling. Just to give an idea of the demand, in 2020 an estimated 3 million people took drugs in England and Wales, with around 300,000 in England taking the most harmful drugs such as opiates or crack cocaine. Deaths from drugs in England and Wales recently reached a new height of going on for five thousand and they have been on the rise annually for almost ten years now. I'll halt for a moment in case anyone has contracted statistical indigestion and wants to solicit further clarification so far." He said light-heartedly.

There were no immediate interventions and so he proceeded with his delivery.

"Unless we tackle the way these criminals make their profits and how they remit the cash to London or elsewhere overseas, we can never break the hold of these gangs on this town and nationally and prevent their noxious impact on our citizens and particularly on our young people. That stranglehold, as you describe it, can cost the national exchequer as much as 37 billion pounds a year and the local economy speculatively several millions. Without being indelicate, each captive prostitute earns about twenty thousand pounds a year for the gang. The average life expectancy after capture is roughly four years. Brothels normally have about thirty prostitutes working at any one time. That is a cash profit of approximately half a million per annum from the one house. Here in Ayton at the very least a million if we include the other house known to belong to this gang. But that is not the main source of their income. That most profitable source is by far the drugs trade. With over a quarter of a million people using heroin in 2020 and 2.5 million using cannabis in 2019, the market is massive and is mounting radically each year. Seizures of cannabis, powder cocaine, crack and heroin have increased but supply of all drugs has increased as has the non-medical use of opiates. A major issue is how does the gang get its ill-gotten earnings out of the town? To escape from the country and from this town, all of the gangs' earnings from the sale of these drugs have to go through a multitude of separate channels. What are those channels and how can the cash flow be efficiently and quickly interdicted? Hopefully this raid and its successor next week will help us to begin to find at least some of the answers to those questions and to disrupt both the trade and its profits. But we need to disrupt the acceptance of dirty laundry by, often blind, so-called enablers sitting on quite legitimate jobs in such metropolitan centres as London. So anyway, just an initial point about tackling the very complex fiscal side of this criminal gang's activities and some of the links with other gangs and legitimate businesses. I'll reserve my case there for the moment in deference to the Deputy Chief Constable. Ma'am the floor is yours"

Deputy Chief Constable Heather Compton Jones addressed the meeting next.

“It is very apposite that Mark has raised up front the issue of the illicit financial flows side of the crime we are discussing today. I am very pleased to see representatives here today from the local authority Social Services Department. Most of the people, who will soon be released by the raids will be traumatised and in need of immediate and sustained counselling and mental support, some will be in need of medical treatment as well. Some may come within the definition of what we call children and the care of these children is a particular concern. I have to say that some of them were enticed or seized from already existing care home placements, sometimes organised by local authorities in places miles away from their homes, families and friends. Whatever their past location, however, some of these children already involved in the drugs side, often as county liners. They are likely to be loners at school, alienated and sometimes deliberately distanced from their families and friends and exiled into distanced and insecure accommodation provisions. We cannot solve all the problems at once, but surely this is one issue which must be given the highest priority for the sake of the future of so many of our next generation of young people.”

One of the beat Constables, Sergeant Julie Harper, made the next contribution speaking about the risks that officers faced in operations like those being discussed.

“The operation this week could be hazardous to officers to put it mildly. My officers have of course practised the procedures to be adopted endlessly. But they will not be armed. We know that some of the local criminals are trading in illegal weapons and are only too willing and able to use them. What happens if my officers are confronted by violent criminals, who show that they are willing to use their weapons?”

The reply from the Chief Officer was immediate and unequivocal.

“They must be tasered without further ado to incapacitate them, if that can be achieved without danger to the officer. If not, the officer should straight away withdraw to safety and summon the armed officers’ squad. I have to say that is the case of the operation being discussed here today, a back-up squad of armed officers will be in reserve but immediately available on the spot. Having said that, we do not expect violence. But if it is threatened or occurs we are fully equipped to deal with it and maintain the safety of all our officers and the public. Our retaliation to any such threat will be legal, swift and decisive. The safety of our officers is amongst our highest priorities.”

Superintendent Rajiv Gundara then spoke to the meeting.

"I would just like to endorse what has just been explained. The procedure is quite clear and the safety of all our officers is its major concern. If an adversary is armed, is instructed to put down his or her weapon and raise his or her hands and when instructed is still adopting a threatening stance and cannot be reached for one reason or another by a taser, we need to make sure that our officers withdraw and leave it to the armed unit to deal with that person."

The Chief Constable nodded his head vigorously in agreement and stated his concurrence conclusively.

"Agreed! This is normal procedure and all officers, not just armed squad officers, have been trained to adopt exactly the procedure that you have quite rightly and accurately just described for us and that for the safety of the individual officer and his colleagues as well."

June Browning, a member of the local authority Social Services Department raised a potentially knotty issue about a potential clash between the requirements of the police and those of Social Services, especially in the case of the innocent and traumatised victims of crime.

The Deputy Chief Constable responded robustly and clearly.

"My departments wish will be to remove the cruelly maltreated victims from the scene as quickly as possible and to get them quickly into a safe and caring environment, so that any immediate needs, such as medical, counselling, food clothing and cleanliness, can be addressed as swiftly as possible. Of course, you are quite right in your statement, that the police will wish to interview such victims as soon as possible, seeing their potentially critical importance as possible witnesses to felonies of one kind or another. The issue you raise is how can these two perfectly legitimate objectives be reconciled? What is the procedure there? Which has precedence? And the correct reply is that all officers will take the advice of social service colleagues and social services officers will be invited to attend with the person concerned in any police interview."

The Chief Officer then gave official endorsement to what his colleague had said.

"Thank you June for that absolutely critical and legitimate question. I just want to add my own confirmation on behalf of the police that the official procedure of this force is as just described. But I wanted to emphasise that the policy applies to all officers and it has my personal support and the official support of the department. As you can imagine, I have pondered about this issue at some length prior to this meeting, and I have consulted my senior officers about this very issue. The policy is clear and unequivocal. The right to care of these terribly abused and traumatised innocent victims comes before any consideration of the need for them to be swiftly interviewed. On liberation, they will immediately be handed over to social services to be transported to a safe and secure location for their immediate needs to be attended to, subject only to their own wishes. And that will happen during and at the conclusion of the raid this week. We shall, of course, seek access to them the following day or when advised that they are ready and willing to be interviewed and in a fit state to be questioned by police officers. In any case, the interview will take place in a safe and secure environment, and not necessarily at a police station, usually rather in the safe house, where they have been housed with an adviser of your choice from social services in attendance or if they wish a legal representative as well. If the victim is a child, the same will apply except that a member of the children's department would be invited to attend as well. On the police side all interviews will be conducted by two appropriately trained police officers, one female and one male. It is the human and legal rights of these persecuted and innocent people that are absolutely paramount in all cases and all officers will adhere to these guidelines. Personally, I would have it no other way."

There were individual expressions of agreement with what the Chief Constable had spelled out from many members of the audience.

One of the beat Sergeants, June Chapman, raised a new issue.

"Chief Constable. The issue of language could be crucial to the smooth execution of the raid. Some, possibly all of the guards in the premises involved in the raid will be Albanian. Will the initial calls to surrender be bilingual and will an Albanian speaking interpreter be available during the whole of the raid. Linked with that point, is the fact that many of the women, who have been trafficked and coerced into prostitution, have been transported from Romania and elsewhere in the most appallingly cruel and inhuman conditions and some of them come from far afield. After arrival in this country, their suffering has not ended and they are traded like commodities for a further brief life as prostitutes elsewhere, awaiting only the end of their short lives every day to end their seemingly endless misery. What provision will there be for these women, some of them even still children by our standards, for caring for them in an appropriate manner and in their own mother tongue?"

The Chief Constable attempted to reply to both parts of the question.

"Well, there are clearly two well defined but separate issues in that overarching question. I am going to reply to the first one, which deals with the raid. Then I shall invite one of my colleagues from the local authority Social Services Department to speak to the other issue of mother tongue provision while in care. So first of all loudspeaker instructions to the guards in the premises to be raided will be in English first with a second back-up announcement in Albanian containing exactly the same material. If the raid goes peacefully there will be close involvement of the Albanian interpreter to prevent any misunderstandings. Obviously we shall not put any civilian interpreter in a situation, which is or could be life-threatening. Should that occur at any stage in the raid the interpreter will be withdrawn straight away until the situation is peaceful and fully under control. June, do you want to respond to the second part of the question concerning mother tongue availability in the care of the local authority."

"Yes, thank you Chief Constable. Basically the second issue in one, which concerns the aftercare of the liberated women and children and it is quite complex because of the demand is for so many different languages. But in outline, we shall be doing a review of the language of communication of each individual. On the basis of the results of that process, and if needed, further interpretation will be obtained by the local authority, which is used to this type of situation and has a long list of interpreters covering a wide range of different languages on its availability books. With regards to the care itself, and especially medical attention, subject to the permission of the individual, with great care and sensitivity for social and religious reasons, it will be available to all from day one of their stay."

John Casey from the National Financial Fraud Squad followed the last response by returning to the issue of the flows of dirty money from their criminal origins to external locations.

"Chief Constable, if I may with your permission, return to the major focus of the National Squad, namely the comings and goings of the gains from criminal activities to overseas locations by devious and complex routes and in the case of this particular operation from such institutions as brothels and county line business exchanges to the bosses on the continent and particularly in Tirana via a laundering process, after which they reappear as clean money in investment sources in this country and abroad from places such as The Gulf. That is the other side of the money chain, namely the way in which those laundered funds are invested in many different parts of the world, facilitated by the so-called enablers, including in some city of London markets. Of course we shall not be taking part in the actual raid. But once pacification has been imposed, so to speak, we should appreciate an opportunity to speak with and interview the prisoners and insofar as possible examine the accounts and any other financial documents turned up by the raid and be able to assess their relevance to the issue of money transmission and laundering. Will it be possible for us to carry out those checks for and on corrupt money, where necessary and relevant to our investigations national investigations?"

The response from the Chair was clear and unambiguous.

"The involvement of the National Financial Fraud Squad has already been cleared by Senior Officers here with senior colleagues in that organisation and guidelines established for that to happen smoothly. For our part, rest assured that we shall be doing all we can to support your work of suppression and interdiction of the flows of illicit cash from the Ayton region, whilst of course guaranteeing your safety. No problem!"

Heather Compton Jones, acting as the Deputy Chief Constable, asked the Chief Constable whether a recap of the details of the raid might be useful and helpful.

"Sir, do you think it might be a good idea just to go over once again the arrangements for the raid on the brothel in Baker Street, which is situated quite close to the city centre in the company of a street of similar Victorian houses leading down to the old town of Ayton? It is not a main thoroughfare, but there is often a trickle of people using it as a short cut to the town centre."

"Yes, thank you, Heather. Please do continue." Chief Constable Horace Lashley invited her courteously.

"Well you have already received the details relevant to your particular function in the raid. But just to repeat: we meet here at police HQ at ten thirty on Thursday this week all ready and kitted out. We shall then proceed in convoy in the order already specified in your instructions to Baker Street with a small detachment taking up position at the back of the property. The road will already have been sealed in advance by some of our officers and parked cars will have been cleared with the permission and hopefully assistance of the owners. Earlier in the day, once the road has been sealed other residents will have been alerted by leaflet to remain indoors during the raid. As is now usual, a loudspeaker warning will be given in English followed immediately by the same announcement in Albanian requesting the peaceful opening of the front door and for all current occupants to come out with their hands above their heads. If the door is not opened after our instruction five minutes will be allowed to elapse and a further final warning will be give again in both languages. If after a further three minutes the door has not been opened, a squad of officers will approach the front door and with a ram if necessary they will break the door down and the squad will enter the building. Any men encountered will be detained, searched and handcuffed before being passed back to colleagues for temporary location in one of the detention vans at the front of the house and transportation to the police station. If all goes peacefully any women and children encountered will be cared for by female officers prior to being handed over to social services personnel, who will be invited to enter the building and look after the women and any children found there. After any immediate after care, the women and children will be taken in private buses waiting outside to a safe house or houses. It will be at that stage, Mark, that you will be enabled to enter the house to look for documents and any other relevant artefacts. Any men captured on site will be detained and transported in the detention vans to HQ, where they will be assessed before commencement of a formal interview with legal representation, if they so wish, after which the preparation of any charges will commence. That in a nutshell is the plan and please make sure that you are discreet with these details to anyone outside this room, including your own kith and kin. In fact, the major reason why this meeting has been called so late and fairly soon before the actual raid itself, is to avoid any leakages of this information to the criminals themselves. Any questions?"

"Yes please! How are we going to determine whether the men we arrest are just availing themselves of the women or they are part of a criminal conspiracy to organise a brothel or other crimes and thus part of the criminal network?"

Officer Kahn, one of the beat officers present, asked.

The Chief Constable Horace Lashley replied succinctly and specifically.

"We shall leave that to the interviews and whatever specific forensic evidence emerges from documents, artefacts or cross examination results. On the basis of the collection and consideration of that material in all individual cases, charges will be prepared against the different categories of criminals for submission to the DPP, Department of Public Prosecutions."

Officer Kahn put a second question about the results likely to accrue from the cross-examination of those detained and arrested.

"Sir, how much useful intelligence do you think we are likely to obtain from the interviews with the men captured by officers during this raid? Especially given the omerta-like vow of silence, which is a part of the inherent culture of the Albanian mafia gang, supported by the social consequences of breaking the besa for the criminal and all his relatives. One can understand and to some extent sympathise with their potential approach to cross-examination and this could lead to very little insight from the interviews? Also, are we likely to obtain any material of value towards prosecutions of malefactors from frightened and traumatised women captives that we have freed in our raid?"

The Chief Constable gave the only reply he could to the two-part question.

"All of that remains to be seen and I don't want to speculate in specific cases. To some extent it will depend on the skill of the police officers involved in the cross-examination of the subjects. In addition there are local, national and international precedents for accused mafia members breaking the vow of silence. Rare it is true. But not non-existent. So we are ever hopeful for a breakthrough. In some cases as well, I understand that an accord can be reached by the relevant authorities for an alleviation of sentence in exchange for useful evidence. But that is beyond my competence and not in my hands. With regard to the second part of your question, we all have immense compassion for all the women freed in such raids and the cruel and inhuman experiences they have all had to suffer. But again it is not unprecedented for a few very courageous women, who have been freed in such raids, to agree to testify against their torturers and tormenters, especially if they are accorded suitable and water-tight security guarantees by the appropriate authorities. But there are never any certainties in any of this."

With that response the Chief Constable made it eminently clear that ne regraded Constable Kahn's intervention as the final one of the session and that his own reply heralded the closure of the meeting. He expressed his warm appreciation and thanks to all attendees and all organisations, which had facilitated the attendance of their staff.

"Thank you everyone for a very informative and useful meeting and for sharing with us in such an open and forthright way your various ideas and comments. Forgive me if I emphasise, once again, the importance of not divulging any information about the raid and our discussions today with any third party. We meet again at ten thirty on Thursday of this week at our headquarters here, equipped and ready to move. So let's show this malign set of gangsters that they are not immune from justice if they commit serious misdemeanours in our town. I look forward to seeing you all here promptly and I wish everyone good luck and success for this, our very first major blow on behalf of all those persecuted by this vicious group of felons."

And so the scene was set for a clash of the Titans between the forces of Law and Order on the one hand and, on the other, a powerful transnational criminal gang in the streets of a small, historic town in the English Midlands.

Chapter Three: The Deal

"Come in Sam. Good to see you and Joel." Jack Burnley Crowder was using his personal interpretation of their names and his normal 'hail fellow well met' business approach to greet them cheerfully to his financial services business office in the town centre. He had just completed his usual Sunday round of golf with the Chief Constable, Horace Lashley, which had gone well for him. He was a man, who planned his meetings well and his aim today was twofold: to squeeze some more money from them and to find out what they were up to.

"Sit yourselves down and let's have a nice strong cup of coffee and some biscuits together and talk turkey, as they say.

"Good day, Jack. How's things?" The two responded sequentially and in a friendly manner.

"Well, help yourselves to coffee and I have just put out a selection of my best biscuits for you. Personally, I never eat between meals, but please help yourselves. So go ahead and indulge yourselves. Anyway, tell me the reason for this meeting today. We can then see in what ways I might be able to help you with your business and how you can assist me with mine too. Mutual assistance it's called!"

Jack proposed humorously. He sometimes fancied himself as a bit of a jester to lighten the leaden atmosphere of some business negotiations. Wanting to get straight to the point, however, in the way of the business man that he was, he had to admit to himself that his business was basically about making money and he saw this as a very promising money-making opportunity.

As the senior member, Samir spoke first emphasising the immediacy of the next supervisory visit from London and the pressing need for it to be successful.

"Well, Jack, as I have already told you, we expect a visit from our London friends, including a financial expert, in this coming week. It is highly likely to include the most senior man in the firm in the UK, in fact the boss of bosses for the UK, Tristen Rexhepi. With him will be a financial adviser almost certainly with an expertise in financing to inspect our books. We do not know exactly when, but we thought we would consult you to see if we could recruit some more co-workers from the local police force and the local community, business people like yourself. We're looking for a replacement in the light of the arrest of one of our key players in the local police force Harry Hamble, but additionally we want to enlist others from the wider sphere of public and political life in Ayton. We could perhaps consider raising the payments we make to our collaborators, especially within the police. For example, some of the people that you meet up with in your clubs and who are active in public and political life in the town, might be interested in earning themselves a few extra quid easily. Similarly we are planning to increase the county-lining of our cocaine and other drugs and we want to recruit a few more ten to seventeen year olds, possibly even younger if need be. They will act as couriers to take care of the expected growth in trade that we confidently anticipate and that the men from London are going to propose."

"Well Sam, I might be able to help you with the first of those requirements. On the other hand, I do not see how I can help on the second, namely recruitment of youngsters for county lining." Jack parried Samir's request for a two-part shopping list and countered with a request. "But what are you offering in exchange?"

Dissatisfied with the way the discussion was going, Xhoel intervened and sought to put pressure on Jack more directly and brutally, or so he thought. But he could never have anticipated Jack's tough reaction.

"Well, nothing, unless we receive something. You'll understand that as a good business man. We could offer something for each collaborator recruited but only after they have signed up and given evidence of their worth. And unless you feel able to assist with finding some youngsters to transport cocaine for us, there is nothing there either for you."

"Well, in that case we have nothing further to discuss gentlemen. You are welcome to complete your tea and biscuits and then I must be going back to my family at home, having been away from them already far too long today."

Xhoel again misjudged the man, as he tried his best to match Jack's tough rhetoric with the same rather aggressive approach of his own.

"Now don't be so hasty, Jack. Your honoured position in the community could suddenly collapse if the rumour got about that you were dealing with and earning money from the local mafia, don't you think?"

But Jack's next comment was even tougher, as he thought, somewhat irritated to himself, what a foolish and insufferable upstart this young man was. He decided to respond by teaching Xhoel a hard lesson

"Joel, my friend. I will take your last comments as a crude attempt at blackmailing me. So let me advise you of something you need to know and obviously don't. When you try that sort of extortion on someone, you need to be very sure of your ground and the strength of your position and the contrasting background and experience of your opponent. In this case, at the first whiff of such a betrayal, our brand new local Chief Constable will receive a report with a copy to the local paper and the national Press about your activities in Ayton and the locations of your properties in the town and further afield. That would of course include your rather secretive 'private enterprise' massage parlour in the shopping parade on the outskirts of town."

Jack paused only momentarily to increase the impact of what he was about to say.

"It seems to me that your young friends in East London would be very interested in that 'beauty' business, don't you? And their friends in Tirana as well! Moreover, I should reveal all to our enthusiastic new local Chief Constable, a friend of mine, by the way. I play golf with him regularly. I did so, this very morning. I am certain he would clear out you and your set-up in a couple of days, given the high grade intelligence that he would receive, as I have said today. Let me emphasise that this is not just an idle threat. The release of documents already lodged would be triggered by my demise. So if you want to talk business, go ahead and begin. If you don't, then I bid you a disappointed good bye. But one thing. Don't ever try to play the intimidation card with me again."

Samir tried rather clumsily to reverse the tide of acrimonious interaction between the two men and Xhoel's threats, which he considered were leading to a business cul-de-sac. That was the exact opposite of what he wanted from the meeting. He tried in vain to excuse Xhoel's approach.

"Now Jack, don't be so hasty. Xhoel was only trying to make clear that we pay you for performance. Without performance, we cannot pay. But of course you yourself are a valuable and valued asset and we shall of course be continuing our financial support for the regular receipt of appropriate reports from you. We value your cooperation highly and are willing to continue to pay for it. No problem! Nothing has changed there."

Jack responded sharply seeing an opportunity for additional earnings from Xhoel's inept outburst and Samir's somewhat weak attempt to steady the boat again.

"In view of the abrupt and discourteous threat of termination, it looks like I am going to have to acquire additional insurance. So given the apparent the threat to my livelihood, I would like to propose to you here today a 20% uplift in my regular payments for information. Agreed?"

Samir swiftly took over the negotiations from Xhoel, and suggested a less expensive but still attractive alternative.

"Oh, I don't think we could manage a twenty per cent boost, our bosses would not accept such an increase when the books are examined. But absolutely I do agree that you merit an increase and we could offer you probably five per cent in exchange for the names of a couple of your friends, who might be susceptible to help us in our business. Payment on delivery of course as always."

"No deal, Sam. At a squeeze and as a generous gesture towards you personally, I could accept ten per cent. Less than that and it is just not worth my professional time and the risk involved in dealing with someone like young Joel here. I can rapidly earn what you offer in other ways from my own business. So let's agree in a friendly way at ten per cent."

Very reluctantly Samir found himself snookered and he tried to introduce a new dimension to justify what he felt he had to agree to, namely the ten per cent proposed by Jack.

"Well, I think that we might be able to manage that given the right contribution from your side. By the way, I hear that your granddaughter is doing well at the college. Elected head girl we hear from one of our couriers. Do you think she or some of her friends might be interested in joining us for some extra pocket money? You could introduce her to us or us to her some time, but soon. We have never met her or your good wife either."

Jack saw this as a further attempt to put pressure on him and he responded sharply and very hard.

"Any pocket money that my granddaughter needs is readily available from my wife and myself. My wife would not be interested in meeting you either. But just a word of caution and advice. Do not try to involve my granddaughter, my daughter or my wife in our business dealings ever again, or our cooperation is finished and there will be consequences. I assure you"

"In that case Jack, just reply specifically to this question. What exactly is it that you are offering? How are you intending to earn your money with or without the ten per cent on delivery that you are now requesting?"

"Information, Sam! Information!"

"Like what, Jack?"

"Like the name of a high up in the police force here in Ayton, who given the right incentive could provide you with the details in advance of what action the force might be planning against your business. You know, of course, that the current Chief Constable has sworn that he will crush you and your business within a year of his appointment. The clock is now ticking. So an insider might just be your salvation. But one tip. Don't try blackmail like you and Joel have just tried with me or you will screw it up completely."

"Look Jack. Let's try to get the conversation back on an even keel. With the arrest of our main collaborator in the police department we are acting blind at the moment and we need to replace Harry Hamble as quickly as possible. So do you have someone we could approach to replace him, or not?"

"Not so quick Sam. First let's clear up the payment side of things. Are you agreeing to my request for a ten per cent upturn in my regular payments for contact names and information?"

Samir's retort was one of total resignation.

"We don't seem to have much of an option. Do we Jack?"

"So do you agree?" Jack shot back.

"Yes, you have my word of honour, my besa, on it."

"OK, then we are making some progress now. I would suggest that you might wish to approach Tony Wozny. He is an Assistant Chief Constable and an avid gambler. He often has problems meeting his debts. He will have full details of future plans for any action against you, which I guess in view of the avowed intention of the new Chief Constable you can expect pretty soon. Try him but do not mention me or repeat what I have told you. As agreed, I shall expect to collect my fee with the additional ten per cent when he signs up. Promptly! Continued support from you will ensure continued information and feasibly even a few more names."

"OK, Jack it's a deal!

"Well now I must encourage you to be on your way. Although it is not a normal work day, I have other commitments and clients and of course as you just mentioned I have business with my kinfolk too."

"Fine, then we shall take our leave and look forward to our next productive business meeting together. Just let myself or Xhoel know, when and if you have any further details about contacts or even just general information for sale."

"Can do. Bye for now."

Jack bade them a rather curt farewell, thinking to himself that he had done a good business deal, but not for himself. Everyone in the police force and even beyond knew of Tony Wozny's gambling addiction, except apparently the two Albanians. So today in a short meeting, he had achieved something for nothing, in a manner of speaking. He felt quite pleased with himself.

When they had left his office, he picked up the phone and dialled a local number.

"Hello Horace. I've just had a meeting with our two friends. Could I call and see you later this evening."

There was a short pause and Jack responded.

"Good OK. About eight thirty this evening then at your place. Bye!"

As they were walking back, Xhoel asked Samir for his reaction to their meeting with Jack.

"Well at least we had one positive outcome to our meeting with Jack today. A potential new recruit within the police Department here in Ayton. How did you feel about it?"

Xhoel responded in a rather critical way, which did not entirely delight his boss.

"Well, judged at this moment, the meeting was not very productive and we paid a high price for what little we achieved, one name. So from that perspective, it was rather costly for us. Jack's a clever negotiator as you'd expect from someone, who has a qualification in both Finance and Law. I have a gentle suspicion, however, that he is taking from both sides. A kind of double agent, so to speak. But we shall have to see how our meeting with this police officer, Tony Wozny, goes and we need to find a way through him of recruiting more members of the police force and, of course, getting more county liners as well."

Xhoel, who normally took a more restrained position towards his colleague, Samir, continued by suggesting a couple of next steps to Samir in view of the urgency, which did nothing to steady Samir's cantankerous nerves after Xhoel's missteps in their negotiations with Jack.

"If you are agreeable, Samir, I would suggest that we split our resources. If you will contact this Tony Wozny from the local police, for my part, I will contact or should I say, touch base with Jack's granddaughter about the possibility of getting her and some of her school friends into the distribution side of their business."

"Yes, agreed! Good idea, Xhoel." Samir responded positively although he was slightly upset that Xhoel, his junior in the business, had made the proposal first, when he considered that it should have come from him. He cast his mind back to previous occasions, where Xhoel had done this, sometimes in front of other colleagues. So he issued a strong caveat.

“But take heed that it is accidental when you meet her and that she is not likely to report back to her avuncular grandfather, our friend, Jack. We do not want any trouble with Jack that could be quite messy and require drastic action from us. Especially at this time with the expected visit of our friends from London, we do not want any upsets. So as far as she is concerned we do not know Jack. Eh?”

Xhoel responded confidently.

“OK, boss. Can do.”

And so Samir undertook to deal with the approach to the local police officer, Tony Wozny, as the further penetration of the local force was planned. On the other hand, contrary to Jack’s specific warning about any contact by them with his granddaughter, the wheels were set in motion for an approach to Andrea and an effort to potentially involve her in the business as well. But what was it exactly that they had purchased from Jack and how might Jack react when he found out what they were planning for his granddaughter?

Chapter Four: The Raid

Chief Constable, Horace Lashley, was a in a particularly good mood that evening. All participants in the raid had assembled on time at the police headquarters and the move to Baker Street had gone quietly and smoothly and without raising unnecessary public attention. The building scheduled for the raid, an old Victorian detached house in a line of such properties in mature, tree-lined Baker Street, not far from the town centre, had only latterly been identified by CID officers as a mafia brothel. So the action was timely.

The house concerned had been sealed since the morning. Plastic barriers had been erected at both ends of the road and all through traffic diverted by traffic wardens. Neighbours in other houses in the street had been permitted to pass, given proof that they were not intending to visit or coming from the raid house itself. The plan was to start the raid at eleven o' clock that night.

Since the end of the afternoon rush hour, a squad of armed police had been in attendance immediately outside the house and no one had been allowed to enter or exit the building. Anyone seeking to enter had been stopped and subject to a police interview. The only attempted entries to the house were by local men, who claimed that they were visiting their girlfriends. From the same time, Social Services staff were in attendance in case of need during the raid by any women or children discovered in the house and officers with first aid training were on hand, although it was thought unlikely that they would be needed. A black maria waited ominously just down the road from the house for any detainees.

Both back and front entrances of the large house were now fully covered. For the last hour, passage of the sparse traffic in the area at that time of night had been totally halted *ad interim* and directed to divert after receipt of an explanation of the reason for being in the area from the driver of the vehicle and any other occupants. No one had so far been detained although a number of both pedestrians and car drivers had been redirected. Deputy Chief Constable Heather Compton-Jones was in charge at the front of the building, accompanied by Assistant Chief Constable Rajiv Gundara. At the rear of the building was a small squad of police officers led by Assistant Chief Constable Tony Wozny in overall charge. All was set for the raid to begin.

At that time of night the area was usually very quiet. It was so when Chief Constable Horace Lashley arrived shortly before the agreed time with the main body of the final group of Senior Officers, to check that all participating units were in place as planned and ready to go at eleven o'clock that evening. The weather was clement and chilly but without precipitation. Not unusually, the atmosphere among the officers was tense but alert, and Chief Constable Lashley was able to rapidly confirm that all was in fact ready for the commencement of the actual raid, the first step in the masterplan. After further consultation with senior colleagues he was able to give the go-head straight away.

A loudspeaker announcement was made first in English and then repeated in Albanian by one of the police interpreters, inviting all those in the house to exit through the front door with their hands held high, instructing any who might be armed to discard their arms before exiting the building and giving them five minutes to respond. Nothing happened and no one came out of the building. After the expiry of a further five minutes, another similar instruction was given and after a brief pause with no response whatsoever, officers with battering rams first tried the front door and finding it locked, used their equipment to force open the door. They then retired and the first squad of armed officers entered the building, where, at first sight, all seemed quiet and peaceful.

The first squad of officers, divided to right and left and began a systematic search of all rooms on the ground floor, where four men were discovered in individual rooms each in the company of a very young woman. The men were passed to the officers waiting outside for questioning and possible arrest. The young women were passed back by female officers to the second squad. They had entered the ground floor to take the place of the officers now engaged in searching each room and thence to the female constables, who were waiting outside. Then the women were placed under the care of local authority Social Services Department personnel for routine checks to health and a meal in a safe and secure environment. That part of the operation seemed to go very smoothly.

Eventually a group of seven women was located in the small individual rooms and again they were passed back by female officers to the female officers of the second squad and thence to Social Services. No children had been discovered so far on the ground floor. The ascent of the stairs to the first floor was conducted with great care and achieved incrementally with officers alternating up each level under the cover of their marksman colleagues behind. With no apparent opposition, the same procedure was adopted for the second floor attics with the first squad covering the ground floor but with a second squad now descending to investigate the cellar below, where a large quantity of drugs and cash was found and confiscated. No further persons were discovered in the cellars.

The upstairs search on the first floor had been extended to the quite large attics, which had been divided into about ten smaller rooms. On the first floor and in the attics, a further two men and eight women were discovered in the various rooms and passed back along the chain, men to police officers and women firstly to female police officers and after brief inquiries about basic details thence to Social Services staff waiting outside.

When all personnel had been cleared from the building, a forensic squad entered and a search was made for evidence. Amongst the other findings, five revolvers and two rifles were found, together with a stockpile of drugs in sachets and a substantial sum of money, principally in five pound notes and still to be counted. More of this cash, drugs and other articles was found in a ground floor room. That room looked as though it was being used as an office with a large wall safe at the back of the room and computers, telephones and desks with comfortable office chairs further forward. There was a modern coffee machine in good working order on a table at the side with half-consumed coffees in plastic cups on the desk. Officers were particularly staggered to find unsafeguarded and in a not very secure hideaway, on shelves in a cupboard in the same room, a small cache of precious stones and a collection of rare postage stamps.

On completion of the search of the building, the armed police Unit was stood down and the house was sealed and the diversions lifted. In the early morning light, all police and Social Services staff returned to their headquarters; the police with their captives and Social Services with the women to their offices in the town centre for appraisal and allocation to a secure place to pass the next few days. All police captives were handed over to a fresh squad of officers for registration and thence to interrogation. After the formalities had been completed they were offered light refreshments for breakfast before commencement of their interviews.

At the end of that afternoon officers, including those who had taken part in the raid, who had been allowed to go home for a sleep, came together to discuss the tentative results of the initial interrogations by their colleagues and the forensic investigation of the evidence collected at the house. The Chief Constable chaired the meeting with the deputy chief and Assistant Chief Constables, who had assisted in the raid also present, as well as all the officers who had conducted the interviews and the forensic examinations.

The Chief Constable opened the gathering with some hint of satisfaction even pleasure in his voice.

"Firstly I should like to offer my sincere thanks to all officers, who have participated, in this raid and the investigation so far for their excellent work and a particularly high level of cooperation and mutual assistance. I have thanked our colleagues from Social Services and they have confirmed that all the women from the house have claimed and most probably are prostitutes in extremely cruel circumstances, who were subjected to trafficking and to prostitution through coercion. They are, therefore, victims, and are not criminally culpable. They are of different nationalities, a majority trafficked from Romania but with some brought from Albania and one young woman from Nigeria. After further medical and personal checks, it was agreed that the women should be subject to police interview before being handed over to the Home Office Immigration Department for further processing and decisions on their futures. I will now call on the deputy Chief Constable to brief us on the results of the interviews with the men. Heather, over to you."

"Thank you sir. Well, without exception, all six men are claiming that they were in the house to meet one or other of the women, about whom they seemed to know nothing. They denied any link to the firearms found in the building. They all appear to be illegal immigrants. They all cited the same legal firm in immediately exercising their right to the presence of a solicitor during interview. We have emphasised that they are not at this stage under arrest but that they are under investigation. We have acquiesced, however, to their right to be legally represented. That has delayed the interrogations somewhat, but nevertheless, we have more or less decided to formally charge them. The problem is that buying sex itself is not illegal in the

UK. So unless we can prove that these men have participated in controlling a brothel for gain or have engaged in sex with an underage minor, we can only hold them on trafficking, drugs and gun charges. For that we shall need some breakthrough testimony from the women, many of whom are deeply traumatised and justifiably suspicious. But we continue to be hopeful for corroborative evidence from at least some of these unfortunate women.

Unfortunately neither of the two top men from the clan were caught. None of the captives mentioned their names and according to feedback from Social Services, none of the women mentioned the names of those men during the interviews either. But these are early days and we shall try to keep going and eventually, who knows? We shall be fingerprinting the weapons and subjecting other objects found to forensic investigation. Finally we are still waiting for a determination of the age of the women, although they all seem very young."

"Thank you Heather for your hard work and that of your team. At this stage we have to be content with modest returns. After all, merely closing the brothel, cuts the funds flowing to the criminal gang and reduces the human misery of so many severely abused and frightened women, although of course they will carry the scars of their experiences for the rest of their lives. But does anyone else have anything to contribute or a burning question to pose about the operation today? Yes, Jagdish. Go ahead."

"As you have mentioned these are the early days in our operation against the criminal syndicate, which has penetrated our community and is doing so much damage to it and especially amongst the youth of this city. Do I take it that there will be further follow-ups from today's operation and that further houses will be subject to raid and closure? And secondly, do our investigations to date give us scope to begin closing down the illicit financial flow routes into and out of this crime syndicate's foul earnings in our midst at least as far as Ayton and the surrounding area is concerned?"

"You are correct, Jagdish, in your first assumption. This is only the very beginning of a very long journey. Senior staff will be discussing the next phases of this operation successively and continually until we have eradicated this menace to the community and not least to the young people of our town and region. Thus, we shall be attempting to cut the county lines, so to speak, as part of the operation in order to protect the youth of our city and surroundings areas. We have a meeting of senior officers tomorrow to continue the detailed planning of the continuation process including the decision where to hit them next. We shall be trying to discover how they are recruiting some very young children for their county lines operation. That will involve dialogue with the primary school and college. I shall be having a first meeting with the headmistress and director tomorrow."

He paused for a while before addressing the second half of the question.

"On the second part of your query about cutting the financial umbilical cords. The National Financial Fraud Squad will be involved in that part of the post-raid investigations. The finger-printing and forensic stages of today's operation are still incomplete. We are hoping that evidence will accrue, however, from them for firmly based charges to be forwarded to the prosecution service as soon as possible for an early decision. With regards to the money trail, we shall be aiming to discover the bank and/or money-transfer organisations where the cash captured today was going to be deposited in and/or transferred out in usually in small packages. When we find the instruments and monetary channels that they are using for transferring their cash, we shall definitely seek the legal authority to close the organisations down. We shall also be consulting with colleagues in other areas about what they have discovered and how the finances of the mafia gang work."

Police Sergeant Brenda Ramsden requested further particulars on the rather complex issue focusing on the areas of sex with a minor or consensual sex and coercive sexual intercourse.

"Sir, do we have any evidence so far from Social Services about the ages of the young women discovered at the brothel? For substantiation of any charges we shall need that evidence."

"Thank you Sergeant Ramsden. I can see where your question is aiming. As the Deputy Chief Constable has already said, we are still waiting for definitive determination of the age of the young women in case a further charge of sex with a minor or non-consensual, that is coercive sex or rape, can be levied against any or all the men. With regards to the consensual side we shall be interviewing the women later with a Social Services counsellor to see if and how they felt coerced to undertake sexual intercourse with successive men and who or which of the captives did the coercing. This is a very difficult time for these women, We are nonetheless hopeful that one or more of them may be willing to give evidence against the men. That has not happened so far. But we are always optimistic and it has happened before in other cases in other dispensations and in our own."

Police Sergeant Rita Howell appealed for further information about the rather strange immediate availability of legal support for the men arrested.

"Thank you, Sergeant Howell, for raising that very important issue. We shall need to proceed carefully on this issue. But we shall be requesting an informal meeting, within the next couple of days, at the solicitors' official office with the firm of lawyers that most of the men seemed to know so intimately and be able to call on so rapidly after their arrest. There is a sense in which the fact that some of the men; a majority, have all requested assistance from the same firm, identified them as more than just casual sex customers."

As all concerns appeared to have been satisfactorily responded to and further ones were not forthcoming at that time, the Chief Constable thanked all the participants and announced a further meeting of senior and key staff the following day.

At that further meeting he declared that it was hoped that further forensic evidence would be available as well as other evidence arising from the interviews. It was hoped that this evidence could facilitate the accurate preparation of formal charges against at least some, if not all, of the men.

He continued giving details of further actions.

"At that time, clearance may be received for the impounding of the money, drugs, guns and precious objects uncovered in the raid. With luck, as I said already, some of the young women might have agreed to identify the mafia bosses organising the brothel. Hopefully they may just express a willingness to testify against them. But we need to be sensitive and circumspect on that issue. Detailed plans will be laid as well for the next raid the following week against a further brothel of the same mob in the town. Further action on the finances side will be undertaken as well. We shall continue for as long as it takes to eradicate the wicked scourge from our society. Good luck to us all!"

So a start had been made to tackling the scourge of Ayton. But the police action was still in the foothills of the mountain, they would need to conquer, and frits part the mafia was beginning to implement its plans too.

Chapter Five: The Encounter

Thump! Someone had crashed into Andrea as she pulled away from school on her bicycle at the end of the school day. Not hard enough to knock her from the saddle or to damage her bicycle, but enough to shock her and to make her halt and look at the offending person, also on a bicycle, with some shocked disdain. In all her years of cycling from home to school and back and to meetings and events in the town, she was very proud that she had never had even the most minor of accidents.

Andrea therefore observed with some contempt a rather handsome young man on a somewhat dilapidated bicycle, casually dressed and smiling at her. She guessed he was in his early twenties or very late teens. She straightaway began to castigate him vociferously.

"What the blazes do you think you are doing riding like that in such an irresponsible way? And on the pavement too! If you can't do better than that, you should go to some cyclist retraining sessions. Or better still, give up cycling all together!"

Xhoel had thought out the strategy for his approach to Andrea very carefully. So he responded innocently, playing a Ukrainian refugee and hoping thereby that his pleas would engage her sympathy.

"Sorry Miss. The brakes failed. It's such an old bike that I borrowed. I probably should have examined the pads before I set off today. My fault entirely. Any damages or injuries? Just let me know, although I have to say, I have no money at the moment. By the way, I'm Joel Melnik. I'm a Ukrainian refugee. Just arrived in Ayton and borrowed the bike from the man I'm staying with. I am trying to see something of the town and get used to riding on the wrong side of the street amongst many other new things as well."

On closer inspection, Andrea found the young man somewhat alluring. He was well-dressed but casually. He was seated with one foot on the ground supporting his rather battered, old stationary bicycle somewhat insecurely. His bike had clearly seen better days long ago, she thought. The two, his clothing and his ancient bicycle, did not seem to go together. A bit suspicious, Andrea thought. So she replied to the man slightly more scathingly than she really intended.

"Well I suppose that does explain your appalling riding … to some extent. But I would think that even in the Ukraine people are expected to adhere to the Law and custom of good riding. By the way, I'm Andrea! Andrea Goral! And your name is?"

"My name, as I have already said, is Joel Melnik"

Xhoel disregarded her implicit enquiry about cycling in the Ukraine. After all, he had no experience of it whatsoever. But he caught on straight away and capitalised of the issue of her surname to continue the conversation.

"That's doesn't sound to me like an English name. Is it? Are you a foreigner or something like me?"

"No. I'm British. My mother is English and my father was Czech. But he's dead now, many years ago in fact. My mother, my grandfather and my grandmother are all still alive though and we are all live together. We are very close, the whole family. What about you? Do you have any family?"

He pointedly took no notice of her query again, apologised and instead invited her for a drink. That might give him a chance to construct some sharp comebacks to her very sharp grilling.

"Well, look. I'm so sorry. Would you like to come for a coffee at the café just down the road, so I can apologise properly to you and perhaps repay you for some of the shock and discomfort? We can talk about our families then, if you like."

"No, thanks. I'm on my way home and I don't accept invitations to coffee from strangers, especially those who are so blind that they ride into the side of my bicycle."

"I fully understand your suspicions and I do understand what a terrible shock this collision was for you. Indeed, I face a similar situation in that everyone here is a stranger, and I have not been able to make contact with anyone since I made the perilous crossing over the channel and arrived in Ayton a couple of days ago. As you have already observed, I am an amateur in picking up social contact with people, especially as English is not my mother tongue."

Andrea contradicted his comment about his English and gentled her tone towards the man.

"Oh. Not at all. Your English is remarkably good for someone, for whom it is not their mother tongue. It suggests many years of learning the language. But you mentioned your journey here and you must have had an awful experience. I'm really sorry for you."

Andrea said, beginning to rebuke herself for the harshness of her previous pronouncements to a young man who claimed to be a poor Ukrainian refugee. As a result she softened her tone appreciably and she now sought to redeem herself by accepting his offer of a drink at the nearby coffee shop.

"Well perhaps I might be able to spare you ten minutes at the coffee shop. But no more than that and I shall pay. I guess that as a newly arrived refugee you are not very well off with money, although it's not very expensive at the coffee house as it is called. It's popular with the youngsters of this town and it serves up an excellent variety and quality of coffee. I prefer hot chocolate myself though. I watch my diet very carefully as a competing athlete. Anyway, yes! I agree to have a drink with you at the coffee shop, but on two conditions: one that I pay and two I cannot stay more than about ten minutes as I have further commitments this evening and a pile of homework to complete before I return to college tomorrow. Is that OK?"

"Well of course it is. In fact it's so kind of you and it will give you a chance to tell me something more about your kinfolk, your school and your town and perhaps about your homework, if you wish. I'd love to get to know more about you and about this delightful place that you are privileged to call home. Without wishing to pry, you might be willing to share with me something about yourself and your school as well. I could tell you about me and mine, whilst we are drinking our coffee and hot chocolate and I can tell you something about the awful war in my own country, Ukraine, at this very moment in time. Indeed as we speak it is still continuing."

Xhoel could feel the first part of his strategy beginning to slip into place and he was optimistic and self-confident that he would succeed in his mischievous aims. The coffee shop escapade would no doubt provide him with some useful baseline information. It would similarly offer him further levers to commence the second part, but being very cautious as his colleague, Samir, had emphasised not to press it too hard to begin with.

For her part, Andrea noted his excellent English with only a slight but pleasant foreign accent, but one that she was unable to identify accurately. She noted his slightly bronzed features as well, which added to his handsome features and spoke of somewhere in southern Europe as his possible place of origin. *Funny!* She thought. *He said he was from the Ukraine and that's in Eastern Europe. Suspicious again!*" She mused.

Anyway, off they cycled towards but not into the town centre with Andrea, as agreed, leading an apparently 'ignorant of the way' refugee and asylum seeker as well. When they reached the coffee house, as it was called, she attached her bicycle with lock and key to one of the pavement metal cycle parking bars, whilst he just leaned his against a nearby wall. She carried her heavy backpack containing her books and other school materials with her as they entered the cafe one behind the other. Straight away, Andrea spied a small two-place corner table near a window at the far end of the room, where they could converse in relative privacy and that is where they took their seats. The waitress was promptly in attendance as they sat down and, their coffee and hot chocolate ordered, they were swiftly served with a latte and a hot chocolate as requested.

Andrea took the initiative straight away after the first sip of her hot chocolate.

“So tell me something about yourself, your homeland and your journey to Ayton. And why Ayton after all? I mean it’s hardly the country’s metropolis.”

“Well, there’s not much to tell really. I was a student studying sciences at university leading a rather dull and ordinary life when all hell broke loose with the Russian invasion. I was evacuated to Poland and thence to the Belgian coast and then to the UK via a small boat across the channel. After arrival I heard of Ayton from some Englishmen that I met after I landed and from what they said, it seemed that this place called Ayton was the sort of place I would like to live my quiet life in again. And, well, here I am! So, what about you?”

“Not very much to tell. I am a student in my final year at college before going to university in the autumn. I have an offer of a place to study engineering at Imperial College in London and in addition to sciences I’m keen on music, sport, games and athletics. I like reading and listening to and playing music on my clarinet. That's it for me."

"Very interesting, but you never mentioned your relatives, except to say that your father died many years ago."

"Yes. Very banal. But if you don't mind my saying so, I just wonder why are you so interested in my family? Anyway, to reply to your question, my mother is an engineer and she works for a national company with a local office in project preparation and monitoring. Both my grandparents are retired, both are local councillors but with different political parties. My grandfather still runs his commercial services business in the town centre part-time. We all live harmoniously together in a modest semi-detached nineteen thirties period house opposite the park. What about you?"

Xhoel hastily made up a mythical background that he thought might satisfy his inquisitor, but at the same time evoke a certain empathy.

"Very sad really. The remaining members of my family were killed in a Russian bombardment on a railway station when they were waiting for a train to carry them away to freedom in Poland. Now I am the only remaining one, so to speak and my home is most probably either occupied by Russian soldiers now or demolished by a Russian rocket or bomb."

"Oh. I'm so sorry. Who is it that you are living with in Ayton at the moment? I might know them or their children if they're at the college I attend."

Xhoel immediately sensed the danger in that issue and he had some initial difficulty in conjuring up a response, as he lived with Samir in the Clan's second brothel that had not yet been raided. Yet! So his imagination raced into rapid creativity mode, but again with the ambition of soliciting compassion.

"Well for the moment I'm staying in an old, rundown Victorian house in Bright Street. I think the man that I am staying with is Polish. I know him only as Sam and his surname is something like Miaso. I think he receives a payment from the government to take me in. He's very old and does not converse much, so I do not have much human contact, although I have to say that he seems to have great sympathy with the current plight of us Ukrainian refugees escaping from the war."

Andrea was beginning to feel that she had exhausted her stock of everyday queries and that she had spent enough time with this Ukrainian migrant. In any case she had work to do at home, helping the others in the house and doing a mountain of schoolwork. Later there was a meeting of the school athletics club to prepare for the school's summer games. As head-girl, she was involved in assisting with the organisation of the event on the playing fields adjoining the school buildings and with the prize-giving at the end of term.

"Well, Joel Melnik. It was a real pleasure to speak with you. I sympathise with the current fiasco in your country and your own dire position. But I must go as my gran will be expecting me home early. She knows that I have a meeting this evening. So, I'll say cheerio and wish you a very bright future here in my hometown of Ayton. I'm sure you will find people helpful here."

"Well thank you. But I do not yet know anyone else in Ayton. Do you think we could meet again for a coffee … err and a hot chocolate, if you wish?"

"Sadly I'm not sure that I can make a commitment to provide you with the kind and quantity of social interaction you are looking for. There must be a migrants group that could provide you with that. Apart from which, I'm not so keen on excessive sweetened drinks, as I stick to a strict diet routine."

But then a mood of compassion took hold of her replacing her previous toughness and she thought sympathetically of what appeared to be his dire captive situation and his apparent loneliness. She rapidly changed her attitude and her approach. After all she felt that she had been rather callous, an attitude that annoyed her. It was not her way.

"But on second thoughts." She said in a quiet and gentle voice. "I may be able to manage a hot chocolate *rendezvous* here at the same time next week. So OK. But not this week. Let's say after school on the same day and at the same time and place as this week in this coffee shop next week. Not outside the school. But be more careful next time how you are riding your bike. Sorry must dash now. Bye. Hopefully, shall see you again next week."

"Bye and thanks. Same day, time and place next week. Hot chocolate. Not coffee"

As she cycled back home, Andrea thought over her conversation with the man called Joel and how she had first encountered him. She wondered how genuine he was and thought the mode of their encounter somewhat artificial even perhaps fake. Was he really a Ukrainian migrant or something else? Her gran, Emily, ever concerned for her sole granddaughter's welfare, had said that she and her school friends needed to be careful in Ayton nowadays as there were so many criminals and other rogues in the town these days. Quite a different place from the one she had grown up in, Gran affirmed. So Andrea determined to mention the incident to her mother, Izzy, and her grandparents, Emily and Jack, when she returned home.

Gran was busy in the kitchen, when Andrea arrived home a little later than usual. She was preparing the evening meal and fortuitously her mother and her grandfather both returned about an hour later, which meant that they could all be together for dinner.

Her parents and Gran were always interested in what she had been doing during the day. She, for her part, was always interested in what they had been doing. After some time discussing Gran's political meetings and a meeting of the Ayton Ladies' Club and some of the business conducted by her grandfather at the office, her turn came. In addition to all the other things she had done during the day at school, she mentioned the incident with the collision of the bicycles and the subsequent invitation for coffee.

All three of them were immediately alert and her grandfather's suspicions were immediately provoked. This was exactly the kind of thing that Jack had referred to at his last meeting with the two mafia gang leaders and against which he had threatened consequences. He could not reveal to her his role with the Albanians and local police, but he could definitely make sure to warn her.

"What did you say this man's name was?" He inquired somewhat anxiously.

"He said that he was called Joel Melnik and he was from the Ukraine and that he was lodged at the moment in a house in Bright Street in the old town area with an elderly man of Polish extraction, called Sam Miaso. He seemed very socially isolated just longing for social contact. I must say I felt a lot of human sympathy for him when he told me of the tragedy of his family and his own experiences. So I agreed to meet him again next week."

With the mention of the name Joel, Jack's alert self-warning system sounded straight away. He recalled his previous conversation with those two mafia rogues, Samir and Xhoel, whom he referred to as Sam and Joel. He shared his suspicions with Andrea, his wife and their daughter Izzy, carefully avoiding any mention of his own connections, and the operation with the police that he was currently involved in.

"I am sad to say that your Ukrainian young man Joel is very likely an imposter. It sounds very much to me as if he is not Ukrainian at all, but an Albanian member of the local criminal confraternity here in Ayton, called Xhoel Gegaj. Otherwise you wonder why he has not contacted the local Ukrainian Association in the town or registered as a Ukrainian asylum seeker. It's an old established community of post second world war Ukrainian refugees, who organised it themselves shortly after the end of the Second World War. Lately they have all been very active in receiving and housing the newly arrived Ukrainian families and individuals and providing them with support, contacts and information. This whole farrago that he is feeding to you sounds decidedly suspicious to me if not totally fake!

"Well that's very interesting. How exciting!" Andrea responded.

"Yes, maybe. But beware of these people." Her grandfather warned knowingly.

"They can be very dangerous and sometimes very violent. If this Joel is really the Albanian gangster Xhoel, he is wanted for questioning by the police suspected of various criminal offences including violence against women and minors. He is alleged to be engaged in people trafficking, drugs and prostitution and probably much more besides. It sounds to me that he's looking to recruit youngsters like yourself or other students in the college for what is known as county lines work, transporting and delivering drugs to other areas outside the town."

Andrea responded quizzically.

"Do you really think that is the case? Sounds shocking to me. But why me? Do you really think he was hoping to recruit me to this county lines affair that you mentioned, granddad?"

"Yes, it's highly likely to my mind. At least if not you yourself, then hoping to use you as an entrée to other students at the school to attempt to recruit some of them to trade drugs for these gangsters. Some such couriers have been recruited from schools elsewhere, it is said, some as young as the age of seven. But in this case, from what you say, I think that is his objective rather than to hook young people into drug addiction *per se*. I'm afraid we shall have to report this to the police. I know the Chief Constable well and I could raise this issue with him, or gran could do it through her Ladies Club or political work contacts. What do you think, Emily? Izzy?"

"I agree that there is unfortunately a need for great caution in this town at the moment." Emily began, repeating a prosaic theme from the discussions at the Ayton Ladies' Club at the moment. She continued anxiously addressing her husband.

"From what you are saying Jack, this man seems to be a member of a criminal syndicate active in this town at the moment , of which there appear to be several at this time according to some of the ladies at the Club. Although I must say that our new Chief Constable has vowed to crack down on all of them. Not before time, if you ask me. But he is quite new and I'm not sure whether the police have started on that yet. If this man is a member of a criminal gang in the town, we should undoubtedly report this to Chief Constable Lashley or one of his staff and you could best do that, Jack. After all, you do regularly play golf with him. Afterwards I think that all of us should meet with Horace Lashley or his head of terrorism. Without doubt, the police will wish to commence some follow-up actions before your projected meeting next week, Andrea, and perhaps put a tap on your mobile in case he tries to approach you directly beforehand by that means. But what do you think, Izzy? Andrea? How do you see it? What do you think?" Emily invited Andrea's mother.

"Well, unusually I agree with the analysis of the situation so far and the proposed action. Andrea will need to exercise great care from now on. In addition, it seems to me that she should report any further attempt at contact to us all, so that we are well briefed before the meeting with the police. Additionally she might wish to reconsider her agreement to meet with him next week."

"Jack, when you speak to the Chief Constable's secretary, could you please emphasise the time line and thus the need to get together as soon as possible before this thing gets out of control."

Emily exhorted him earnestly.

Can do!” Jack confirmed. “And I shall report back to the next meeting of this ‘committee.”

He commented jovially smiling at Andrea’s Grandmother.

So the first part of Xhoel’s plan had not gone entirely to plan and the meeting with Andrea had set in motion other outcomes than those he had envisaged. But how would this all work out when it was discussed with the police and how would his colleague, Samir, feel about the delay in implementing the plan that Xhoel himself had proposed?

Chapter Six: Visitors from Barking

First thing on Monday morning after the raid on the mafia brothel on the Sunday, two visitors arrived from London at the Clan house in the old town of Ayton. The London boss of bosses, Tristen Rexhepi, was accompanied by one of the Clan's chief auditors, Noel Shkodra. They were in the mood to ask hard questions and do hard business. Samir Pecic and the young Xhoel Gegaj had been up since the early hours digesting the results of the raid and the closure of one of their bordellos. They were wondering how they were going to explain the incident to their visitors, who would surely have learned of the raid already.

What were their losses and how could they minimise the damage to the firm accruing from the raid to their London bosses and thence to the supreme bosses in Tirana, Albania? Given the consequent reduction in remittances to Tirana, which were sure to follow this disaster, how could they credibly explain it?

This was a very serious situation and they were worried about possible lethal consequences for them both. Samir, the senior member, was deeply anxious about any traces of their off-accounts beauty parlour-cum-brothel in the town. A further worry was that the rather slapdash junior partner Xhoel might inadvertently have left some details about this free enterprise endeavour in their somewhat chaotic account books or supporting documents.

Even as they were sitting down in the lounge of the so-called 'ladies' house' with their two visitors, Tristen Rexhepi began to set out his hard line objectives for the visit. He commenced ominously but not unexpectedly with the raid and closure of the only other ladies' house formerly in the Ayton branch of the business, the only one as far as he knew apart from the one they were meeting in. There was plenty of further bad news to follow and not a few implicit threats and some explicit ones from the domineering and inscrutable boss of bosses.

"Our colleagues in Tirana, confidently appointed the two of you as a safe pair of hands and a new broom to oversee and improve activities and profits here in Ayton after the disastrous previous management had departed. On the basis of your previous progress, I myself took the hazardous step of recommending you both in recognition of your achievements in Barking in East London over the last couple of years. On sober reflection, it might not have been the wisest of steps for me to take. Maybe it was even a precipitous step too far, too soon for the both of you. But tell me."

At this point, he began to mount a vicious tirade against the two Ayton colleagues.

“I understand from sources, that one of the business’s brothels that existed at the time of your appointment and which you inherited from the previous management team, has been subject to a raid by the local police and for that reason has had to be closed. Is that correct? How did it happen with you two unaware and unable therefore to take avoidance measures and mitigate the enormous loss to the Ayton business? And what precisely are your calculations of the negative consequences in terms of workforce, stock and treasure? I believe that my bosses in Tirana will want some pretty convincing answers to those questions.”

Samir tried to respond in as composed a manner as he could muster, utterly floored by the financial interrogation. He, his junior partner and account keeper, Xhoel, had not yet considered in detail what action to take responsive to such matters. He tried his best to focus his mind. All the time conscious that, whatever he produced would be a poor best, and his life could be on the line.

“Boss, that raid took us completely by surprise as our precious pair of ears at police headquarters had been arrested only a few days earlier and charged with collaboration with us and snitching vital evidence to a criminal organisation. Various other things were also laid on him. They obviously intend throwing the book at him. So we have just begun to assess the cost to the business but not yet in gross terms. Needless to say, we have not had the time to seek a replacement."

Tristen Rexhepi interrupted him abruptly and impatiently.

"Just reply to the specific questions please, Samir. Or let your young colleague have a go, if you are unable to!"

"Yes, of course, boss. I was just setting the context. In terms of workforce, four of our locally recruited co-workers have been arrested and are in prison pending charges. There will be additional and unforeseen costs associated with the legal assistance for these men and for support for their families, either here in Britain or in Albania or Kosovo, probably for some considerable time. We have lost twenty women, including two madams, and the loss in property and equipment is incalculable. At the last count, the cost was approximately three hundred thousand pounds and counting."

He explained making a wild guess on the basis of no calculations whatsoever.

"Recurrent income and therefore remittances to London, overseas and eventually to Tirana will be substantially reduced this year. Oh and I forgot, we have lost some fifty thousand pounds in cash, one hundred thousand pounds worth of drugs and precious objects such as stamps and gems. We have not finished the exact calculations yet and those estimates include only capital losses and do not include the impact on recurrent income." He hazarded fearfully and numerically creatively with that caveat.

Tristen was swift in his very sharp return. He turned to Samir and Xhoel and with clear threat in his authoritarian and strident voice, he looked them menacingly in the face.

"Pretty disastrous then, wouldn't you say Samir? Xhoel? And all because you were totally unaware that a police raid was in the offing. As you yourself have said, you had no ears at police headquarters. You must tell me later, what steps you are taking to fill that gap soonest. Although I agree it is a little bit late, isn't it? Oh and by the way, how many brothels do you really have in total in this area?"

He broke off, and looking at Samir with cold threat in his gaze, as if he knew something that Samir hoped he didn't know, he spoke.

"I'll leave you time to formulate a response to that last one. In any case, we shall have full details once my colleague and finance officer here, Noel, has had a chance to examine the books and has calculated capital loss and likely recurrent loss up until you are able to establish a replacement brothel. He will be examining your county lines sales and profits and reconciling your drug receipts and stock with your income from those substances that you have received from East London, or in some cases directly from one of the channel ports at the behest of my colleagues in Barking."

Tristen lingered for a few seconds as if thinking of his timetable for action. "I estimate that, knowing how quickly my colleague Noel works, we should have the particulars from him later on this morning and we can then have a further meeting say at 12.00 noon to decide action. Then he and I can start the long journey back to London mid-afternoon. At least that is the timetable we are hoping to work to. In the meantime I should like to have a look around this house and to meet your other staff and some of the women. Alright?

"Yes, yes, of course. Anything you like, Tristen." Samir reacted obediently debasing himself to try to appease the big boss from London."

"By the way, I should just like to mention that when we entered this building I noticed that you had two of your four guards on the front door. Unarmed, looking rather loutish and scruffy and lolling against the door jambs at either side. They probably need some updating on standards, if you could please undertake that soonest. And if they are not already weapon-trained, get it done straight away."

Samir shot back swiftly, seeking to exculpate himself.

“Yes, they are new recruits engaged from the asylum seeker hotel in town and I accept that they are not by any means fully trained yet. But in accordance with your suggestion, we shall expedite that process and make sure that they weapon-trained.”

Tristen ignored what he regarded as a weak and fuzzy response from Samir seeking to free himself from blame for another instance in the long line of mismanagements in this mafia business in Ayton. He made other demands.

“Anyway, perhaps I could meet the rest of your staff and some of the women first. Do you have any customers in at the moment?”

“Yes and no. Yes you can meet with the other colleagues and some of the women and no we do not have any customers in at the moment. Although we did not hear about your visit until early this morning, we were able to put off the few customers that we might have at this time of day to maintain the confidentiality of your visit. In any case and for the most part, the customers tend to come in the evening or late at night. But of course there is now additional demand on this house in view of the closure of the other one and we are planning for four or five additional women in the next few days."

"Of course that additional client demand that you mention is possible, that is unless our present clients go to our rivals." Tristen observed abruptly.

Whilst his colleague and chief auditor, Noel Shkodra, was busy giving the books a detailed examination, with Xhoel in attendance in the same room, at the same time, Samir conducted his London boss, Tristen Rexhepi, around the premises. He introduced his two other locally recruited co-workers and some of the few madams that helped with the organisation and control of the prostitution side of the business and all the provisioning of the women prostitutes.

When noon arrived everyone was crowded in the small lounge for the final meeting of the day with the two visitors from London. Tristen Rexhepi called on his colleague, Noel Shkodra, to give a report based on his initial and rapid examination of the accounts and the stock cupboard. Samir and Xhoel waited in great trepidation. What was going to come next in the onslaught of this domineering old man?

"Noel could you please brief us on the outcome of your examination of the books and if possible relate those results to the state of the drugs store cupboard, if you have had time to examine it."

"Surely, Tristen. I have looked at all the results of the past few months and examined the somewhat chaotic and incomplete documentary evidence such as invoices. And I have to report, rather worryingly, that the cash earnings are well below the results achieved under the previous incompetent management. The main reason is clear, when you look at the state of the store cupboard, there is a very large accumulation of drugs received from London or from elsewhere on London's say so, that has never been marketed. Returning to the books, payments and receipts for so-called county lines activities have fallen since the arrival of the two new managers and payments to couriers have also declined, due apparently to a reduction in the number of couriers and the poor record in recruiting replacement ones."

Noel hesitated and sighed deeply as if tired with the task of listing bad news after bad news all the time.

"Payments to informers and collaborators of one kind or another have declined slightly from a very low level. According to the books there only appears to be one community collaborator at the moment, although he seems to be earning well, judged by the normal rates of payment for such services in the rest of the firm in England. One only hopes that he is worth the extra money, although to say that one has serious misgivings as he does not appear to have provided any advance notice of the raid. Another rather strange aspect to the financial figures is that while the so to speak retail level of consumption has grown in society as a whole, the wholesale has declined. That in turn raises the issue of whether some other organisation is hiving off a portion of our normal wholesale market or, heaven forbid, someone here is hiding some major sources of income."

He grimaced at the two men for a couple of seconds to let his last statement sink in.

"Only the income from the two houses, which the business owns in Ayton, have been reported. This source of income has increased very slightly and remittances from those two sources, the two brothels, had risen up to yesterday. With the closure of one of the houses in the raid yesterday, projected income is likely to be halved at least depending on the number of workers in the other house. So remittances of some million and a half from that line seen over the past year will likely be reduced to some six hundred and fifty thousand pounds over the coming fiscal period."

He halted momentarily to prepare his audience for his next point.

"But that of course is speculation, which would only occur in the absence of rapid and drastic remedial action. In brief, the picture is far from rosy and Tirana is unlikely to be happy with our financial report on the Ayton business. Finally, I have to report that I have found no record of income from brothels except from the two known to us at this moment, one of which has now been closed. I have found one or two haphazard references in the supporting correspondence to the accounts to a beauty salon, but no income."

Tristen responded swiftly and negatively to the report.

"Thank you Noel. Well a pretty damning report, which our bosses in Tirana are not going to like at all. Their reaction could be pretty damning or even worse, unless an upturn is seen straight away and evidence is advanced that the management has a plan of action to tackle the basic problems identified by Noel pretty swiftly. I just fear for your health if you do not achieve those goals. Do you have a response ready and more specifically do you have a plan of action to address these devastatingly bad results?" Samir? Xhoel?"

In fact the two men were almost struck dumb by the thoroughly damning report from Noel and the supplementary comments from the London boss of bosses, as well as the dictatorial and domineering manner in which the presentation of the demands had been made. Shuddering from the shock, Samir tried to cobble together any reply at all to placate Tristen, while Xhoel looked on dumbstruck and trembling with anticipatory fear as well and totally unable to help.

"Tristen, we have had a succession of bad luck, but Xhoel and I have already formulated a plan of action, including recruiting a new informer high up in the local police and rapidly developing the number of our couriers." His mind then seized up as he could think of no further action but fortunately at that point Xhoel seemingly came in in to assist his boss, or did he? You could never tell with Xhoel.

"We're intending to open a new ladies' house as well. We have a property in mind that would be suitable. Additionally we are in the process of recruiting additional youngsters for the county lines operation. This will, of course, reduce the over-large accumulation of drugs pretty quickly. So we are moving forwards from what our unsuccessful predecessor managers left us."

"Without wishing to be negative, it all sounds pretty airy-fairy, scrappy and *ad hoc* to me and I suspect that it will do to the bosses in Tirana. So I'll tell you now what you need to do to maintain your good health. As soon I depart this afternoon, you need to start on the preparation of a plan for a comprehensive recovery strategy for the whole business and let me have a copy soonest. The plan should be costed in detail and the steps indicated should be concrete and not imaginary pie in the sky. For that reason, I intend to lend you Noel's services for the next few days, which you will of course pay for. You are also obliged as a matter of Clan courtesy to provide him with comfortable and safe accommodation appropriate to his important status as my senior finance officer for the period of his stay here in Ayton"

There was a look of deepest alarm on the faces of Samir and Xhoel, for they knew what that meant. Noel would not only be helping with costings, he would be spying on them and reporting back to his boss in London. From this point forwards they knew that they were on probation. They would need to be very careful.

Tristen continued to tighten the screw.

"When I receive your proposals, I emphasise again I need to receive them as soon as possible, I shall then consider the plan. After any possible amendments required by me, I shall send it to our bosses in Tirana with the London office's comments and you must pray that it satisfies, nay convinces, Tirana to continue your tenure here.

He regarded his two colleagues intimidatingly for a few seconds with a perplexing sardonic smile on his face.

"Well, that is my advice and so you know what you have to do and the timescale that you have to do it in."

Now I must leave you and look forward to receiving your plan within the next day or two. Mark my words carefully, your report is a matter of great urgency for the business and even more so for your own good health. Now I must hit the road. Make sure that you look after Noel for me. Good luck and goodbye!"

And so the groundwork was set for a major upturn of the performance of the criminal gang's enterprise in Ayton at exactly the same time as the Forces of Law and Order in Ayton were aiming to put the whole mafia business out of business. What would, what could, the result of the contest be?

Chapter Seven: The Second Encounter

And there he was. As she entered the coffee house at the time agreed previously, Andrea spotted him instantly at the same table they had occupied on the previous occasion. This time he had a latte and an inviting hot chocolate already on the table in front of him. Joel, if that was really his name, smiled broadly as she entered and stood up politely as she approached him at the table and then sat down again at the same time as she did.

"Nice to see you again, Andrea, and more or less on time. I'm so pleased you could come. Have you had a busy day at college?"

"Yes, very busy. Things become ever more hectic at school as we move towards the final days of the summer term. I have to do quite a chunk of homework this evening too and, earlier in the evening, I have a meeting of the athletics club at seven o' clock. So I cannot stay for long. Just enough time to drink a nice hot chocolate and the chance to continue our exploratory conversation for a short while. Thank you, by the way, for the advance purchase of the drink. That should speed things up a bit."

After the discussion with her family and the suspicions expressed by her mother and grandparents, and with the prospect of a meeting between police officers and her family about this man at the weekend, her purpose in accepting a further *rendezvous* was to try to find out more about him. He might, after all, be a man capable of such vile crimes as those mentioned by her grandfather. As a fan of Agatha Christie's novels, that was one of her reasons for coming and she focussed on it without delay. But principally, she had to admit that she had on her mind the issue of the gang that had killed her father as well almost twenty year ago now. She recognised now that he was literally trying to take her for a ride with his fantasy about being a Ukrainian refugee newly arrived in Britain. The main question for her now was who was duping who?

"Joel, last time we met you mentioned that your kinfolk had been killed in the war and that you had fled Ukraine. Where did you and your relations live and where did they die and which university did you study sciences at in the Ukraine?"

Joel was hard pressed to reply to that question and open himself up to more detailed grilling about a country and places that he had never visited and knew little or nothing about. So he tried an evasive approach.

"Andrea, I think I spoke over much about myself and the perilous situation of my country last time. Don't let's talk about that sad place this time. I must say, it's a rather painful for me to talk about it. What about you? Have you been lucky enough to live in Ayton all your life?"

But Andrea was not going to be fobbed off by such a weak excuse and repeated the question after she had confirmed her residence in the town all her life.

"The answer to your query about my length of domicile in this toon is yes. But where did you and your close family live before you came here. And where were you studying and which sciences were you studying?"

Again, Joel was astounded by Andrea's tenacious perseverance. He was not used to dealing with such stubborn and repeated probing, particularly from a woman. He recognised that he had to respond now and rapidly conjure up some name or other to avoid revealing himself as an imposter. Bearing in mind that his overall knowledge of geography was negligible, and the only place in the Ukraine that he had ever heard of was the capital, Kyiv, where there would surely be a university and which had been subjected to Russian rocket attacks, he decided to go for it.

"The answer to both questions is the capital city, Kyiv. I've never been out of the city before. It is there at the University that I studied general science as well. Anyway look, I thought, when we've finished drinking our coffee and chocolate, we might go for a little walk by the side of the canal without, of course, delaying your return home overmuch. We can talk about each other's backgrounds as we walk along that beautiful stretch of water there. What do you think, Andrea?"

"Well I shouldn't really, Joel. As I told you I have a heavy schedule this evening. But as you are a newcomer to the town, I suppose we could spend a few minutes to walk from the lock in the city centre to the first lock after that and back. But tell me first how you know that the canal is a beautiful stretch of water. Have you perhaps spent some time there already?"

"Yes I have." He retorted lamely.

There was to be no respite for him and Andrea had another bombshell that she decided to try him with. In any case, she wanted to try to draw him out about his real background.

"By the way, have you contacted the Ayton Ukrainian Association, which is organising the registration, support and care of Ukrainian refugees newly arrived in the town? It is an old-established organisation dating from the period just after the end of the Second World War. It was established by Ukrainians, who were themselves refugees just like you, fleeing from communism at that time."

Again Xhoel found himself off-sided by the question and he did not, nay could not, go there. So he tried to dodge the likely suggestion of a visit to the Association, whilst keeping the conversation going.

"Well, no. Not yet. But thank you for that helpful suggestion. On the issue of the beautiful canal, I went exploring almost immediately the day after I arrived and the canal was one of the places I visited. I'm quite interested in nature and there is lots in the fields and woods around and on the canal. Now, if you've finished your hot chocolate, let's get going as you are very committed this evening and you have so little time to spare for a refugee in your busy life."

His comment was intended to make Andrea feel guilty about her treatment of an allegedly freshly arrived migrant and he wanted work on that, if he could. So he quickly swigged his coffee down and began to stand, pushing his chair back noisily.

But Andrea had not finished yet with this increasingly blatant fake of a man allegedly from the Ukraine, so she appeared to acquiesce and stood up regrettably leaving some of her hot chocolate in her cup.

"I know a short cut to the first lock of the canal just quite close to here. So let's start there, shall we." He proposed.

Andrea noted that he had said that he only arrived a few days ago in Ayton, so his knowledge of a short cut to the town lock seemed at the least very incongruous or even once more very dubious. But in spite of her suspicion that he was not a Ukrainian at all, she wanted to be absolutely certain. She would squeeze him for whatever further details she could, as she was very annoyed at this obvious attempt to bamboozle her for his own nefarious purposes no doubt, although she was still unclear of exactly what his intentions were. On the other hand, she was clear in her own mind of the danger of a young woman walking by the side of the canal with such a man, even though the part of the canal they would be walking along was usually fairly busy especially at this time in the late afternoon. Nevertheless, she needed to be careful.

"Ok! Let's do that, Joel. But only to the next lock up from town and back."

"Ok. Let's go! He proposed, satisfied for the moment to have got his own way.

So off they set for the town's midtown lock, which was only a short walk away. As they walked they remained in a rather embarrassed silence, except for Andrea deliberately saying hello to lots of people that they passed, whether she knew them or not. They progressed into the town centre and then up from the town lock towards the first lock outwards. People, she hoped, would remember her and the handsome young man accompanying her and he would note that she was well known in the town. When they reached the canal, she opened up another avenue for him to try his hand at. If he was really Ukrainian he would jump at the chance. If not, well what further proof was needed of his mendacity?

"Joel. It just occurred to me that we have a few students at the school, who are, or whose parents were, refugees from the Ukraine. If you like, I could try to arrange for you to meet some of them at the school in a group with a teacher present of course. That would mean that you could have a chance to speak Ukrainian to someone else. And I believe some of them are, or their parents were, from Kyiv. With your excellent knowledge of English as well, you could help them do some translation perhaps. What do you think? It would be under the supervision of one of the senior teachers of course and I would have to formally request permission first."

This lead-in seemed to her a yardstick for the accuracy of what she considered to be his fabrications about Kyiv. It was a really telling question and she waited curiously for his reaction.

But Joel was no fool and he saw the danger at once. Yet on the other hand he perceived a possible entree to the school that he had been angling for from the very beginning. It was a matter of pros and cons. But no, the danger was too great. So he camouflaged his response with a suggested delay.

"Yes, sure. Sounds like a good idea. But I'm quite busy at the moment with all the bureaucracy of signing in as a refugee at the Centre and so on. Maybe we can talk about that idea at our next meeting."

Andrea had anticipated that he would use a delaying tactic so she accepted his suggestion temporarily but with some noted interest.

"Certainly, and if I can help with the bureaucracy at all, just let me know. British bureaucracy can be a bit bewildering for foreigners and even for British people, you know. Just let me know."

She logged his lack of full compliance again, regarding it as just one further indication of his spurious claims.

"So Joel, what on earth have you been doing in the last week since I saw you, then?"

Andrea probed further, trying to keep the interrogation going, but couching it in pleasant terms of a conversational exchange as nicely as she could.

Xhoel felt that his back was more and more against the wall with her consistent series of pleasantly phrased inquiries, to which he had no convincing rejoinders and in which he appeared to see dangers to himself. He began to wonder if she was a member of one of the immigration committees or something worse. He quickly rejected the idea, thinking that her inquisitive approach to normal conversations could derive from the fact that both her grandparents were involved in local politics and she was used to this interrogative style of conversation, for which she had a certain flair. So he quickly cobbled together a halfway convincing reply and at the same time reinforced the reply he had given to her about the canal earlier.

"Well, I have been busy trying to put together the documents required for registration as an official refugee and trying to see a little of Ayton at the same time. That's how I knew of the short cut to where the town lock gates were."

Clever answer, Andrea thought. *But still not very convincing.* By this juncture she was more than ever convinced that he was an imposter, a fake! So she would mention this at the meeting between her, her mother and her grandparents on the one hand

and the police, probably CID, on the other. In the meantime, she intended to trail him along, as she wondered whether he might be a new young member of the criminal gang that had killed her father all those years ago.

By this time, walking briskly they had already reached the first lock-gates, where they had agreed they would turn round and return to the town.

"Well, here we are. That went quickly, didn't it? But I must get back now. So let's go back smartly. No sauntering. I need to go back to the café to pick up my bicycle and school books in the pannier. I just hope they will still be there!"

She wanted to convey her urgency to him and he agreed, although reluctantly, and still feeling a bit uneasy by this time with his own inability to respond satisfactorily, to what seemed to him, to be a highly focussed and well-directed quizzing.

"Well I had hoped that we might just go a little bit further. You know how beautiful it is further up the canal and we might have been able to see the swans and the cygnets."

Andrea sensed danger and immediately found the necessary words to put him off, although in a way, which would not deter him from a future meeting, if that was required, after the meeting with the police CID officers. It could be in the following week. After all, there was still much to be discovered about this handsome young imposter.

"Well maybe next time." She retorted firmly.

"But for the moment I must get back to the café, pick up my things and get home to help grandma with the evening meal or she may be worried about me. In any case, it's not fair that she has to do the cooking by herself all the time. Is it?"

"No, I suppose not." He concurred weakly.

As they turned to walk back Xhoel tried to put his arm round her waist and she pushed it away gently and politely, and very firmly. Next he tried to take her hand and she resolutely refused that too.

For a short while, he was silent and then he asked her.

"Why did you do that?"

"Do what?" She demanded irritably.

"Push my arm away from your waist and even refuse my hand?"

"Well I considered both those attempts to be precipitate, given that we have only met each other briefly on two previous occasions. In other words, your actions were, in my opinion, too forward for circumstances in this country. I don't know about your country. Perhaps later when we have got to know each other better it may happen but not on the second brief occasion of meeting. Understand? Happy?"

"Oh, OK. Just so as I know." He responded as humbly and remorsefully as he could.

By this time with many intervals of silence they had reached the inner city of the town and were on their way back towards the cafe, when he made a further request.

"May I walk you home?"

"No I would prefer not as it is not very far." She responded adamantly. "But if you behave yourself, I may invite you over to meet my kin sometime in the future. In the meantime, I think I would like to meet you again and get to know you a little better. I suggest we meet a week today, same time, same place and this time the drinks will be on me."

By this time, they had reached the café bike park and she was checking her things ready to start cycling home, when he tried to give her a farewell peck on the cheek but she turned her face away and said.

"Too soon again! Well I shall say *au revoir* to you until next week."

With that short farewell salutation, she turned and began to cycle away rapidly as he called after her

Bye, see you next week, Andrea. Same day, same time; same place.

When she arrived back home, over dinner she narrated the events of her second meeting with the alleged Ukrainian man calling himself Joel and claiming to be a refugee. She itemised the more or less evasive replies he gave to practically all her questions.

“With the apparent falsehoods that he seems to manufacture to each succeeding question that I put to him, I became more and more suspicious. Now I am convinced that he is not Ukrainian at all, though exactly what he is, is not yet clear. Indisputably a phoney refugee!”

“I think it could be help in our discussions this weekend with the police, if you could just briefly jot down whatever you can remember of your questions, his responses and what you think about them to help to illustrate the nature of this bogus Ukrainian refugee.” Emily suggested and Andrea agreed with her Grandma’s suggestions in spite of all the other college work she had to accomplish.

Her mother agreed and added some sensible advice.

"Yes and if you meet him again, you must be very careful. He could be very dangerous. But I think Granny's idea of an overview of the issues you raised and his responses could be very informative especially for the police, when we meet up with them."

Her grandfather, Jack, added a contribution to the strategy, which was beginning to emerge for their meeting with the police at the coming weekend. He issued a sincere and loving warning to her to be extra-cautious at all times and in all places.

"Joel sounds like an Albanian name to me. If so, he could really be one of the mafia criminal gang active in Ayton. I advise great caution and no trips to any out of the way places or anywhere in fact off the beaten track. Keep in populated areas and do not accept a vehicle ride with him anywhere and at any time whatsoever. Every time you are with him you are putting yourself in great danger. Take heed. I beg you my love!"

So all of them were of one mind that they should share all this information with the police and CID at their meeting probably at the coming weekend and see what the reaction and advice of the police was. On the basis of that, a family decision would be made about how to continue, if at all.

So Xhoel's plan was about to be used against him. But could Andrea gain any further useful information and would the police suggest continuing the association or not?

Chapter Eight: Police Headquarters

As they walked together through the town to police headquarters on that quiet Sunday morning, there was a certain sense of fearful excitement shared by all members of the family and perhaps, especially, by Andrea. They knew what the meeting was about. They hoped it would throw some light on the strange man, whom Andrea had encountered seemingly quite accidentally on her bicycle outside her college at the close of a college day. They did not know what to expect in terms of information, advice or other outcomes. Yet they felt that somehow, they had entered a new phase in their normally so close, almost humdrum, lives.

On arrival at the central police station, situated in the old nineteenth century neo-gothic town hall building, they were clearly expected. At reception, one of the two clerks made himself immediately available and led them to the rather large and official-looking office of the Chief Constable, Horace Lashley. There they found four other people that the Chief of Police courteously introduced them to, after first welcoming them to his office in the police headquarters in Ayton.

"A warm welcome to you all. Please do sit down around the coffee table and make yourselves at home. Coffee, tea? Anyone? Help yourselves to biscuits."

They all politely refused as it was not very long since their ample and leisurely Sunday morning cooked brunch.

“Well in that case let’s get started. This is the chief of the local CID (Criminal Investigation Department), Felix Brigstowe,”

He pointed to a middle-aged, distinguished-looking man, clean shaven, smartly dressed and in civilian clothing.

“At his side is Detective Inspector Maria Clarke, his assistant and specifically in charge of a major investigation into a lucrative drug and prostitution set-up, organised and run by a major transnational crime syndicate in this city. Further details of that later. Next to her is Sergeant David Berger. He is the beat officer in the area of your house. Through him, you will be able to contact us at any time, night or day. He will share the details of how that works later in our meeting.”

Both the preceding officers were in uniform, as was the Chief Constable, Horace Lashley.

“As you probably already know, I’m Horace Lashley, Chief Constable of the local Ayton Police Force. All right thus far?”

He smiled and halted briefly in case of any initial questions. Receiving none from any member of the family, he continued.

"I thought in this initial meeting, the first of a number maybe, we could begin by hearing from Andrea concerning the charming pretender, whom she has encountered and who alleges to be a Ukrainian refugee and asylum seeker. Then Maria will fill you in, in confidence, about the reason why we are so interested in this man, allegedly called Joel. Finally, David will detail how you can contact us at any time, including at a time of emergency for advice or assistance. Before you leave this morning and if we are agreed, there will be a plan of how to proceed and the contribution of all sides to your safety, Andrea, and that of your close relatives. Would that seem like a logical and helpful way of proceeding?"

All four members nodded their heads and consented to the plan for the meeting and expressed it confidently and succinctly.

"Agreed. Yes, sounds a very sensible way to proceed." Emily endorsed the proposal.

"Then it's over to you, Andrea. If you could briefly fill us in on your meetings with this mysterious young man on a bicycle. Sounds almost like the beginning of an Agatha Christie novel, don't you think, Andrea?"

Andrea wondered how he knew about her enthusiasm for that particular author. She dismissed the matter and proceeded to describe the first and subsequent encounter with the man. She outlined the evasive and obviously bogus statements that he had made posing as a Ukrainian asylum seeker and refugee, who had recently arrived in the UK, and more specifically in Ayton.

She gave the Chief Constable a copy of the questions that she had posed and the clearly doubtful responsive information he had furnished. She explained why she thought that the answers were fabricated. As she was handing over the hand-written paper, she emphasised what she genuinely believed, namely that the notes had been based on her memory of the two meetings and it was of the nature of human recollection, that the recollection would be imperfect.

"Of course, I cannot guarantee that every question and response is exactly as it happened in every way and correct in every detail. The memory of all of us being what it is, frail and faulty, there may be some minor errors. But the general feel of the meetings with him and the manifest dubious nature of so many of his replies has not been deliberately exaggerated in the paper. On that I have done my best to be accurate."

The Chief Constable responded graciously.

“Thank you very much for that Andrea, for all that information and for the account of the questions and responsive details from this man during your meetings with him, that you have drawn up. Warm thanks to you for the precious time you have given to this task in what I understand from your Grandfather is a very busy time of your young life.“

He nodded towards her and smiled broadly at her and she immediately realised from where he had obtained the particulars about her reading choices. Her Granddad!

“Well, next I think we should hear from Detective Inspector Maria Clarke, Maria to us all. Maria over to you.”

“Thank you sir. Our interest in this man Joel, is derived from our belief, that his real name is Xhoel Gegaj. He’s believed to be an Albanian mobster, who, together with the other major figures of a nationwide criminal gang, is a key focus of a nationwide investigation into the activities of an Albanian mafia clan in Britain and particularly, as far as we are concerned, in this town. Not without challenges from other mobs to its hegemony, the Albanian mafia would appear to be a dominant force, maybe even **the** dominant force, in the fields of drugs, prostitution, arms and people smuggling in the UK. Whitehall is determined to crush this international criminal syndicate at least in the United Kingdom. Although, we are working with the cooperation of Interpol and Europol, and through their offices with other countries, which are likewise involved in the pursuit of this criminal syndicate, which in some cases they undoubtedly are. Some of these mafia-like syndicates are transnational and there is especially one in this town, which is of particular interest to us and which we believe this man Xhoel Gegaj manages. We think he actually is one of the managers or leads it. Our task here is to take down that dominant local mafia gang and to end its criminal activities in Ayton and the surrounding area. The gang is currently headed here in Ayton the two gangsters, Samir Pecic, who is the bellwether of the gang, and the much younger Xhoel Gegaj, who is the man we think you have encountered, Andrea. They also have a number of assistants recruited almost exclusively from the small Albanian satellite community in the UK or from the ranks of young asylum seekers from Albania presently resident in asylum seeker hotels, including the one here in Ayton. They are directed and coordinated from Barking in East London by the boss man in the UK, who is called Tristen Rexhepi. He in turn is responsible to his bosses in Tirana, Albania. Sorry it's so complex. Any queries so far?"

Emily was curious about the apparent involvement of her granddaughter, Andrea in tis massively complex international criminal set-up.

"So why, in all that complexity of organisations, tasks and personalities, some of which are international, as you put it, do you think that, put bluntly, this man is busy making up to my granddaughter?"

Maria gave a very clear but somewhat chilling analysis responsive to Emily's point.

"Well, there are at least two possible reasons. Firstly this man is hoping to recruit your granddaughter as a courier or prostitute. Just a short while ago they already had over sixty women in two houses in town that we know about. But they are always on the look-out for more! Of course there may be other reasons as well. So, secondly, and more likely, they see her as an entrée to recruit more youngsters as couriers from amongst the students at her college for their county lines, drug trafficking set up. I would personally go for the second, whilst not ruling out the first, once she has been hooked on their drugs. In that respect, Andrea, be very careful not to accept any treats or drinks from this man and watch over your drink very carefully if you are in a café with him."

"So, what do you expect of my granddaughter then?" Emily appealed rather pointedly.

"Well, I'd prefer to leave that to the conclusion of our discussion, if you don't mind. But always on the understanding that you are here voluntarily and it is your choice to continue attendance here today or not. Clearly, the choice is yours not ours. In any case, we are extremely grateful for your assistance so far in coming here today. Andrea's experience has given us a seminal lead, which we did not have before."

Sensing that there were no more questions for Maria at the moment, the Chief Constable made an effort to advance the meeting.

"Given that there are apparently no more questions for Maria at the moment, I'm going to invite the chief of the local CID, Felix Brigstowe, to share with us whatever he can safely do about the overall investigation. Although, he's here in an observer capacity. Felix, it's over to you"

"Thank you very much Chief Constable Lashley. I should like to begin by endorsing your thanks to Andrea and the members of her family, who are present here today for this very important get-together. Firstly, I must emphasise what the Chief Constable has already said about how important it is that we all respect the confidentiality of anything that is said in this gathering today. The international criminal syndicate that is at the heart of our discussions today has antennae all over the world and of course throughout the organisation here in Ayton and the surrounding region. It specialises in outguessing law enforcement agencies across the globe. It's organised as a kind of international business corporation with headquarters in Tirana, Albania. These criminal enterprises achieve their goal of untouchability on the basis of advance information or intelligence about our intentions and plans for their future, as we would call it. It's fed to the gang bosses by planted informants or collaborators in business, the legal and law enforcement organisations and some social groupings. For example, they have collaborators in the legal ranks of legitimate Law firms, police forces and corrupt local politics, about which, for the moment, and for the purposes of our discussions today, I shall remain silent."

At that point he smiled knowingly and looked at his small audience to see if anyone had any comments.

"Like all successful business corporations, the criminal cartel that is the focus of our attention here at the moment is highly adaptive. Gone are the days of the iconic leaders of the past. Instead, you have much more nimble corporation-like structures concentrating on doing their illicit business in our town. Sometimes several criminal cartels will form a network for production, supply and distribution in a cooperative deal and, at the conclusion of that phase of the business, they disband the network. As with the businesses that they seek to mimic, staff, who do not perform are got rid of, sometimes by drastic means. That penchant for violence underlies their business approach too, if they consider it necessary, or it helps them to achieve their objectives. Any questions so far from anyone?"

There was a stunned silence from all present, expressive of their amazement at the almost unbelievable extent and complexity of his revelations. He had even more to tell.

"As far as the UK is concerned, the major Albanian cartel under investigation is more or less dominant in the illegal importation and sale of drugs. But it is similarly involved in people trafficking and prostitution, sometimes in co-operation with the Kurdish or Italian mobs, sometimes in competition or even violent conflict with them. Nationally, the mobs make millions here from drugs and prostitution. So they also undertake the subsequent money laundering for the cleansing of the earnings and their use in legal investment vehicles, such as sovereign bond issues, many here in London. This is sometimes dubbed the international dirty money launderette."

"Any questions yet? If not, I'll proceed.

"So this crime organisation is international with interests and influence in all four continents. Its interests spread from Lebanon in the east to Buenos Aires in the west, taking in most countries of Western Europe. The mafia bosses in Tirana,

Albania, direct and have overall control of it. The various national subunits, like the one in the UK, are controlled through an all-powerful boss of bosses, call it a company director, in each country including in this country. The supremo in the UK is based in Barking, East London. He currently goes by the name of Tristen Rexhepi. He's actually the lieutenant of his bosses, the mafia top brass in Europe and especially in Tirana. He was seen down here in Ayton only a few days ago because of the perceived poor performance of the Ayton office. We understand that the two local bosses have been placed on notice to improve otherwise there will be trouble. The implementation of the nefarious business is delegated from the supremo further to the regional or city level, such as here in Ayton. The two men responsible here in Ayton, and the surrounding counties, through a system called county lines, are, as I have said Samir Pecic and the much younger Xhoel Gegaj. The latter is the man we believe has waylaid Andrea outside her college and is making efforts to achieve a foothold in the local secondary school cum college to recruit youngsters for the trading of drugs or as recruitment of young girls for prostitution after being hooked on the mob's free drugs. I think I have spoken long enough to give you an overview of the vile enormity and insidious spread of this organisation that we are discussing here today. Hopefully, you should now understand the size and threat of its international links here in the UK, nationally and locally, especially to vulnerable young people."

"Thank you Director." The Chief Constable offered his thanks on behalf of all present. "A very helpful overview. Next we shall hear from police Sergeant David Berger, who as I said a moment ago, is the beat officer for the district where your home is situated. His district includes the school, or college should I say, which Andrea presently attends."

"Thank you Chief Constable Lashley. My function in the scheme of things and that of my colleagues, Sergeant Frank Balbinski and Constable Lucy Wainwright, is to ensure your safety, Andrea, particularly if you agree to continue with the work you have started. The choice is of course yours, and yours alone."

"Thank you Sergeant." The Chief Constable said.

"We now want to share with you all, what we are proposing as our further cooperation. At all times, you have the option not to participate further if you so wish. We should like you to continue further with your meetings with this man Xhoel. Be very circumspect in the relationship. Do not go into lonely places with him or to residences other than your college and your own home. If you find him getting over-familiar or aggressive, cease the contact immediately and let us know. Try to get him to allow you to take a photograph of you and him side-by-side and pass the result to Sergeant Berger. We undertake to delete you from the photograph before we use it. On the next occasion when you meet him, we should like you to wear a wire and record what he says. Under no circumstances accept a drink or food from him and of course never accept a manifest drug from him let alone consume one. Try to get him to talk about his work and colleagues, if you can without alarming him. We need to know where the main premises of this gang are in the town, for example. Let us know when you are meeting him and where. After the meeting, we shall arrange a further debrief here at police HQ. That is what we are proposing. What do you think?"

Andrea was the first one to respond.

"Chief Constable Lashley, thank you for inviting us here today and for briefing us so frankly albeit in confidence on the on-going investigation of this criminal mafia clan internationally and locally here in Ayton. I have listened very carefully to the scenario of international, national and local criminal activity that you have described and my own intrusion into that world by dint of my chance encounter with this man called Joel. Or was it chance? I now understand more clearly and fully why he deliberately met me outside the school and what his and his organisation's intentions were. I understand that you are inviting me to assist in draining more information from him about his aims, the locations and the projected plans of his organisation. In response to your question, I should like to discuss your proposal with my family, not least because of the element of danger involved for them as well as for me."

Emily spoke instinctively and supportively.

"Well, I think that your suggestion for us all to discuss it amongst ourselves at home is very wise. But as a courtesy we should offer the Chief Constable a day and date by which time we will let him know our position on the issue."

Her mother, Izzy, keenly supported Andrea's suggestion too.

"With the addition of Emily's point about giving the Chief Constable a date by which he could expect a response, I agree."

Jack came in last and accepted the suggestion with Emily's appendix about a deadline date by which a decision could be given.

"I agree with what has been proposed so far, but I should like to hear more about the security precautions for my granddaughter either from you, Horace, or from the Sergeant. Not least because it's my understanding that our granddaughter, Andrea, has arranged to meet this man after college on Tuesday of this coming week. Will she be covered for that encounter?"

Sergeant Berger replied to what had been implicitly requested by Jack's question and then explained the protection arrangements.

"The answer to your question, sir, is yes. Definitely that meeting will be covered and we can take your statement today as an official notification for our action."

He then turned to the Chief Constable.

"With your permission, sir, perhaps I could explain to the family how the protection would work. You let us know when and where you will be meeting this man, and we will put an inconspicuous tail on you both for as long as you are together. Advance notice would be welcome, but in an emergency, if you ring the emergency number on this card we shall do our very best to comply. Always carry your mobile with you all the time."

He held up a business card with a confidential police number on it and then distributed a card to each one of them.

"Please keep this handy at all times and feel free to contact me immediately, if an emergency should arise day or night or you believe that you are in danger. I should add that we will institute permanent surveillance of your house, most probably in the form of two detectives in a car opposite your front door."

The Sergeant subsequently reiterated his initial point in an encouraging way. "Do not hesitate for one moment if danger arises. Act straightaway! Contact us on the number on the card and we shall be at your side soonest. Any questions?"

There were no further issues raised and at that point the Chief Constable, perceiving that the meeting had run its course and achieved its initial purpose, drew the meeting to a close, saying:

"Thank you everyone for your participation today. We shall wait for Andrea and her relatives to respond before calling a further meeting. Again, very many thanks for coming today. There has been a very useful exchange of views, from which I believe we have all learned a great deal. I am sure we shall meet again and I wish you all a pleasant evening. Take care."

Thus the first steps had been planned for an important source of information about the entity, which was the object of the major police action in Ayton at this time. But could Andrea succeed, given that the particulars gleaned so far were mostly bogus and told the police nothing about the plans of the local crime syndicate.

Chapter Nine: London Takes Over

It was mid-morning when he suddenly appeared at the large Edwardian house on the fringe of the town centre, which was used as a sort of central office and lodging place for the gang's official visitors by the Albanian criminal confraternity in Ayton. Tristen Rexhepi, the chillingly driven and tyrannical London UK supremo of the Albanian crime syndicate in Britain, appeared as a total and wholly unwelcome surprise to his colleague subordinates in Ayton, Samir Pecic and Xhoel Gegaj. They were all the more taken aback, because normally he contacted them in advance, or at least one of his minions in the Capital contacted them for him. This time he had just turned up.

Their shock and horror was amplified even more when Noel Shkodra, his financial and business 'wizard' followed him into the room at a respectful distance. The two visitors were both shown by one of the guards from the front entrance to the small office. The office was used by the gang's senior members for collecting and collating the cash from clients at the brothels and in part to store the cash from the county lines sales. In particular, it was used for preparing the cash for transmission abroad or for use for the running costs of the gang's enterprises in Ayton. These running costs included, in addition to such normal expenses as food and lighting and heating, the bribery of senior figures in the social and political life of the town.

The office was a central administrative and commercial hub and it was there that the preparation of the cash, earned locally, took place for transmission of the money directly or vicariously by intricate and diverse methods and pathways to the bosses in Europe, Albania and in some cases via Chinese handlers to North and South America, and the Gulf. Once even partly laundered, some of the cash would be reintroduced into markets far and wide as clean money, usually through the so-called monetarist laundromat of London.

"Good morning gentlemen. Noel tells me that you are not making a great deal of headway in putting the business here in Ayton back on track and into a healthy profit. I know that Tirana is pressing for this business to move more swiftly into profit, a healthy profit mind you. They are profoundly disquieted by the seizure and closure of one our most lucrative brothels in this region. So they and I were wondering what planning has gone into tackling the avoidance of similar problems in the future. Additionally, they wish to know whether you're planning to replace the women's house, which was raided, with another equally money-making house elsewhere. If so they want to know where, when and how much will it cost their business? For all these reasons, and in spite of my extremely busy schedule in London and abroad, your patch is so important to the bosses that I have come down here to try to help you to put these matters in order."

Tristen declaimed his oration in a very cool, calm, unemotional and business-like fashion but in an authoritarian and menacing manner as well. He continued tersely.

"Now, down to business! Firstly, tell me what the situation of your planning for a second women's house is after the closure of the first one; what plans you have to protect or move the second house; and what you have done to make up the immediate deficit in stock and recurrent income from the closure of the first house. Do you need to import some new stock, for example? Or do you need some more of our friends in the small local Albanian communities or from the local asylum seeker hotel to replace those guards and other men you lost in the raid. Where are you going to get the money from for those initiatives? You could co-operate with one of the Kurdish or Italian gangs, but if you shake hands with them on a deal, take heed and look at your fingers afterwards."

He gave a harsh laugh and pressed on.

"We have had experience of such co-operations elsewhere in the country, where the resulting income is shared and though I say so myself they were relatively successful, provided that you let the other party know who the boss was and what the consequences of default were. Secondly tell me what efforts you have made to increase the number of couriers for the powder cocaine and crack trades, which seem to be diminishing over time, though numbers of addicts is escalating every year to something over a quarter of million in the UK, I estimate. What steps have you taken to reduce the vulnerability of Clan premises and stock by moving to safer havens? The massive store of drugs you have in this building are in Noel's view, are susceptible to another raid where they are currently located. In addition I should be interested to learn how many informants you have acquired in the local police force, the business community and political parties since I last visited you. Take your time. No rush at this moment!"

Samir was outraged but also dumbfounded at the accusations of this 'odious little man'. In fact he was totally lost for words by the long list and its threatening mode of presentation by his domineering boss from London. He was flabbergasted at the detailed knowledge of the failings of the Ayton business and the caustic manner in which they had been presented. He immediately began to focus on who was likely to have been the snitch that had revealed such detail rather than trying to stitch together a suitable response. He could think of only one name, Xhoel, his insufferably disloyal snitch. Wrong move!

Similarly he recalled that in the previous meeting he had already found himself on the back foot with regard to the performance of the business but with the added worry about where the source of the detailed information had been. Even if it was Noel, it had to have come originally from Xhoel, his ever-treacherous assistant. Whoever it was they would pay the price for their treachery. But later! For the moment the biggest issue was how to deal with this monster threat and get him off their backs and back to London as soon as possible.

Samir squirmed and quaked and he was stunned into an embarrassing silence. Only after a couple of minutes was Samir able to face up to the fact that he had to say something and bit by bit his brain slowly began to create some kind of hesitant reaction. Nonetheless he tried to speak with a confident voice.

"We already have a further collaborator in the police department here, an Assistant Chief Constable called Tony Wozny and our collaborator in the business sector, Jack Burnley Crowder is urgently searching for further suitable collaborators in that sector and in the political and business sectors too. We are making plans at this very moment to move the second house to a safer location in one of our properties on the outskirts of town. Xhoel is already engaged in arranging for a young woman to help us recruit further youngsters from the local college and primary school for the county lines work and we should be pleased to consider whatever additional measures you yourself might propose besides."

Tristen riposted curtly and cold as an iceberg.

"Tell me about your plans and the timeline for their implementation."

"Well the engagement to penetrate the school is already well underway and Xhoel will tell us more about that in a minute. In addition to that we have plans to move the house tomorrow and we have already identified a senior police officer to approach and that is scheduled for tomorrow as well. Xhoel, can you bring us up to date with the progress on penetrating the college? Then I will fill Tristen in on the house move. "

"Not good enough! Too much delay, indefinite and inadequate planning for action to have an impact on the cash flow of this business quickly enough to satisfy our bosses in Tirana. I am not trying to take you for a ride, but you two could lose your heads on this if you do not improve the financial performance and economic situation of this business quickly. Tirana wants urgent action now, not tomorrow, to prevent further disasters that we cannot manage and the further draining away of so much cash."

Samir squirmed and finally muttered a formulation of obedient surrender.

"Xhoel and I will accept whatever plans you think we should implement. We shall work through the night if necessary."

"Good! So immediately after we finish this session today, I want you to begin the move of all personnel, furniture, cash, drugs and equipment from the women's house. Needless to say that includes any cash or other valuables, such as stamps or precious stones. To avoid awakening any suspicion all the work for the move must be done in the darkness of night, inconspicuously and quietly. Arrange for the whole exercise to be completed well before dawn. If you have them available, leave a couple of surprises in the house for the intruders, after the last person leaves. Keep them on their toes!"

"I'll get the lads on with that straightaway." He agreed obediently.

"We need to respond to this attack on our business or we shall lose face with the other gangs. That could become another disaster if they begin to understand that we are weak. So first thing tomorrow morning you should put out a contract on the Chief of Police. You could get one of your boys to do it, I could bring in someone from the Capital or you could put it out to contract, although

I would stress that whichever one you choose, it is going to cost you money, big money, that you presently do not have. But do it quietly and make sure it cannot be traced back to us. If it is, on your head be it and you know what that means."

He enunciated his words carefully and once again mounted a menacing glare at his two subordinates, who were literally horror struck by this time at his words and the accompanying facial expressions. But there was more to come.

"Yes, you could have access to one of my boys in London or to the Kurdish lads, who are quite expert at this sort of thing. Both would cost you dearly in cash you do not have, although that might be the safest path, but it would cost you mightily for either. Anyway, that action alone should make our opponents pause, as I say, so that we can have the time to reorganise our assets and strengthen our protection of the business's assets and get the business back into profit."

"Consider it done, boss." Samir answered pathetically and Xhoel nodded his head in total agreement but interjected.

"Excuse my asking. But don't you think, my friend, that chopping the Chief Constable could cause a furore, which could result in even more vigorous pursuit of us and impede our activities further? And at this delicate stage, do we really want to get entangled with that incompetent Kurdish mob?"

Tristen metaphorically went for Xhoel's throat and responded adamantly and dismissively.

"No. From previous experience over a long period of time in many different countries, I am fully convinced that taking out the top man will make them pause maybe even halt permanently their persecution of our business and furthermore it is required by Tirana because of the financial loss that this man has caused us already. It will thus be a kind of repayment for the damage this Police Chief has already caused us. Under the Kanun it would be considered as an eye for an eye. On the matter of the person, who you chose to carry out the job, let me say that whether you use the Kurds, or not, it is entirely up to you, as are the consequences of your decision. The Kurds have shown themselves very astute in becoming the dominant group in the cross channel asylum seeker trade. But the decision is yours. Let me remind you, however, that your position is presently excessively precarious."

Tristen continued sneeringly.

"But take heed. If you don't have the stomach for this decision, you may leave the business forthwith. Of course there would be consequences for you both in that direction too."

He then turned swiftly to the rest of his agenda.

"Then during the morning, call in your contact in the business sector that you mentioned earlier, so that we can all have a word with him and tell him what we expect him to do for the substantial sum of money that he is regularly receiving from us. He needs to know that he is at our beck and call and not we at his."

"Agreed." Xhoel interjected and in a face-saving effort he added, "A good idea. I was thinking of doing that this week. We have honestly been much too lax with Jack so far."

Tristen passed over Xhoel's comment in a distinctly aloof manner and pressed on.

"Later in the morning I want you to bring in the police collaborator that you mentioned. I need to meet him soon. I also want Xhoel to speed up his contact with this young school contact woman. If you need to, threaten her that we are tired of waiting for a further batch of couriers for the county lines work. If that does not succeed, tell her that she will be abducted and put to work for her keep in the house with the other women. In the afternoon we shall meet up again to appraise the progress we have made."

“Where shall Xhoel and I meet you this afternoon? And what time is convenient for you?”

A dejected Samir solicited the specifics dolefully.

“Well not here definitely!” Was the curt response. “This place will already be known to the sharp-eyed officers in the local police. No. I shall be moving upmarket to one of the clan’s new houses on the other side of the Portway, near but not too near to the place that I recommend you should move the women’s house to in the newer suburbs. I’ll leave you two to organise that for me. Oh and I shall be taking my colleague Noel with me. So make sure it is comfortable and well stocked with the necessities. I do not like camping and neither does he.”

Finally, let’s help some of our couriers to earn a little extra. Get your boys to offer them fifty pounds to draw in a friend to the county lines work. Additionally there is local authority provision for children in care, separated from their families and housed in this town, where a more rapid access to additional couriers could be achieved quickly and efficiently as well. That is a strategy we have used successfully in our other businesses in the UK because so many local authorities are messing up child care placements by posting some of those youngsters, supposedly in care, miles away from their habitual homes, friends and relations. Maybe you already have some youngsters from the hostel here and, if so, what are you doing about using them to get more?"

Samir responded to these recommendations briefly and weakly.

"No, we have not used that method so far. But it seems to me to make good sense and I shall get a couple of my boys on with it quickly, today in fact."

Tristen then turned to his own personal requirements and those of Noel, his financial and business assistant and adviser.

"Well you have quite an arsenal of jobs to tackle today, so I had better leave you to get on with them. Get one of your boys to help me move my things and Noel to move his, both to the same best property on the outskirts of town and away from any of the rest of you or your remaining brothel."

"Tomorrow morning I want a report, which tells me that you have moved the house. With its large store of powder cocaine, opiates and crack cocaine because of the inadequacy of your county lines set-up and the size of its business, it would be a prime target for the coppers. It and this office need to be moved like yesterday.

Noel gave a sycophantic nod of his head to confirm his agreement as Samir made a totally unsuccessful attempt to quieten the situation.

"Surely! It shall be done."

Xhoel intervened likewise and sought once again to curry favour with the big boss from London.

"I could help you out with that, if you wish, Tristen."

"No! You need to work with Samir on the many changes that are required in the business in a short period of time. Just make sure that I have one of your boys and the transport needed for my change to more suitable and safer accommodation. You never know how long Noel and I will have to stay. The outlook here is not very propitious at the moment."

Samir supported that rejection and Tristen's request for assistance with a staccato expression of agreement.

"Both items agreed and done."

"Well you two had better move on now and start on with all those little jobs you have agreed to. I'll wait here for your removals man to come … soon mind you. And by tomorrow you can report back on all your achievements."

With that heavily laden salutation, the meeting ended and Samir and Xhoel departed ditheringly afraid and thoroughly down-hearted for their night of hard work and their dubious future careers.

But the planned counter-attack to local police actions had been formulated and agreed for early action.

Chapter Ten: An Emergency Meeting

"I have called this extraordinary meeting of the planning group because, for a change, I have something very positive to share with you. I'm delighted to be able to be able to inform you that the department responsible for public prosecutions has worked swiftly and has today agreed to formal charges being levied against all four men arrested in the raid on the mafia brothel last week. This is a great step forward in our fight to crush the criminal gangs, who are plaguing our town at the moment. Of course, the men remain innocent of the charges until proven guilty in a court of Law. So it is a welcome beginning not an end."

With a beaming smile on his face Chief Constable Horace Lashley was clearly elated, when he addressed the second meeting of the planning group. It had been assembled urgently to review a previous raid and to consider plans for further action against the major Albanian criminal syndicate based in Ayton, which was selling and plying drugs and prostitution in the city and spreading well beyond. He mentioned that seen nationally this criminal syndicate was beginning to co-operate more collegially in trading with other criminal gangs and this was happening in Ayton and its environs as well. On top of that they are becoming more and more involved in gun running and use in inter-faction disputes. This shows, he argued, that even groups like the powerful Albanian criminal syndicate are working in close cooperation with groups like Italy's dominant 'Ndrangheta mafia clan, which controls much of Europe's cocaine trade. The effect of this new mood of co-operation appears to be an increase in the supply of drugs on the market. It is thus helping to keep prices down nationally and locally and contributing in turn to increasing usage.

"Just casting a glance for a moment back from the drugs side to the prostitution business, in fact it is beginning to look like the CPS is intending to throw the book at all four men. All are now facing charges of conspiracy to arrange or facilitate people trafficking and to control prostitution for gain. They all face further charges with regards to trading in illegal drugs and weapons. Two of them face additional charges of sexual activity with a minor. Without revealing any details, I should pay tribute to the very brave women, who have agreed to give testimony in some of these cases. Needless to say they are in safe police protection at separate secret hiding places. I understand that the Prosecution Service Witness Support Unit will be contacting them soonest to offer whatever support is needed. This success of ours is now in the hands of the staff of the appropriate prosecution service. But additionally and at this stage I should like to recognise and compliment all of you, who in one way or another have contributed to the successful outcome of our work so far. It is a good beginning!"

The chief of the local CID (criminal investigation department), Felix Brigstowe added more cautiously.

"Of course as the Chief Constable implies this is only the very beginning, the charges stage, and the whole process has to go through a number of stages before a potential conviction. It has to go firstly to the Magistrate's Court and if approved, it will be sent to the Crown Court for example. It will take time, but at least here in Ayton we have given the process an initial impetus. But do remember, as the Chief Constable has already stated, that under English Law all the men are of course considered to be innocent until proven guilty."

Detective Inspector Maria Clarke, in charge of a major investigation into drugs and prostitution, such as was organised by the major Albanian crime syndicate in Ayton and the surrounding region, added a sobering rider.

"Yes, I do endorse what the Head of CID has said. It's important to remember that this is just the very first step in a long process that we have embarked on. This is just one of the many hundreds of such criminal syndicates, active in the UK and the several in business locally in Ayton. But I agree it is a beginning. It will take many moons, however, before we can see the completion of that road with some real satisfaction at having completed the job. In the meantime, there will be very many setbacks and disappointments. One of them has just occurred. The planned raid on another of the mobs' brothels has been delayed. Somehow the mob guessed or was informed that we would follow up the first raid with a second one. As a consequence in the dead of night they moved their entire red door exercise to another location as yet unknown to us."

The Chief Constable inserted a footnote in amplification.

"From inside information, other actions by the group tells us that as a result of the first raid and the consequent reduction in income, the top man in London, Tristen Rexhepi, has come down to crack the whip and sort out the business here in Ayton. That doubtless happened at the behest of the mobster chiefs in Albania. This man and probably more so, the main bosses here in Ayton, have probably been placed on probation to boost their game. It is sheer speculation on my part, but I do not believe that he wants to stay long. He has lost a couple of his top men to the Calais group, where there are very lucrative cross-channel illegal migrant runs, but most recently very violent on-going knife and gun fights with the Kurdish mob too. As a consequence of Albanian success there is an ominous increase in the cross-channel migration of young Albanian men, some of whom will be presumably engaged by cognate ethnic gangster groups here, often as forced labour on indoor drug farms. So I would guess that the supremo would like to finish the job here and get back to his own patch as swiftly as possible. That may cause him to overreach himself as he has done once already with the issuing of a contract on the Police Chief's life. By the way, that reminds me, Sergeant Berger, what further developments do we have in the saga of Andrea and her so-called suitor, Joel?"

He smiled broadly at his own quip and added.

"They did say they would confirm with us their decision as to whether Andrea felt able to pursue the further contact with that man, Xhoel, and keep us informed."

Police Sergeant David Berger's reply was brief and in a sense negative but nonetheless intended to be reassuring.

"Well, none is the succinct answer. There has been no further contact with or from Andrea since the last meeting, when she first alerted us to the subterfuge this guy was trying on. But that was only a couple of days ago. She is not due to meet this man again until next week, when we have arranged to commence backup protection to monitor her safety. Andrea has, however, as agreed at our meeting with her and her family, communicated the unanimity of herself and her kinfolk to the effect that she should continue the surveillance of this man called Joel by meeting him occasionally and reporting back to us. In the meantime, we have put a tap on both her phones, although it would appear that the man is using burner phones all the time. But no further approach. That track appears to have gone cold for the moment, possibly because the group has been preoccupied with responding to, no doubt, numerous demands for reforms from the big boss in London, who is now active here in Ayton."

"Thank you Sergeant Berger for that report. I think that covers everything that has happened since our previous meeting and we can now turn to our next moves."

He then addressed DI Felix Brigstowe.

"DI Brigstowe, do you know what advance we have made in tracing the new location of the second brothel and the new main headquarters office of this criminal fraternity?"

"Not quite but nearly. I believe that we have located the district where both establishments are located. It's only a matter of time and resources before we find the exact address by tapping users of the brothel facility for that information as they come and go. We know that a central office has been set up for the man from London and for meetings with the gang members, as also for lodging their stocks of drugs and cash from local activities. We're close to identifying the exact location of that one too. The location of the latter premises is a more difficult task because it is exclusively ethnic Albanian members of the gang, who are permitted to come and go and they are all part of an omerta-style conspiracy. But I'm sure we'll find it, and soon."

He halted as if considering the delicacy of his next statement but eventually continued.

"Additionally there is a rather mysterious sex facility, euphemistically called a beauty parlour. It seems to have existed for only a short time and is, in effect, a clearing house for women trafficked for prostitution and for sale, after an induction phase, where they are available for the local trade. We have the address of that facility but the ownership is still somewhat vague, although we believe it is owned privately, off the books so to speak, by the mob's two top men here in Ayton. Thieving from the gang in that way is considered to be a capital offense by the mafia bosses, if and when discovered. Anyway it may be that, as we have still to trace the location of their other brothel and their headquarters building, this so-called beauty salon could be a good next target with damaging ramifications for the gang members. Relatively easy I would think and it would hit them directly and immediately in their pockets. Moreover, if we make enough of a fuss about the closure of that establishment, it may be that we could indirectly encourage the descent of the wroth of the bosses on the two gang members, who have indulged in an off-the-books enterprise, even possibly the London boss of bosses as well. But more of that later."

Deputy Chief Constable, Heather Compton-Jones, wanted to know more about the headway that had been made in closing the financial channels used by the gangs to transfer their gains outwards to destinations external to the UK.

The response was given by DI Brigstowe.

"Our financial colleagues in the CID have also made progress in identifying and closing some of the channels used by the mob to export their ill-gotten gains. There has been some criticism of blind bank managers in the past. But I must say that the banks that we have been approached are being very co-operative. Of course, as always, there is still much more we can do. One noticeable development, is the use of precious objects such as gems or vintage and valuable postage stamps to transfer the loot from Ayton for cashing in at the other end. It is then invested as clean money in such instruments as sovereign wealth funds or other offshore private equity companies in distant countries or territories. Some of it finds its way back to London as clean investments, a bit like the funds of the so-called 'oligarchs'. In fact in the last decade, this criminal syndicate has had a heyday in profits, now estimated at some thirty billion per annum. The whole process is a very clever and complicated economic morass, making it difficult to trace the origin and pathways of laundered money, which is followed by the cleansing of dirty money earned here from criminal activity by mafia gangs. After various cleansing measures, such dirty money becomes the investment for those same funds as clean money in legitimate activities on the stock market, for example, or in some foreign sovereign wealth funds in areas where supervision is lax or hardly existent."

At that juncture Chief Constable Lashley broke into the dialogue.

"I should like to pick up the issue of the so-called beauty parlour again. It seems to me that without slackening our efforts to find the other mafia locations, not currently within our reach so to speak, it would be a good first strike to close that facility. I suggest that, resources being available, and I will take advice from you on that Maria, we should plan a hit for some time early next week. I think that we shall need the local authority's adult social care people to accompany us, not to take an active role in the raid naturally, but to take good care of the cruelly traumatised women that we are likely to find there, some of them underage.

Maria, what do you think? Could we arrange that for Monday next week? Or is it a little bit too tight or over-ambitious? I'll take your advice on it."

Detective Inspector Maria Clarke responded immediately and positively

"Chief Constable. Subject to the availability of staff from the local Social Services Department, I would think that the beginning of next week is wholly possible and indeed desirable. The quicker we do it, the less chance there is of a leak, which could disrupt our plans or completely sabotage them. An early strike would keep up the momentum of our campaign against the criminals, cut their income again and keep them on the back foot as well. Personally I think what you are suggesting is perfectly feasible but I shall check with our colleagues in Social Services, whether that is OK for them as well. On another issue, I just wanted to know whether we shall need an accompanying firearms unit or, at the least, some authorised firearms officers. Just in case? That seems to me to be especially important given the threat against your own life. A short time ago intelligence about it was leaked out to us from an inside source. In addition, the increased trade by the local gangs in firearms appears to be the beginning of a tendency to use them freely in inter-gang conflicts and competition for markets."

"Thank you for that question. I have pondered this one myself. We are without doubt dealing with a gang, which has proved itself to be capable of extreme violence. The numbers of members of the gangs carrying firearms with them is presently on a sharp rise. Funnily enough they seem to always carry them in the back of their trousers. On the other hand, this beauty parlour is unlikely to be secured by armed members of the criminal gang. The guards are more likely to be inexperienced new recruits from one or other of the Albanian satellite communities in the UK or in very recent times from the local asylum seeker hotel. So it's a bit of a toss-up. Personally I come down on the side of being prepared for anything and everything in a raid like this one. All in all, I think it would be prudent to have an armed unit available to us even if we never make use of it. But if other people have other opinions, do speak up. Finally I just want to say that the threat against me personally has not influenced my view on this or any other matter of police work, although, of course, I shall take every precaution to frustrate the plans of these evil criminals, including this particular threat."

"Does that mean that we shall also be accompanied by a police medical unit?" Detective Inspector Maria Clarke asked apprehensively. "Just in case!"

"The answer to that one is a definite yes, not just in case of injuries to our officers but equally because female colleagues with medical training in the unit may be needed for immediate care to the abused women working under duress in this so-called beauty parlour. Let's not forget as well, that some of these may be minors, of whom hundreds are trafficked into the UK every year. So for that reason we may need specialised child psychological staff from the Social Services Department of the local authority in addition. That may of course be a second stage measure. Could you please raise that with the Department when you speak to them about our proposed arrangements for next week?"

Detective Inspector Maria Clarke nodded positively and came back again with a question about the drugs side of the mafia gang's business.

"I also wanted to emphasise the drugs side of this evil group's activities and to remind us that over a quarter of a million people, male and female, young and old, are estimated to be addicted to heroin and crack cocaine in the UK. These are the most lethal drugs together with opiates."

She paused in case of any questions.

"That's over a quarter of a million ruined lives and a massive bill to health and social services for detoxification each year. This gang of criminals is at the centre of that trade, earning billions each year from their evil business. We are not just facing a prostitution racket here in Ayton and the surrounding area but equally a real money spinner for the criminals in illicit drugs. Somewhere in one of their houses there is bound to be a stash of drugs, transported from London or one of the channel ports, sometimes hidden with other products in containers and we must aim to find that store as well and impound it."

"I couldn't agree more. Thank you for raising that issue and we shall certainly be seeking that treasure chest of drugs in our investigations. So we are looking for coercive prostitution, child molestation and drugs. Maybe we shall uncover some guns in our raid too. Let's say on Monday in the early hours of the morning as agreed today. Thank you all for your positive contributions. See you on Monday at approximately, no exactly, one o'clock in the morning. Sleep well!"

But Heather Compton-Jones, a stickler for the small details, was not quite ready to endorse the timing of the planned raid as stated by the Chief Constable.

"Chief Constable. If I may, I should like to request a small change in the timing of the raid."

"Please do go ahead." The Chief Constable, a little disturbed by what the change could be, after all the planning had taken place, replied courteously.

"Well we are proposing the commencement of the raid to be at one o'clock in the morning. This timing is because the premises is situated in a major and very busy shopping area and the property itself is in the middle of a parade of shops. We are proposing that time to avoid expensive claims for compensation from shopkeepers about potential and actual interruption to their businesses. But in addition we need to take into account the need for completion of all work and inhibitions such as on the movement of traffic in the area before the opening of some of the stores. As you know newspaper vending will start from six o'clock the following morning and indeed the delivery of some items to stores will be even earlier. For that reason, and to give us time to complete the necessary work of the raid and the follow-up investigations *in situ* as well, I would personally feel more comfortable with a commencement at eleven o'clock."

The Chief Constable responded in a very reassuring manner.

"Well, that seems to me a very reasonable and well-grounded proposal, Deputy Chief Constable. But what do other officers think? Would there be any dissent from the Deputy Chief's proposal?"

Obviously everyone found the amendment not only reasonable, but an insurance policy against police work still continuing when the shops were opening for business or early deliveries were being made, because no one dissented from the proposal.

The Chief Constable confirmed the amended arrangement and closed the meeting with a slightly humorous quip.

"In that case, for the second time, I declare the meeting closed and I look forward to seeing you all promptly at eleven o' clock on Monday night, kitted out and *in situ* and ready to go. Good luck and sleep well!"

Thus the next step in the campaign against the local mafia syndicate had been agreed and would be implemented forthwith.

Chapter Eleven: Waylaid

It is fair to say that Andrea was shell-shocked as she left the college gates early the following week to see the man, whom after one bicycle collision and two very brief coffee shop meetings, she knew as Joel. He was outside the school grounds apparently waiting for her. As he crossed the road pushing his ancient bicycle to approach her in a rather hurried manner and with a broad smile on his bronzed face, she moved towards him pushing her bicycle and addressed him somewhat irritably.

“I thought we had agreed to meet next Tuesday not this afternoon. Why are you here today?”

Joel reacted somewhat shamefaced.

“Yes, you are right, but I wanted to see you again after our delightful conversation last time. In the same context, I wanted to correct a false impression that I may have given last time and to invite you to see where I live here in Ayton and perhaps to meet my mate Sam and our Polish landlord, who is likewise called Sam, Sam Miaso.”

The alarm bells began to ring straight away at that invitation. Andrea recalled the advice that police Sergeant Berger, the beat officer, had given her at the meeting with the Chief Constable at Police Headquarters only a few days ago. She was particularly wary of the invitation to see his lodgings and to meet two of the characters there.

On the other hand this could be a good chance to try to find out more about this proven charlatan and his activities in Ayton. It was on the tip of her tongue to challenge him. But she had other objectives presently. So she parried the question and curiosity about his confession took precedence and stimulated her to add a little gentle coaxing.

"I am afraid that I have something on this evening so a visit to your residence would be impossible for me. But if you're paying, I could spare a few minutes at the café for a brief hot chocolate to give you a chance to unburden yourself about the bogus facts you have been giving me so far in the two short sessions of our extremely brief acquaintance. So let's go. Time is short."

In spite of the hard-hitting comment by Andrea, Joel jumped at the chance for a further meeting in the café, hoping to persuade her to advance the date of their next meeting and agree to come to his place, even if he had manifestly failed in his bid to entice her there for this evening. He had a longer term goal in mind. He could afford to be a little patient, although he knew that his colleagues could not. So he confirmed his acceptance of her terms.

"Sure I would be happy to pay such a small price for the pleasure of your company and we can have a good talk. I don't know about all these falsehoods you refer to. But I could correct one inaccurate impression that I may have inadvertently given. So come on let's get started."

They both cycled the short distance down to the coffee shop with Andrea in the lead. On arrival at the cafe Andrea anchored her bicycle to one of the stanchions erected for that purpose and Joel casually left his as usual leaning against the cafe wall. Whilst he was getting rid of his bicycle, Andrea surreptitiously sent a pre-prepared text to Sergeant Berger about the meeting, after which they entered the rather crowded café.

Their usual table had already been occupied, but Andrea found a place near the window where she could observe her bicycle and from where she hoped she could be observed by any police constables shadowing her as promised by Sergeant Berger, although she realised that it was very short notice and they probably would not have arrived yet. As they sat down and ordered their drinks from the waitress, Joel began by politely thanking her for joining him; arguably too politely it seemed to her. So she opened up the probing to set a sprat to see what kind of mackerel she could capture this time.

"I just can't wait to hear these new and especially corrected personal details that you want to share with me. Is it by chance about your real nationality or identity?"

Joel was knocked back by the accuracy of her guess. *But was it a guess?* He asked himself. Could she have access to information from somewhere that he had not even vaguely imagined she possessed? Inadvertently she had alerted him, and he recognised that he would have to proceed with caution in what he told her from now onwards.

"Well it's not an earthshattering revelation, but I may have given the impression that I was a Ukrainian national from the Ukraine. But I am not. I am a refugee from Kosovo, expelled from my homeland a couple of years ago by the loathsome Serb paramilitaries."

Andrea responded quite harshly.

"Well that's really not surprising to me. I guessed as much, when you refused the idea that I put to you for meeting a group of Ukrainian students from school. Interesting but not earth-shattering, I agree. So, let's start again. Where in Kosovo did you originally come from?"

He had been to Pristina a few times from Albania on drug-trafficking journeys for his mafia bosses there and so he cited the capital of Kosovo. He hoped that it might prove a cul-de-sac for the particular direction of the current discussion.

"I lived and was schooled in the capital of Kosovo, Pristina."

"Let's go back over the issues I raised with you before and check your apparently newly formulated re-creations. Where in Pristina did you live, where were you schooled and which university did you study what at, and do your family and relatives, if you have any living kin, still live there?"

Joel was becoming ever more disconcerted by her penetrating grilling and yet he felt impelled by some force, other than gain, to continue the conversation constructively. At all costs, he knew that he must avoid showing his irritation about her cross-examining him. After all he had a purpose in their meetings way beyond what she could perceive at the moment, unless of course .... So he sought desperately to provide a response which could probably never be verified. He had only ever stayed in Pristina occasionally and briefly and that was in one of the mafia's houses. But she would surely have heard of Mother Teresa. So he stumped hopefully for that option.

"I don't know whether you have ever been to Pristina but we lived in Mother Teresa Street, a dingy, downtown area not far from the Catholic cathedral, dedicated to her after she became a saint. On your question about my relatives, I am afraid that I lost them all during the Kosovo war."

Hm! How very convenient. A likely story! Andrea thought to herself. *I'll come back to that one a little later when I have had a chance to do a little more research.* So she tried a different line of questioning.

So that's now mainly Albanian speaking isn't it? I believe almost all the Serbs were expelled at the end of the war. Were they not? Is Albanian your mother tongue and have you ever been to Albania?"

"Brief visits only earlier in my life, usually to Tirana on school trips. And yes, Albanian is my native language."

Andrea decided to switch tracks again to keep him off balance as long as possible, memorising his replies for any relevant facts that would be worth transmitting to the police later.

"So where are you getting your money from here in Ayton, seeing as you gave me the impression that you have never registered for refugee welfare support in spite of having lived here in the UK for several years according to your newly revised curriculum vitae? Especially when you seem able to pay for expensive cups of coffee and hot chocolate for a new acquaintance, just like that?"

Joel found that that one a real stunner! Once again she had skilfully put him in an embarrassing situation, unable immediately to find a watertight and convincing response. Eventually, he found one answer that he thought might satisfy her. Or so he hoped!

"I earn money by doing odd jobs for the man I have found lodgings with in an old house, owned by a Polish man, named Sam Miaso. I live there with a fellow Kosovan, called Samir. We call him Sam for short. Incidentally that was the same way I earned my keep in London by helping with gardening, painting inside and out, repairing fences, clearing out guttering. That sort of work." He lied eloquently.

"How does Sam Miaso earn his money then?"

"He has a business that I know little about. It has nothing to do with me though. When you come to see where I live, I will arrange for you to meet him. If you change your mind and we go today I am confident that you will be able to meet him. I'm sure you will like him. He is very affable."

She ignored his repeated invitation and intended to continue to interrogate him.

"You said earlier that you had lost all your relatives in the war. Were you ever married and if so, did you have any children. What happened to your family exactly?"

This is beginning to seem like an official investigation. Joel thought to himself. *I'll try to bounce the cross-examination back to her.*

"Oh, for goodness sake, Andrea, why are you asking me all these questions? Our intended friendly conversation is beginning to feel more like an official police interrogation."

"Not at all, Joel. By the way is that your real name?" She explained deflecting his retort. "We are supposed to be getting to know each other and that involves asking each other questions about our backgrounds to see what we have in common. In any case, I spoke to my mother and grandparents about my chance encounter with a stranger outside school, who after crashing into me had then invited me for a coffee. In reaction they put to me some of the worries about you that I am putting to you this afternoon. At the moment, you know a lot about me and I know almost nothing about you and what your interest in me is. By the way, you have not drunk any of your coffee. It must be going cold by now and you haven't answered my last question yet. Do you have some additional dark secret to hide?"

Andrea smiled and winked at him mischievously as she addressed him.

"No dark secrets, unfortunately, Andrea."

He returned her smile similarly.

"But dark memories of how my relations perished, the details of which I prefer to try not to recall."

He waited for a few seconds, thinking how best he could proceed without alienating her, but eventually proceeded, having mustered his thoughts again.

"And the answer to your other matter is that I have never been married and have never had any children. I should like to settle down here and I am actively looking for a likely partner. Nothing wrong with that, is there, Andrea?"

Andrea felt the advantage in their exchange slipping away from her and decided to seek to regain ascendancy in their interchange again.

"Joel why did you come to Ayton of all places after living in the metropolis all those years?"

She had incautiously let slip that she knew that he had been in the UK several years, and he recalled never having told her that. *Clever!* He thought to himself. *But not clever enough for Xhoel.*

"It was really quite by accident. I found London an unpleasant and sometimes violent place to live. Too big for me, given my small town, small country background. So I looked round for somewhere quieter and safer where I could pick up the threads of my life again. I met some people, tourists from Ayton, in a café in London one day and the way they described their town made me feel that this was the right place to try to start a new life and seek a partner to settle down with."

He explained surprisingly convincingly.

"So, have you met or sought out those people you met in London since you came here?"

"No sadly I did look for them but I had rather foolishly never taken their details and have never seen them since that encounter in London".

"What did you say their names were?"

"Unfortunately it was quite a brief meeting and since then I have had much more on my mind than remembering their names. It's also a while ago now. But to the best of my recollection, their surname was a very prosaic English name, something like Smith. Or feasibly it was a colour, such as Grey, Black or Green. I just can't remember."

"What a pity. So what do you do in your spare time? Do you have a hobby and do you have friends that you can invite for a drink, of coffee sometime after work? Incidentally are there many people from your country living here in Ayton at the moment?"

"I just ride around on my bicycle and sometimes listen to music. But Sam keeps me pretty busy. So I don't have much free time. Apart from me and Sam I do not know of any other people from Albania living here in Ayton. Do you?"

"No unfortunately not. How would I? Do you have a religion? I read that most Albanians are Moslem."

"No, I don't have a religion. And yes, most Albanians are Moslem at least theoretically, although many are Christian. But a rising number are irreligious. They just do not have a religion."

Unusually Andrea felt herself flagging and her stock of subjects almost entirely exhausted. So she decided to finish the meeting, not completely satisfied with the results of her multi-facetted interrogation.

"Well, I must get on home now. Grandma will be expecting me to help with the preparation of the dinner and after that I have a hockey club meeting."

"Can I walk home with you perhaps?"

"No thank you. I have a bicycle, I know the route and I shall be going fast. On the other hand you appear to be inexperienced in cycling in a big town, as you put it on the wrong side of the road. So cycling home with you would delay me overly. It would be far too slow. And of course by the same token, we might be involved in a further collision." She winked at him and he smiled back.

So, no thanks I prefer to cycle home as I normally do. I have already spent rather more time here with you than I intended to. Cycling will be swifter than walking in any case. I assume that you still want to go ahead with our meeting next Tuesday. Same time and same place. Not outside school please! That sets the other students chattering. So let's meet here please and bring your bicycle."

Joel decided on a last rather clever throw for information. Her mobile phone number perhaps.

"OK! Agreed! See you next Tuesday. But how do I contact you if I am held up or can't make it?"

Andrea immediately saw through his clever ploy and responded in a similar vein.

"You can't, but if you are not here, I shall wait for a quarter of an hour and then go. Same for you if I cannot make it, unless you want to give me your mobile phone number."

Touché! Joel thought to himself. *Careless I can be sometimes, but stupid I am never.*

"You may not believe this, but as a poor immigrant I don't have a mobile phone."

This was strictly speaking true as he only used burner phones, which he discarded after use.

"For that reason I can't give you my mobile number. But if you don't come, I shall wait until you do. So see you next Tuesday, same time, same place, same drinks I assume?"

"Same time, same place, next Tuesday and as you are the one, who is inviting, it's on you for the drinks. Bye now." She jested playfully."

With that final salutation, she cycled off into the cool early evening air, pondering what she had gained from their conversation. She was also wondering who she should share it with and whether it was worth sharing it with anyone at all. She waved to him cordially as she rode away.

For his part, Joel tried to work out what she really knew about him and how she might have acquired that information. Several of the matters she had raised indicated that she knew more about him than she was revealing. He would need to proceed with extreme caution. He was equally conscious that this task, for which he had volunteered was taking much longer then he had anticipated. He knew that there was a real danger that his boss, Samir, would be growing impatient. His impatience would be reinforced by that tyrannical boss of bosses from East London, if he did not move this thing along more rapidly.

But the next encounter was already scheduled for Tuesday. That was only a couple of days away and he reassured himself that there would be a breakthrough at that meeting. He needed to be a little bit tougher perhaps and not humour her so much. That was all.

Chapter Twelve: A Reckoning

There was an air of furious and menacing anger in the office that morning, when Samir Pecic and Xhoel Gegaj met the head of the Albanian mafia set-up in the UK, Tristen Rexhepi. He was accompanied by his close assistant and financial wizard, the devious but avuncular Noel Shkodra. This was not their usual or normal weekday meeting, which had regularly and normally occurred by conjoint agreement since the two visitors had arrived from their base in London a couple of days ago.

This time it was a special meeting. It had been called with some haste by Tristen on the advice of his finance assistant, Noel Shkodra. Noel had been auditing the books for the mafia fiefdom of Ayton and region and had found some seemingly suspicious entries in the chaotic and slipshod accounts.

Tristen Rexhepi began the meeting as if he was conducting an investigation and he opened the meeting curtly.

"Firstly I'm going to let Noel share with you the details of his findings based on his scrutiny of the books for the Ayton office. Afterwards I shall tell you what you have to do. Noel, will you please share with our friends the worrying results of your audit."

"Thank you, boss. Well, I have spent some considerable time and effort putting together the very untidy and incomplete accounts, based on the wholly inadequate fiscal records and economic performance of the Ayton office. Indeed, judged by those accounts, the performance of this office is way below what the bosses would customarily expect from this level of social and monetary investment. Even taking into account the unsatisfactory financial performance of this office, transfers to the authorised sources in cash or kind are also below routine business expectations, as measured against other areas in the country of a similar size. Moreover, there appears to be a larger than normal cash surplus mostly in five pound notes rotting away in the firm's safe deposit bank account here in Ayton. That money could be easy prey to an aggressive police surveillance and result in total loss to the organisation. Indeed, I'm astounded that the account has not yet been closed by the relevant authorities with consequent forfeiture of the organisation's money. I would suggest that this is all indicative of poor accounting, budgetary monitoring and commercial decision-making. Overall very poor fiscal management. I think I should pause there briefly for our two friends to make their response to the contents of my report thus far."

Samir winced at what he saw as a blatant attack on himself. To give himself time to think through the implications of Noel's findings, he cleverly passed the buck to his young assistant, Xhoel.

"Xhoel is responsible for keeping the firm's accounts here. He is therefore better acquainted with the why and wherefore of those accounts than I am. For that reason, I am going to request him to respond to your report first. Xhoel, could you take Noel's points up from here."

"Yes well, of course your comments in your report have to be seen against the background that we have no trained accountant here as you do in London and to some extent in a few of the other firm's offices. The task of keeping the books is usually passed to the newest and youngest member of the team, and thus to the least experienced and financially trained. In my case I took the books over from the previous grossly unsuccessful management team. So some of the blemishes of presentation are, to my mind, attributable to our predecessors and conceivably even to their predecessors as the close monitoring of regional offices is relatively new. Thus the issues you identify were not discovered in the past as there was no previous monitoring or auditing. So I admit to my lack of experience and appropriate training opportunities. I'm sure, however, that with Noel's capable assistance and goodwill all these imperfections can be quickly rectified and the accounts put in order to your satisfaction."

Tristen reacted piercingly and in a highly personalised manner to what he considered false claims and excuses aimed at clouding the issue by blaming the lack of regular auditing or even that incompetent bunch, which had preceded the present management. He addressed Xhoel directly and spoke plainly.

"Xhoel, as I understand the situation, Noel's criticisms do not just relate to cosmetic presentational matters or even gaps in the supportive paperwork to the accounts. Those imperfections, as you call them, are far outweighed by the identification of major policy choices that have been made and have resulted in the general underperformance by this office over the period of time since you came here. It is these failings, which have resulted in financial losses to the bosses in Tirana. How would you explain those? Do you ever or have you ever before requested an audit of your accounts by a neighbouring office for instance?"

Xhoel was stunned by the onslaught and seemed to retire into a cocoon of silence for a while. Slowly he responded as best he could and tried to pass the buck back to Samir.

"Well, no, now that you mention it. I did not know that such training might be available if requested. But policy issues and decisions are always the scope of authority of the Chief, so if I may, I'm going to pass you over to Samir to respond to your assertions."

Samir received his commission from what he considered his inferior subordinate, Xhoel, with bitter resentment to say the least. In any case he was shocked rigid by the clever way that Xhoel had played the same game as he had. He recognised full well that because of this action he could be fighting for his life.

"Xhoel is right that policy decisions are exclusively in my hands. To respond to the criticisms at the underperformance of the Ayton office, I can only say that to rectify the errors and improve the performance of this office after the acknowledged underachievement of the previous team, is to climb a mountain with your hands tied behind your back. I might describe the situation here when we arrived as an unsupervised financial shambles of the last management team. It's proving to be a more lengthy business than either you or I would have ideally wished for. Remember that when the previous management team were replaced, there were no collaborators in the police service or political life, whereas we now have several. There were no county liners, whereas we now have quite a number. Monetary remittances to authorised outside sources were at a pathetic level and they have improved consistently since Xhoel and I took over, though they may still be temporarily below the astronomic monetary returns of the other regional offices. Purchase of precious items for alternative transmission modes abroad were non-existent when we first arrived and we now have several proven transit arrangements for precious vintage stamps and gems. Progress can sometimes be slower than we would wish. But it has to be recognised for what it is however modest."

The tyrannical and domineering Tristen mounted a vicious and sustained counter-attack to the array of what he considered puny excuses that he had been presented with thus far by both men. He was similarly irritated at their weak attempts to park the issue at his door by alleging lack of supervision. His ranting words were brutally menacing, as if he were speaking with a knife-sharp tongue.

"Just moving on from the inadequate presentational and inept decision-making issues within the accepted framework, which are admitted it seems to me by your responses, there would appear to be a bigger and for you more life-threatening anomaly in the accounts to explain, if you please. Noel please elucidate."

"Well thank you, boss. On a very few occasions both incoming and outgoing, there is a very brief reference to a beauty salon, almost as if someone had slipped up in the very fact of including that item in the books. There is no constant income or expenditure in the books relative to that investment and that plainly requires a satisfactory explanation, especially as there is no other mention for example in the office's list of holdings of property. Not that a beauty salon is a not good idea, Samir, but only when it is accounted for and the transactions recorded in the books, showing a good income and profit for the firm. I believe we shall require a swift and detailed explanation from the two of you, before a decision can be made about what further action to take on this matter and whether to transmit my report uncommented by you to Tirana. Remember when you are formulating your responsive document that thieving from the Tirana bosses is a capital offence against our Coda and there is only one punishment. Not that it is within my job description to make such an important allegation. In any case, I'm sure that you recognise that such an action, if it did occur, would be a self-serving failure, even suicide. So make sure your explanation is a fully convincing one, suitable for transmission to Tirana. Go ahead Samir, my friend."

No advance warning had been given of this bombshell about the beauty parlour and so Samir was totally unprepared to respond. Someone had blundered and the obvious candidate was Samir's current hate figure, Xhoel. Samir had always left the preparation of the books to his assistant, Xhoel, and never bothered to critically review them. He could not understand how explicit recognition of their off-the-books commercial enterprise had come to be explicitly mentioned, even if only on a very rare occasion in the books. The slip-up was just beyond belief.

He began his response hesitatingly and uncertain what myth to construct to justify what he knew very well was a capital offence, for which he would be held to be the major culprit. He could only expect the worst from the domineering and tyrannical, irascible old 'bytha'(ass) from London. He needed to get out from under this tricky glitch and palm it off onto a scapegoat. But who? Xhoel of course. So very adroitly and with an apparently masterful command of the facts, he put his mind to constructing and verbalising his escape scenario.

"Well! There is no secret to the fact that a so-called beauty salon, was established a short while ago to fund direct investment in the activities of this office, such as bribery, payments of new recruits from local communities and from the local asylum seeker hotel in order to staff the brothels and the salon itself. It is additionally used to fund the expenses of running our central office here. In addition, the funds were used for attracting and hiring a larger number of county liners for transportation of the goods we receive from London or one of the channel ports to outlying areas. This has meant that it has been possible for all income from our other activities to be remitted in full and without service deductions to authorised external agents. The income has also been translated into precious goods again for safe export to authorised and trusted partner agencies abroad. It is true that in addition my assistant, Xhoel, and I have retained a small amount for our own living expenses and those of our co-workers as well as for the entertainment of potential collaborators in the local police force or legal and political life. Those transactions may have been inadvertently omitted from the books. Conceivably Xhoel Gegaj, who is responsible for the books, thought it unnecessary in the context of an organisation of friends, bound together by the Coda. If that is so, it will be put right at warp speed by Xhoel with my personal apologies to you and Noel. I hope that clarifies the situation and at the same time refutes what was implied in your assistant's presentation, namely that there has been an attempt to siphon off earnings due to the firm for personal gain. That is totally incorrect and indeed it is insulting to loyal servants of the Clan such as Xhoel and myself."

The hot-tempered riposte from Tristen was contemptuous and dismissive.

"Oh, c'mon then. A bit overdone on the hurt pride side of things, Samir, and weak on the rationale. But let us take it that your statement is an honest and honourable statement of fact and intention on the part of the two of you. In that case, three further demands arise. Firstly Noel will need to visit this establishment today to estimate its earning capacity over the period since its foundation, so that we can arrive at a figure which signals the size of the financial gap in the books. Secondly, you two will need to make good any monetary deficit from your own resources and include this establishment in the list of property holdings. Thirdly you will need to correct this and the other failings identified by Noel in the books today. Right now if you wish! And no attempt to influence Noel's work. He knows well how to do it and it is important for you two that the outcome is correct, accurate and convincingly presented. When you have finished that list of tasks, I want you then to prepare a report, ostensibly for me, but which I shall send on to our bosses in Tirana with my responsive comments attached."

Samir tried to continue what he saw as his life-saving efforts and responded swiftly and in a compliant manner.

"I promise that those tasks shall be done today and every support will be afforded to Noel by myself and my colleagues to expedite the work and assure its quality. Given the availability of Noel's assessment of the earning capacity of the beauty salon since its inception, we may be able to complete our report by this evening, when we could meet again to approve a final version of our report."

But Tristen was having none of it and rather ominously, he added a final postscript to his comments.

"Well, we have some rapid movement at last. Remember you two are writing your own passports to continued life here in Ayton or just imaginably anywhere. You have a choice. Make a better job of justifying your decisions than you have done so far on the one hand, or on the other face recall to Tirana and you know what that implies. You still have a choice. But not for long."

"It shall be done and your message is clearly understood." Samir stated dolefully and Xhoel nodded his head in support.

Tristen was silently aware that his own job tenure and even his life could be threatened if the report did not fully justify his own decisions as well as those of his very own subordinates. After all, it was he who had recommended the pair as a good team to take over in Ayton after the debacle of the previous management team recommended by his departed predecessor in London. The current whereabouts of that team and its leader were sadly unknown.

He was experienced enough to know that any incompetence by those he recommended would be reflected badly on him as well as them in Tirana. Thus he had a vested interest in the preparation of a report eloquently justifying the performance of the Ayton office and the probity of the decisions of his two colleagues, although of course they had no means of knowing his little secret deception. He hoped.

With the exchange of sincere good intentions, they all prepared to repair to the beauty salon without delay to begin the work. As Samir was about to leave, however, he was horrified to receive an important and disturbing message which came through on his mobile.

The message was from an inside collaborator and the warning stipulated that police activity had been observed around the beauty salon with some of the roads already barred to traffic and interrogation taking place of all persons entering and leaving the cul-de-sac, where the beauty salon was situated along with several other shops. It looked very much like a full police raid of the establishment was imminent.

Samir sighed and reluctantly acquainted the others with the news he had just received.

Tristen's reaction was a stark reminder of what was at stake for the two Ayton men as he warned them.

"At least we got to know before our visit! But the implications of a second loss could still be devastating and career-closing for you two."

Chapter Thirteen: A Second Raid

The organisation of the second raid on the mafia's collection of brothels, focussed on the one known to the Ayton criminal bosses as a beauty salon. For a number of reasons, preparations for the raid were much more complex and demanding than for the previous raid. In addition, the plan for implementing the raid had to be changed from what had been originally planned. Firstly the Chief Officer, Horace Lashley had tested positive for Covid-19 and had to isolate and withdraw from the planning team and leadership of the operation.

That meant that the burden fell on the next most senior officer in the planning team, namely the titular head of the freshly established drugs and prostitution wing of the police station, Deputy Chief Constable, Heather Compton-Jones. In London and since her arrival in Ayton, she had proved herself an ambitious, capable and effective officer although she was a very recent arrival in the Ayton force. By the same token she could rely on the able assistance of her deputy, Superintendent Rajiv Gundara. Although the fact that they had both arrived a short time ago from the Met was a cause of some suspicions by a few officers, who had been at the station somewhat longer.

The location and lay-out of the premises chosen for the operation had led to further planning complications, including time and space constraints. For example, the building where the so-called beauty salon, in reality a brothel and transit point for trafficked women, was housed was in an erstwhile retail store in the middle of existing retail stores. There were thus six businesses in a row with other shops in close proximity.

The existing stores provided normal and regular daily service mainly to local customers in nearby housing. The shops included off-licence access to items such as alcohol, newspapers and a restricted choice of food locally. The other shops were regularly open from about six o'clock in the morning to catch the early employees on their way to start a day's work. Those shops included a bakery and a small grocers. At the other end of the business day, some of the shops remained open until ten o'clock in the evening. This meant that some deliveries could take place earlier than 6am, whilst others occurred throughout the working day and later.

This location meant that the raid and exclusion zones had to begin predominantly after the closure of the latest closing shops at about eleven o'clock in the evening, be completed during the hours of darkness and total withdrawal had final wind-up well before the opening time of the earliest commencing shops and their deliveries namely well before six o'clock in the morning. The raid was, therefore under time pressure and all activities, including exclusions of traffic and pedestrian passage before and after, as well as detailed forensic investigations, had to be accomplished by early the next morning to avoid closure of stores essential to the local community and consequent claims for compensation by the proprietors of those stores.

Moreover, the design of the construction of the six properties, in one of which the beauty salon was located, afforded a continuous roof space. This provided a potential getaway route in the unified loft space as well as uninterrupted access across all the premises.

In order to accommodate all of these complexities, the raid required extensive advance preparations, which had to be conducted with great discretion and involved confidential agreements with the other shopkeepers. The commencement of the raid was scheduled to begin at one o'clock in the morning with the barring of all entry, road and pedestrian access, to the small off-road cul-de sac as well as the shop front parking spaces for each shop.

After some preparatory dispositions, the raid proper commenced with the arrival of the main body of the raiding party of police from the Ayton Constabulary, including transport such as detention vans, armed unit and first aid units. These were followed by the social services team slightly later and situated in the rear at the beginning of the cul de sac in the parking places there. This meant that social services staff were held in the first instance at a safe distance, but could be quickly available if and when needed. In advance, during the evening two senior officers in plain clothes had gained agreed access from the two shop proprietors at each extremity of the block's continuous loft space to make arrangements to frustrate any attempt at flight and escape. Slightly later, two officers gained access to the yards at the back of the shops to block any escape by that route as well.

On completion of the preliminary arrangements and the prompt arrival of the main body of officers, the usual loudspeaker announcement was sounded in English and Albanian to the effect that a police raid was under way and any occupants of the premises should leave the building by the front door unarmed and with their hands held up. The first such announcement evoked no reaction or movement from the premises whatsoever. Consequently the message was repeated with the additional threat that if people did not comply and exit within three minutes, entry to the building would be forced by the police.

There being no response to the second warning, Superintendent Rajiv Gundara, led a small squad of officers bearing a hand-held battering ram and each carrying routine shields. They approached the main entrance to the property. The locks were swiftly breached and the door swung open inwards. Stun grenades were launched into the ground floor accommodation. Two dazed men, apparently armed guards, were peacefully taken into custody at the doorway and disarmed. After frisking and handcuffing, they were passed back to colleagues to be temporarily lodged in one of the detention vans. The small advance squad of officers entered the premises with caution and then split up into two subunits each of two officers to scrutinise both wings of the establishment. The first squad was replaced at the door by a further small squad of officers to provide back-up for those already inside, if and when required.

Almost immediately two further men were seized. They seemed startled, almost as if they had not heard the warning and remained immobile behind a small reception desk in the middle of what appeared from the furnishing to be a kind of reception area or lounge. The same procedure was adopted as with the first men taken into custody.

There was a drinks counter in the area and a series of bright cushions adorning several sofas with small coffee tables and partly consumed alcoholic drinks still on them. Meanwhile a further man was detained by officers in the back yard of the property as he tried forlornly to escape by that route. The captives were all fed back to officers outside, searched and handcuffed before being placed in the detention van at the front. In the van, the detainees began assailing each other, seemingly for ineptitude in what later turned out to be a northern Gheg dialect of Albanian.

Inside at the beginning of a short corridor downstairs there was a series of small rooms, minimally furnished with bed and some small items. On the right-hand side a larger room fitted out as a kind of office with computers and printers and other office furniture and equipment together with a substantial looking strong box. Two men were pulled in there as well and in the smaller rooms, no more than cubicles further arrests were made and several women released and passed back by female officers to social services staff awaiting them outside. After the office and ground floor were declared clear by the first squad conducting the sweep of that area, specialist forensic officers were permitted to enter to deal more intensively with the office. Other officers went down stairs along a short corridor where there were a series of small rooms in each of which, a terrified young woman was found cowering in a corner or squatting motionless and terrified on the floor or on a bed. It was left to designated and specially trained female officers to deal with the care of these terribly abused women, many of whom seemed to be very young even early teenagers and most of whom did not speak any English. In some of these cubicle-like rooms a number of further men were detained as well, some of them in a state of undress.

The women were gently but persuasively led outside by the female officers and offered light refreshments during which some minimal personal details were recorded. After that they were placed in the care of staff from the Local Authority Social Services Department for eventual transportation to a place of security and safe keeping. Further in the future they would be interviewed with immigration officials on their residence status. After care and attention, they would be further interviewed by police officers in the presence of female Social Services staff concerning their lives in the brothel and the staff who were responsible for their detention and abuse.

Very quickly a call of 'All clear down here' echoed across the downstairs corridors and the tentative approach upstairs began with Superintendent Gundara leading the way. Again upstairs there was what looked like a reception desk with two women sitting at it. The women were clearly alarmed, in terror and apparently frightened into immobility where they sat. On either side of a short corridor there were the same small rooms along the pattern encountered downstairs. In two of these rooms, men were discovered trying to hide behind or under the bed. In all rooms a young woman was discovered and liberated by a female officer. The men were led outside and cautioned before being loaded into the second detention van. The women from the desk and the other ten women from the small rooms were led downstairs, offered light refreshments and handed over to Social Services.

On the final scrutiny, some thirty five women had been freed and seventeen men detained and taken in for questioning. The status of the men was still to be ascertained, but some were clearly visitors using the services of a prostitute, while others were locally recruited brothel guards working on behalf of the mafia gangsters, some of whom were armed. They would face more serious charges. The forensic examination took a little longer and many objects, specimens and samples were collected up for later examination. A large stockpile of a variety of different drugs was found and cash and documentation was seized for accounting and later confiscation.

Notwithstanding the detailed forensic examination, the whole operation on site was completed by first light and the withdrawal of all the police officers and social services staff and their vehicles was effected before the first deliveries were made and shops were due to open. All restrictions on pedestrian and vehicle movement were removed before the opening of any shops and also before delivery of goods such as the morning papers and fresh fruit and vegetables from the wholesale market.

The work was not yet complete, however, for all participating officers faced an initial short debriefing as a group. This would occur straight after arrival back at the station before later release for a well-deserved sleep during the day.

Deputy Chief Constable Heather Compton-Jones had been called away on an urgent matter as she was deputising for the Chief Constable during his continuing absence on sick leave, due to the requirement to still isolate due to positive results on lateral flow tests. Therefore the task of chairing the short debriefing meeting to evaluate today's raid fell to her assistant, Superintendent Rajiv Gundara, who opened the meeting briskly, bearing in mind the fatigued audience he was addressing.

"Welcome back to HQ and congratulations to everyone on a successful operation completed smoothly, on time and without any casualties or violence on the part of either side. Although we do not yet have any forensic results or the results of interviews under caution with the prisoners, the purpose of this meeting is to record any impressions or recollections of use or relevance to the operation while they are still fresh in our minds. Yes, Sergeant Julie Harper you wish to speak. Please go ahead."

"One of my first and most abiding recollections was of the complicated and lengthy preparations that were required before the raid had even started, allied with the fact that the operation was relatively simple and so easily completed compared with some others that I have participated in previously. It may be that the rewards that this raid will yield will be slight and the ultimate findings insignificant in our fight to crush this gang of mobsters. Foremost in my mind is whether the outcome justifies the input? I also took away from this experience a lasting and distressing memory of the trauma being suffered by the women we have liberated today as a result of the cruel and inhumane treatment that they have been subjected to. This, inspired in me a determination to bring to justice those responsible for these crimes, regardless of the cost in resources, even though I understand that none of the top men were captured today. So contradictory recollections but maybe shared with others."

Changing the subject, Constable David Jones then requested clarification about how long this establishment had existed undiscovered and why.

"This brothel was in a very prominent location in a quite large local community with a small but significant local shopping centre not far from one of the local churches on one side and similarly a pub not far away on the other side. It must have been noticed as soon as it was set up. Was it not commented on by members of the local community or had their observations not been taken into account? Or perhaps local beat officers saw and commented on it as well but it was considered insignificant in comparison with the overall fight against crime of the force as a whole. Could I just inquire about how long we have been aware of its existence? And have there been any previous reports or complaints from the public of from our officers about its existence that were not acted on."

DI Gundara tried to respond frankly to the question, which implied a serious lack of appropriate action on the part of the force locally.

"As you know, I am relatively new here in Ayton, so I cannot respond to your request for information with great certainty. My understanding, however, is that this operation was launched to raid the premises at the earliest possible opportunity after discovery, consistent with the resources available, seen in a time scale. The alert came from members of the public and was endorsed by local police officers. According to those reports, the premises were only set up lately but that remains to be confirmed. Thank you for raising this issue and for my part I shall raise this subject with the Deputy Chief Constable."

Another of the beat sergeants, Sergeant June Chapman endorsed the emotional reactions she had felt similar to those of a previous colleague about the women found in the premises and she raised a new issue.

"I had similar emotional feeling about the women we rescued today and I shall never forget their forlorn faces and dejected looks. I was immediately seized by an intense feeling of compassion and a similar intention about the culprits to that expressed by Sergeant Harper namely to catch and bring to justice those responsible for these atrocities. But I wanted to add that this establishment had a bit of an amateur feeling about it in spite of the relatively large number of men we have arrested, some of them no doubt mafia staff. Nonetheless, it did not seem to me to have any of the hallmarks of an officially sanctioned brothel. To me it felt as if it were imaginably a little bit of freelancing on the part of some few members of the Ayton criminal syndicate."

Police Constable Brenda Ramsden spoke next to a similar effect.

"Yes, I agree that it seemed very amateurish in its organisation and furnishings and just maybe understaffed and fortunately for us sloppily guarded. After all, we captured about seventeen men but we do not yet know how many of them were staff. And no definite madams yet! Moreover it did not seem to be doing very well or else someone had informed that place that a police raid was imminent. The place was so dirty and untidy. By the way, one final thought. How will we distinguish between which of the men are mafia gangsters and which are local visitors to the brothel?"

Superintendent Gundara gave a first tentative re-joinder to police Constable Brenda Ramsden's question.

"We shall have to see which of the men request to see their lawyer and if it is from the same law firm as was invoked by previous men from the mafia set-up already captured in the other raid. There is the language issue too. Not many, if any, local Ayton men will be able to speak Albanian. This distinction will emerge through cross-examination and there may even be further charges of sex with a minor after interviews with some of the women, who seemed to me to be well under statutory age."

Police Constable Peter Page raised the issue of the further timeline for the investigation and DI Gundara responded cautiously.

"Do we have any idea when the forensic reports and other evidence from interviews will be available to us and when charges may be formulated against those having been suspected of committing a crime or crimes including the one you mentioned?"

"That really is in the lap of the gods. A lot depends on the workforce which can be spared to address this project. Having said that, this whole investigation is now in the hands of the local CID. I'm hopeful that, by the end of next week, they will be able to give a fairly complete briefing on the progress on that score. But we have the Head of the local CID (Criminal Investigation Department), Felix Brigstowe with us today. It may be that he can give a more accurate estimate of the timeline than I can. Felix do you want to correct what I have said? I do hope I have not spoken out of place?"

The comeback was short, sweet and positive.

"No that's fine Rajiv and I hope to be able to comply with your suggested timeline of the end of this week. No promises, mind you."

It was on that happy note of unanimity that the meeting ended and a group of tired police officers retired to their beds to await their next challenge in the campaign to eradicate the criminal gang responsible for the enslavement of so many young women. But the overall operation was even now, only in its very early stages. There was still a mountain to climb and further ripostes from the criminal gang to cope with.

Chapter Fourteen: A Reappraisal

Roan Prifti, a member of the guard staff from the beauty salon team, had come dashing in almost stumbling into the office first thing in the morning. His entrance coincided with the foursome team from East London and Ayton preparing to go to the salon to audit the accounts and accommodation, with a view to verifying its current earnings and economic potential. They also intended to design measures to bring it over into the normal books and, after examination of the accommodation, to seek to maximise its earning capacity for the firm. His arrival confirmed their suspicions, aroused by the disturbing text from an insider that Samir had received only a very brief time before he arrived.

Roan Prifti spluttered and stammered as he slumped into one of the armchairs in the office exhausted as he tried unsuccessfully to be calm and coherent.

"Please forgive this … err … this early morning intrusion. Err …Sirs. The police are raiding the salon even as I speak to you. In fact, they have been there all night and they have emptied the place arresting the other members of the guard staff, our hired workers and the few visiting men from Ayton and releasing all the women. I understand from local spy reports, that they have pillaged the office, the computer and the safe with its contents and carried them all out to a waiting van. In addition, they have likewise impounded the small selection of drugs and the cash in the safe and cash register. I have rushed here to tell you this as you were, I understand from the boss, planning to come to us this morning, on a supervisory visit. Had you done so, you would probably have been caught in the net like the others. Very sorry sirs to be the bringer of such bad news. Very sorry."

Tristen and Noel regarded each other with astounded perplexion. Whilst Samir and Xhoel looked at each other in bewildered horror. Tristen spoke first in his usual splenetic and commanding manner.

"Why don't you have a cup of coffee and then tell us all about it. In fact, we'll all join you in a refreshing cup of coffee, won't we fellas?"

They all nodded in assent and Noel added sycophantically.

"What a good idea!"

They each drew a cup of coffee from the machine and all four joined Roan at the small coffee table in the centre of the room. When they had settled down, Tristen invited Roan to tell them about the raid speaking in a quiet and kindly voice to the man.

"Well, Roan, now you've had a chance to recover a little, why don't you tell us how you managed not to be captured when all the others were taken and what happened at the premises. Then we can go on to assess the damage."

"Yes sure. I had been to the local take-away for our somewhat late dinner. We were all a bit late because we had had a rush of customers. The rush had just eased off prior to my departure about 9.35. We were occupied preparing the books and back-up documents for today's visit by yourselves. Fortunately, I think there were only a handful of customers left when I left to buy the dinner for the three of us. But when I returned almost to the entrance to the cul-de-sac bearing the dinners, I found to my alarm and dismay that access to the cul-de-sac had been cordoned off. So I went to the small copse on the other side of the main road to observe what was going on."

Roan puffed rather short of breath and tried to take a deep breath. He was unsuccessful and Tristen had to advise him to take his time. His account continued after a couple of minutes.

"The raid began very shortly afterwards at about midnight or so. There was some announcement that I could not hear clearly, but I think they were encouraging everyone to surrender and come out with their hands raised above their heads. No one did so, however. I think with the prior arrival of various items of transport and lots of police all kitted out with body armour, bullet-proof vests, shields and so on the police were ready for anything. A second announcement was made in English and Albanian to the effect that everyone inside should come out, unarmed and with their hands held high. Again, no one did, even after the second announcement. Consequently, the police fired stun grenades into the building through the downstairs windows and the main door which they had broken down. The debris fell into the hallway of the premises. Shortly after that they began bringing the men, the guards and visitors, out from the building. After searching them, they were handcuffed and put in the back of the black marias. From what I could observe from my vantage point and without revealing myself, our stock, I mean the women, were treated carefully and solicitously. They were offered a drink and then handed over to what looked like women from the Social Services Department, placed in a coach and driven away to goodness knows where. All the time they were cared for by Social Services staff, who of course were not in any kind of uniform. Various items of furniture and things like documents were all loaded into a large lorry. I waited until they started withdrawing their prisoners to the police station and then I walked here quickly as my car was in the garage attached to the premises for the night and is no doubt forfeit now. I believe that is all."

Tristen continued to demonstrate who was in charge by the tone of his voice at that point in the interview.

“Thank you Roan for that very detailed account. Very helpful. I’m not going to ask you what happened to the take-away meals.”

Tristen quipped and gave a rare smile, while expressing a short and subdued chuckle.

“But you can go now and have some breakfast in the kitchen upstairs and a rest in one of the rooms up there as well, if you wish. I suppose you’re very tired after being up all night. Thank you again for keeping watch all that time. We shall call you if we need you again, but I rather doubt that we shall. In the meantime, you should stay here at headquarters and await redeployment to another task by Samir here.”

So Roan departed hastily, hardly believing the courtesy and concern that had been shown to him. The four men remaining looked at each other with differing expressions on their faces, and Tristen asked Samir what he thought of the incident.

“Well, what do you make of that, Samir?”

“I just cannot imagine who could possibly have snitched about this place. But obviously someone surely did. Roan and his colleagues are the only staff involved, although there are some locally recruited guards as well, and they are all fully trustworthy as you have heard from Roan today. I cannot imagine how we can explain this loss of money, stock and fellow members of staff to the police. At this moment in time, I don't know how it can be placed in the books in a financially acceptable way, or at least a way which your bosses and mine will find acceptable. I'm at a loss to explain it."

"And you Xhoel. What do you think?" He probed.

Xhoel replied once again aiming to shift any blame from himself to his colleague, Samir.

"I'm baffled by this event. It is not as if this is a well-known place as the brothels in the town go. It is fairly freshly established and it is not, by far, the most lucrative such establishment in the town either. But I was always uncomfortable with the idea anyway of its being located as a beauty salon in a small shopping precinct surrounded by other shops and subject daily to the intrusive glances of masses of shoppers, let alone the likes of other shopkeepers and delivery men. As far as I am concerned it was always just too public. So, I'm not disappointed that one way or another we have rid ourselves of what had a short time ago become an embarrassment and a threat to our relationship with our friends in the Clan. But, in sum, I must say I smell a rat. I strongly suspect that someone was bribed to reveal the details of the existence of this place. The big question is who?"

"Noel. What do you think?"

"Well boss I see this as a minor pinprick. The location, as Xhoel has already pointed out, always made it a bad choice and rendered it vulnerable and financially weak. According to what we have heard from our two friends here, it was never a big earner. From what our two friends have said about it, it was always going to be a write-off. That's what it should be, a write-off in the accounts and institutional memory. On the other hand, I always try to look for the advantage that such an apparently disastrous event brings with it. I must say it seems to me an un-missable opportunity to erase an embarrassing anomaly in the books of the business here. That is where we should be looking to deal with this unfortunate event. Not looking back or at each other and reflecting negatively on the happening. That's my view."

"Thank you Noel. Words of wisdom as usual. So I agree that this is a god-given opportunity to quietly and totally erase an unfortunate and even inexplicable blunder investment by the Clan officials here in Ayton from the books and from any other documentation, the like of which I have never encountered before. I hope I never will encounter such a foolish investment again, namely the establishment of a dubious off-the-books facility. We have already spoken about the effect that this could have on the careers of our two colleagues here, if it remained in its present form. So I suppose one could argue that the Local Constabulary have done us all a favour. Who snitched the information about this establishment is the important issue to me. That is, if anyone did. It could have been that the original decision to place it there always was flawed and the site was just unduly public in the first place."

Actually Tristen could possibly have been more concerned, in what he was thinking, about his own future in the eyes of his bosses in Tirana and his possible fate if he were to be associated with an illicit action according to the Coda. In fact he was glad that this establishment had been closed down and was seeking a way to erase it from the organisational memory and the financial books and any other documentation of the business without himself being responsible. So he decided to pass it over to his assistant. But how to frame it so that the result was the ever loyal Noel's proposal and not his own?

"Noel. How would you yourself suggest we deal with this new situation, if possible so that it is effectively a non- occurrence in the organisational memory?"

"Well boss. I would erase all of the mistaken entries in the books, and there are only a few anyway, erase them from the accounts that Samir and Xhoel send to London and which we then transmit to Tirana with our comments. Secondly, I would check all documentation and correspondence and any documents, where the existence of the beauty salon is mentioned and dispose of them. Thirdly, we would need to discuss with Samir and Xhoel, how much of their, let me call them, extra-curricular earnings, should be paid to us as a once and for all penalty for the work involved in the cleaning up of the accounts and the avoidance of some rather nasty consequences for our two friends. I'm sure they will be generous."

Splendid, Tristen thought to himself. *Now to make these two idiots formulate their own punishment.* So he suggested.

"Well we must ask Samir and Xhoel what they think about that idea. Samir you start as senior office keeper here."

"Well, I agree with Noel. I think his proposal offers everyone a clean and painless break from what, with hindsight, appears to have been a little bit of an oversight in supervision, I believe. I would suggest we adopt his proposal in full and leave to him and myself the decision on how much will be paid as a penalty for the inefficiency, err

lapse, and how that can be incorporated into the accounts in an invisible manner."
"Good and Xhoel?"

"Well I cannot see how I can escape from the logic of Noel's excellent proposal. But at base, as he intimated, this was a policy mistake from the start. I did not make the decision and I was forced by the besa to go along with it. I was not the one, who made and implemented the policy and that continues to be the case. So I think in terms of any policy decision about culpability, my modest payment of compensation should reflect that fact."

Samir was horrified and furious at what he accurately saw as a blatant betrayal by his colleague on top of the spiteful rant of his boss, Tristen. Before he could respond, however, his boss came back in to impose his concept of unanimity and conclude that part of their discussion of the issue at that time.

"Well it seems that we all have a friendly accord and we shall leave the implementation of this solemn agreement to Noel and Samir and add a rider to the effect that they should take account of Xhoel's point in assessing his payment to Noel and myself. All agreed?"

No one objected, but it was evident that an existing irritant to the bond between Samir and Xhoel had been further exacerbated, for which Samir promised himself there would be timely retribution.

Tristen then proceeded to the next item he had had in mind to deal with this morning.

"Well, with the time that has been liberated for us this morning, let's have a comfort break and another nice cup of coffee and come back for discussion of how far we have got with our agenda of change, agreed a couple of days ago."

The foursome dispersed and returned with fresh coffee and some business-like haste.

"Well, since we have some unexpected spare time, I thought I would go through some of the outstanding actions that we agreed on and the advance achieved in implementing them. Xhoel, my friend, can you share with us what progress you have made in recruiting those urgently needed county liners?"

"Well, to cut a long story short, movement forward has been painfully slow."

"Yes please do give me the shortened version of your excuses. Do you mean slow or non-existent Xhoel?"

Tristen demanded imperiously.

"I wouldn't say non-existent. There has been some progress in attaining access to the school via the young lady I mentioned, but not much. I'm due to meet her again on Tuesday."

"Xhoel, you have to understand that this is a mainstay of one of our central policies for the economic repositioning of this branch of the organisation and the rapid achievement of profit again."

Tristen angrily barked an ugly warning at Xhoel.

"You must get a move on. Otherwise I shall have to bring someone in from London, who can do the job and you would be recalled to Albania for an uncertain fate. Understood?"

"Yes, and I shall renew my efforts to succeed rapidly in this matter."

"Samir let's move on to another current and pressing issue. What do you have to report on the issue of the contract to take out the Police Chief here in Ayton?"

"Good progress, insofar as we have an agreed a contract with one of the men in the local Kurdish organisation, with whom we sometimes co-operate. I met with the proposed sharpshooter yesterday and I understand from him, that he has already been scouting for a secure place, from which to achieve his goal. Although there has been no opportunity, as the Chief Officer has been absent from work on sickness leave for a few days. But the Kurd will continue to keep a look-out and let me know when the contract is completed. We agreed that the full fee will only be paid on successful completion with a small starter payment after engagement. That is a deal already done, and we have agreed a fairly reasonable monetary deal, which Noel has endorsed."

"Good, at last. You will also be engaged with Noel in cleansing the accounts of the beauty salon and allocating and agreeing the pecuniary fine to be paid by yourself and the lesser one by Xhoel to myself and Noel. Such payments to be entered into the books as earnings from the brothel. They should be used partly to support one of your locally hired men, who was arrested this morning and for the upkeep of his family. We do not want to put ourselves in bad odour with the local kindred minority community, from where we recruit a number of our soldiers and the majority of our guards, do we now?"

"What advance have we made in finding new premises for the office and safe accommodation for visitors such as Noel and myself? Oh and how is the similar search for suitable accommodation for the opening of a second brothel, Samir?"

"Well we have not had much time so not very much quite honestly. We have all been focussed on the likely consequences flowing from the now deceased beauty salon."

"What you actually mean is that there has been no progress, Samir. So say so! Please make sure that this is attended to this week, starting today. It is urgent with the local police hunting for our establishments everywhere at the moment. It is urgent so it can form part of the recovery plan for submission to the bosses soonest. Do you understand the reason for the urgency?"

"Yes, I understand and I agree."

"Do you understand the consequences for the two of you if both of these issues remain unresolved for much longer?"

Both men humbly nodded their heads in silent agreement.

With that menacing interchange he stood up peremptorily and left the room followed swiftly by Noel. The dye had been cast and Samir and Xhoel knew that the decisions and their aftermath could not now be changed or halted. Moreover it was not solely their **jobs** that were on the line.

Chapter Fifteen: Supermarket Encounter

As Andrea and her grandmother, Emily, were about to enter the supermarket in town to do the week's shopping, who did they see there, but the young man Joel? He was nonchalantly leaning against the wall next to the supermarket entrance. Immediately he saw them, he smiled broadly and he straightway approached them. He addressed them both in a friendly and polite manner.

"What a pleasant coincidence seeing you here, Andrea. It would seem that we both have something else in common. We use the same supermarket more or less on the same day and time. I guess the lady accompanying you is your grandmother. Hello there! How do you do? My name is Joel and I know from Andrea that yours is Emily. I have heard a lot from the other immigrants here in Ayton about the good work you are doing for refugees. Thank you very much for what you are doing for us. As to me, I'm from Kosovo. I wondered if you both might like to come for a cup of genuine Kosovar coffee and a look at where I live. I have my car here in the shop car-park and I could drop you off back here after you have visited my accommodation. It would not take long and if you come today, you could meet my colleague, Sam, with whom I am currently living and for whom I do odd jobs and my Polish landlord, Sam Miaso."

Based on the discussions at Police Headquarters and reports back from her granddaughter, Emily immediately recognised that this apparent coincidence of meeting at the supermarket was a pretext for his real nefarious intention, whatever that was. She consequently responded first by rebuffing the offer and querying rather frostily why they should accept his proposal.

"Thank you for your very kind offer, Joel. Why should my daughter and I want to visit your accommodation, which has no doubt been approved even feasibly supported by the local authority for accommodating the many immigrants that the town is now welcoming and supporting? I suppose, indeed I hope that your housing is very comfortable for you. At least I hope it suits your needs. If not, there is a very easy mechanism available in town for you to complain. I'm very sorry but neither my granddaughter nor I can take up your kind offer today. After the shopping we both have firm and longstanding commitments for this evening and indeed for the weekend. They were arranged some considerable time ago. Anyway it was so nice to meet you and we shall no doubt see each other again by chance the next time we are shopping. Bye now!"

Emily turned quickly to go to the nearby trolley park but Andrea hesitated for a moment, sufficient for Xhoel to hastily seek to continue the conversation.

"Yes, I hope so and next time maybe you can accept my coffee invitation. It might prove useful feedback about the condition of immigrants in Ayton at the moment and the problems they face. By the way, what day do you normally shop here?"

"There is no normal day for us. We both have very busy lives and shopping is often just a spur of the moment decision."

On hearing the reply, Joel changed his mind about how to react to the stark rebuff of his proposals.

"On second thoughts I could simply wait for you to come out of the supermarket and take you for coffee then. Yes we could have a brief coffee together in the supermarket coffee shop after you have finished shopping so as not to take up an unreasonable amount of your valuable time."

Andrea intervened swiftly in an attempt to keep open the option of a further conversation, during which she would hope to uncover useful information about this Joel and his activities and those of his mafia criminal mobster gang in Ayton.

"Well the day and time we come to shop and the time we take to shop vary a lot due to our crowded schedule of other commitments and the amount of shopping we need. That is particularly so as my grandmother is an elected councillor, a dedicated and conscientious politician and chair of the local authority committee on migrants. I'm not sure at the moment whether we shall have time for a coffee when we have finished shopping. Sometimes we do. But today is a big shop so it will take quite some time. If you care to wait and see if we have time afterwards to sit together for a short while over a drink, that is up to you. But I'm sure we shall bump into each other again soon in any case. We must get started with the shopping now. Bye and see you again, perhaps later today."

With that allusion, Andrea and her grandmother disappeared into the supermarket pushing a large trolley and chattering to each other in a spirited manner about the strange approach by this rather pushy young man. Emily asked her granddaughter about the man.

"Andrea. Is that the strange man, who collided with your bicycle outside school the other day?"

"Yes Gran he is. That's the man who first told me he was a Ukrainian immigrant and then changed his story to say he was really from Kosovo. That fits with what Granddad had said about his real name and criminal background and objectives here in Ayton."

"I think we should report his efforts to track you to the police. I don't like your being associated with a criminal. Jack says that these people can be very violent as well. And you have to ask yourself very seriously what he really wants from you."

"Well, Gran, don't you remember that we have already done that when we met the Police Chief and some of his staff a couple of days ago at the Police Station? For security, I now have someone from the police station tailing me at all times, probably watching us now and maybe following us into the supermarket. I was told to take my mobile phone with me wherever I go and given a special secure phone number to ring in case of emergency. The purpose of our speaking to this young criminal charlatan is to find out more about the crime syndicate, of which he is part and to pass that back to the police. It is not to sign a treaty of friendship with him or a liaison of some kind. As we know, his purpose in wanting a coffee with us is very different from our own intention and indeed his is most probably quite malign."

"Oh, I see. I now recall what the Chief Superintendent and his colleagues said when we met with him at the police station. What you are suggesting bears out what we all agreed at that time. Thank you for reminding me. I am afraid I am getting a little forgetful nowadays. And I have been so busy this last couple of weeks with so many meetings and commitments and such a flood of newly arriving migrants that I had clean forgotten. I don't know whether I'm coming or going at the moment. So what are you suggesting about today?"

"Well I fully expect this young man to be waiting for us when we finish our shopping. I further expect him to invite us for a coffee, which he will offer to pay for. We should accept the offer and use the opportunity to speak with him to find out more about the evil organisation, to which he belongs and which caused the death of my father."

"Andrea what is it apart from the death of your father that persuades you to engage in what could turn out to be a rather dangerous game?"

"Well apart from assisting in the destruction of an organisation that killed my father, I feel that I have a civic duty to assist the police and prevent this evil gang from contaminating any more school children with their criminality and drugs. I know of the detrimental effect these drugs can have on some of my fellow students at the school, who have had to go for mental health treatment as a result of using the stronger cocaine supplied by these guys. The drugs appear to be getting stronger as they get cheaper and I understand that there have been some fatalities amongst young people linked to the newest version of crack, but not yet at my college."

"Ok! I understand. So let's do it, but what concerns do you think we should pose to elicit the kind of particulars you are seeking for the police?"

"Well we need to put some easy non-threatening ones to him at first to settle him down and put him at his ease. Ordinary everyday things you might inquire about from any stranger. For example, you could solicit from him details of his schooling in Pristina, about his teachers and the subjects that he liked best. That would be one. Does he have a hobby and what he does in his spare time would be another. Getting more to the point, we could then enquire what his employment was in Kosovo and whether he trained for a trade or profession. And so on, getting more difficult to cover such issues as, does he know anything about the use of drugs in the immigrant community and about those who are pushing them in Ayton, where the drugs are coming in from and what the price is today on the street. Or does he know or associate with any other people from Kosovo who are currently here in Ayton? Why not or if he does who? If you get the idea it would be helpful if you could test him with some of the starter topics first please, gran."

"Yes of course. Anything legal to help you … and my friends the local police!"

Andrea and her grandmother spent over an hour shopping and putting their shopping through the automatic check-out as there was a long queue. Painfully slowly they moved with their heavily loaded trolley towards the store exit. As they moved towards the store exit, Andrea invited her grandmother to go for a cup of coffee in the café, the entry to which was on the right.

"Well, gran, we have now finished our shopping here and paid at the self-service check-out system. So would you like a cup of coffee at the café even if that young beau is not there to pay for us? We can take our trolley with us, gran, so we can keep an eye on it and its contents while we have a drink and a natter. I shall have a hot chocolate, I think."

"Yes well but …"

"You look a bit shaken up? We can go home now, Gran, straightaway if you would prefer not to have a drink."

"No, that's fine. I'm just a bit tired after a long shop nowadays. But we can have a coffee and meet this young man as well, just as you suggested, and I will try to help you, if I can. Yes let's do as you are suggesting, love. I'll help insofar as I can."

When the two emerged from the supermarket shopping area an hour and a half after they had entered, intending to take a cup of coffee, the young man, Joel, was hovering about at the entrance to the café. They nodded acknowledgement to each other and he followed them into the café, and offered to buy them their drinks, to which they agreed and they sat down at a table of their choice to await the arrival of their coffee and hot chocolate. He returned to their table bearing two cups of coffee and one hot chocolate, some brown sugar sachets and the accompanying biscuits. When he had distributed the drinks and sat down, Emily opened up the conversation innocently as suggested by her granddaughter.

"Thank you very much for the drinks. Very nice and always welcome after a shopping expedition. Did you do any shopping?"

"No not really."

"Andrea tells me that you attended school in Pristina. Some of the asylum seekers here in Ayton now, come from Pristina as well and they have spoken about their experiences there. What was it like to live there and which school did you attend in Pristina to have learned such excellent English and good manners to boot?"

She remarked semi-humorously.

"Well there is a very famous music school in Pristina and that's where I wanted to go. But I failed in my application and ended my education, just before the beginning of the war, at the Dr Ali Sokolij upper secondary school in Pellagonia."

The reason for this quite specific formulation was that, accustomed by previous sessions with Andrea, Joel had anticipated this subject arising and had looked up a suitable school on the internet.

Unhappily, Emily overloaded her next question somewhat.

"What was it like? What were the teachers like, what was the curriculum and your favourite subjects and did you specialise in any subject or skill area? Was it in the city centre?"

"Well, I'll see if I can remember all those questions. If I forget one or more, please feel free to remind me. The location of the school was more or less in the central part of Pristina. But remember, that was before the war erupted. There has been lots of investment in the country and its education system and lots of construction has occurred, including in the education sector since the war. So I don't know what it is like now. It may even have moved to new buildings in the suburbs."

"And the subject matter and your area of specialism?"

"Well the curriculum was a general secondary school one. But as you guessed it had a stream, which specialised in English language and I took that branch of study."

"And the teachers?"

"Well they were all very distant. They considered that it was their job to give their lesson and then go. There was very little contact, almost none, between students and teachers outside the classroom. So you didn't get to know them at all."

"What was the language of instruction at the school?"

"Albanian."

"So, are you an Albanian or a Kosovar?"

"Definitely Kosovar but Albanian speaking as well and proud of it! With a little English of course!"

He joked weakly.

At this point and after the overloaded and quick-fire efforts of her grandmother, Andrea took over the task.

"Did you have a specialist qualification when you left school and what trade or profession did you train for?

"I did not have a specialist qualification when I left school and I did not have a trade qualification either, because at that point the war with the Serbs erupted."

"So that was about 1999, when you left school then, wasn't it, which makes you about twenty three years old. What was your job before you came to the UK?"

"I was a general labourer in Kosovo and that is what I am here."

"We have a small number of refugees from Kosovo, have you ever made contact with any of them since your arrival here in Ayton?"

"No! Sadly I have honestly never met any of them except my colleague, Sam. I haven't really had the time or inclination. Anyway I preferred to try to get to know some of the locals instead as I intend to make this place my home and settle down here."

"Why not?"

"I think I have answered that already. I didn't need to and the opportunity never presented itself. But primarily I intend to make this place my home, so it is people like yourselves that I prefer to get to know. Do you understand my reasoning?"

“Yes, of course. The police have ascertained that the main drugs market in the town is supported and fostered by several drugs cartels, but that the main contributor to the trade is an Albanian criminal gang. Do you know anything about that?”

“No, sorry. I don’t know anything about that.”

“Have you met any other refugees, who were pushing or hooked on drugs and have you bought, sold or taken any illegal drugs yourself?

“Good question!” Joel suggested jovially. “The answers are no, no and no!” He suggested rather genially.

“How much do you earn from odd-jobbing for your mate and how many hours a week do you work for him?”

“The number of hours varies from week to week and so does the pay.”

“Do you pay any deductions, for example for national insurance or tax?

“No I do not earn enough.”

“Emily intervened as she could see that Andrea was getting tired at the constant stone-walling.

"Joel, if that is your name, as one of the people responsible for the welfare of asylum seekers, I would be intrigued to know why you have apparently never registered your presence here in Ayton with the authorities, like all the other refugees have done and especially in spite of the many benefits of doing so. And the fact that you have never met any of your co-nationals from Kosovo except for your friend Sam. I must say, I find it rather extraordinary and unusual in comparison with all other asylum seekers, who appear to cleave automatically to members of their own ethnic community. Moreover registration of your status would have entitled you to free health care and other economic benefits as well as free accommodation."

"I feared being deported." He offered.

"Why?"

"Not sure. But the fear was enough."

Emily intervened with a further rather critical remark.

"You seem to me to be a sort of social isolate and yet you have sought Andrea out as a companion or at least for company."

"Correct. But there is no law against that, is there?"

"No!"

"But to clarify, I did not seek Andrea out. It was a happy accident. And now I like her company and, I have to admit, being with her also gives me a chance to use and improve my English, the language of my new homeland."

There was a momentary pause and Joel interrupted the fast-flowing stream of investigation coming from the two women and eventually demanded.

"Have you two finished the interrogation or are there any answers you would like to clarify further? Otherwise can we just get on with a normal interchange about ordinary everyday things like life in Ayton?"

Emily responded enigmatically.

"Well conceivably on some future occasion we might have the time to do so if we see you again and do as you suggest. For the moment, however, Andrea and I need to get back home, unload our shopping and start on the evening meal. So, sadly we must postpone further discussion until later and possibly accept your kind invitation to see where you live and to meet your landlord and employer and even put a few more questions a little later. You never know!"

"The offer remains on the table and you have a rain check on a coffee or other drink next time we meet. You can store up any further queries for our next meeting. See you on Tuesday same time as before in the café after school, Andrea."

Andrea did not respond but nodded nonchalantly at Joel. Emily began to rise as did Andrea and they regained their trolley parked at the side of the table and quickly exited the supermarket for the car park. They left Joel still sitting at the table, feeling rather pleased with his performance of the art of creatively stonewalling.

For their part Emily and Andrea departed feeling rather despondent and totally devoid of any feeling of success whatsoever. Would there be another opportunity and if so, how could they play their cards differently next time to obtain more of a better quality of information?

Chapter Sixteen: Time to Reflect and Plan

In the absence of the Chief Constable, due to continuing positive lateral flow test results for Covd-19, the regular planning and evaluation meeting was chaired by the Deputy Chief Constable, Heather Compton-Jones. The meeting was a further session in what had become a series of such regular planning and review meetings since the commencement of the all-out campaign against the Albanian criminal network in Ayton. Its overall aim was to assess the headway made in the local operations against the foremost local mafia syndicate in the Ayton area and to plan the next moves aimed at taking that group completely out of business. The Deputy Chief Constable began by greeting the usual attendees.

"Once again good to see you all back for another of what have become our regular meetings to assess how we are doing, so to speak, in our objective of closing down one of the major perpetrators of criminal activity in our community. Of course this is merely a first step to closing down drug and the drug and prostitution criminality which blights our community at all levels and ages. I'm going to invite Superintendent Mark Brownlow from the National Crime Squad to update us on the present state of our initiatives in the town and the surrounding area set in their wider context of national effort with the same aims. Superintendent Brownlow over to you!"

"Thank you Deputy Chief Constable. Well, first of all I want to thank you all for this opportunity to share your experience. Up and down the country there are groups like yours, having meetings like yours and sharing their aims with you as you are with me. This is an important aspect of your, their work and our work. You are not alone in your effort and we can learn from each other how to be even more effective and efficient against these monsters because of that solidarity. Now ma'am perhaps I could give you some feedback on my own impression of your work today. Today's raid was focussed on what was called locally a beauty salon, but was in actual fact and in practice a brothel and centre for the a cruel and inhuman exploitation of trafficked young women. I should say that this is not the first time in my travels around the country that I have come across brothels described or better disguised as beauty salons. It is not a new idea! Neither is the heart-breaking link between such premises and women trafficked under the influence of illusory expectations or coercion and cruelly abused as commodities in lifelong prostitution. Seen in the context of the national scene, these are major and continuing features of this kind of criminal exploitation of women. Next the raid. The raid was planned to take place during the hours of darkness in deference to the need and the wish not to disturb local businesses and their customers and delivery drivers. I'm happy to tell you that in my view, this aim was very successfully and sensitively achieved. The premises are now closed and that is a good achievement too. The release of at least twenty five young women from criminal and abusive bondage in thrall to a mafia gang making millions off the backs of these women is a praiseworthy achievement too. All of these successes are an integral part of a national effort to put these gangsters out of business and into gaol. It is true that the haul in terms of captured criminals was meagre indeed, perhaps even disappointing for you. But it did strengthen the hypothesis that this establishment was an 'off the books' adventure rather than one fully part of the gang's plans. The fact that it was almost totally undocumented and only lightly guarded by newly recruited men from the local kindred minority community and from local asylum seeker hostels, including one such hostel in Ayton, also endorsed the idea of a less than formal set-up, again encountered elsewhere in other regions. In fact, as you already know, only two members of the criminal gang was captured and has been charged with profiting from prostitution, people trafficking and illegal sex with minors. Another unrelated arrest has been made of a man associated with the criminal syndicate in a minor role and that man has been charged with possession of an offensive weapon and criminal property. This man at first hearing seems likely to be willing to sing in exchange for some relief in his period of imprisonment. So there is hope that somewhere down the line a successful prosecution will result as well in a by-product of useful information on the functioning of this gang and its monetary dealings including links to national traffickers, suppliers and receivers of dope, etc. That is a commendable outcome as well and not to be underestimated. The other men captured and incarcerated were locals enjoying the favours of the women on a paying basis. They have already been interviewed, bailed under caution and may yet face criminal charges. There are too some signs that one or two of the women released from captivity may be willing to testify against the men who abused them and there is a hope that they may be able to help illuminate the national links of the trafficking business. It is significant, for example, that some of them have said that they were trafficked across the channel as refugees, trade routes that are predominantly under the 'ownership' indeed in the stranglehold of Kurdish criminal gangs. This is a very lucrative trade for these gangs as on average they earn some sixty five thousand pounds for one boat crossing and such crossings are catering at the moment for a minimum of twenty thousand refugees a year. Very approximately it is estimated that such a business could yield the gangs a steady income of over ten million pounds a year, excluding of course, the profits from the sale of the trafficked young women in this country. Looking back on the raid, the haul from forensic examinations is likely to be scant. But then you never know. Some fifty thousand pounds is now out of the system rather than in the gang's pockets, together with some valuable vintage postage stamps, and a small collection of precious stones. All of these items, small in their own way, further deprive the gang of funds and are matched by similar deprivation in other parts of the country. This must mean that in total these people are hurting, financially speaking. It was disappointing that little was discovered in the way of incriminating documentation, with no links even to the local gang let alone to the hub of these gangs in East London. So you may think the results of the raid were skimpy, but when added together with similar gains of your colleagues across the country, you can see how really successful you have been together. All the time you are draining finance from the gangs and their criminal activities. This reduces or eradicates any potential remittances to the syndicate's bosses abroad in Albania and elsewhere and payments to Chinese middlemen for stocks of drugs from South America. So warm congratulations on your achievements and here's to the next one. I think I should halt there now and if there are any concerns, I should be happy to respond to them."

But after that very long presentation, the Deputy Chief Constable had other ideas than further interrogation this stage of the meeting and she intervened to move the meeting along.

“Thank you Mark for that excellent and very honest overview and scene-setting talk and especially your critical comments as an observer on our own efforts in the context of the national efforts of our colleagues elsewhere in the country. It is very helpful and refreshing to us to see our own efforts set in that national context. If you are agreeable, I think that we can leave any questions until later in the meeting. I should now like to call upon the Chief of the local CID (Criminal Investigation Department), Detective Superintendent Felix Brigstowe, to fill us in with regards to the financial side of our investigations. Over to you Felix.”

“Thank you Heather. I believe that we have made good progress with local banks, insurance companies and local private currency transfer and exchange bureaus, etc. The aim is to block off any scope for use by the mafia gang of normal bank accounts or other publically available services such as national and international transfers for the export and cleansing of their ill-gotten gains. It is important to note that it is drug trafficking, which is the most lucrative source of money for the criminal syndicates of which there are some considerable number in the country. On the other hand, prostitution is an important ready cash earner, and the closure of two of their cash earning establishments here in Ayton has effectively closed two major avenues of funding for the local gang.

Although there still exist some minor outlets in the form of private usually ethnic local money transfer services, used predominantly by minorities for transfer of legitimate earnings back home to families. We are currently working on closing that side of things to the criminal gangs as well. It is significant to emphasise that, as has already been mentioned today by my colleague, Superintendent Mark Brownlow from the National Crime Squad, our efforts have to be seen as part of a national plan, which is similarly closing down such gangs in other towns and cities of the realm by curtailing their earning and cutting of their means of money transfer. Crucial to that co-operative effort is the two-way exchange of intelligence and sometimes the coordination of raids etc. For instance, nationwide by that co-operative effort there have been, overall, well over a thousand arrests of criminal gang members and some three million in cash has been recovered with analogous closure of channels of transmission elsewhere or local utilisation. Masses of drugs, vintage stamps and precious gems have been seized and efforts are currently in progress to stem the flow of illegal drugs into the country through the channel ports, often in containers with innocent looking contents, such as pineapples, dried fruit and bananas. In the past few weeks a multinational gang, involved in people trafficking in several major countries has also been taken out here and in Europe. As has been alluded to before today, looked at in conjunction with these other local, national and international measures, these successes are now beginning to seriously hurt these criminal gangs. Well! I think that is it for the moment. But again I am happy to respond to any pressing questions by colleagues or visitors."

"Thank you Felix. Next I should like to request Detective Inspector Maria Clarke, who is the officer in command of the major investigation into drugs and prostitution locally, to outline the next steps for us here in Ayton and the surrounding districts. Maria."

"Thank you Deputy Chief Constable. Just to outline where we are up to before moving on to the next phase of the plans. Two establishments run by this mafia gang involving the abuse of largely trafficked and underage young women have been closed and prosecutions have either been commenced or, I am confident, will commence shortly. The impact of the closing down of these two major generators of cash on the financial position of this criminal gang is likely to be devastating with immediate effect. The co-operation of operative parties, such as banks and insurance companies in blocking the lodging and the channelling of dirty money abroad have now been largely achieved as well. Again the impact on the gang's economic position will be major and demoralising. So much for the past. Now to look to the immediate future. The location of the second brothel run by the gang has been found and is currently under round the clock observation by officers. I understand from the Assistant Chief Constable, Tony Wozny, that the intention is to raid this establishment if possible this very week. After taking out the brothel, we shall be moving on to the central office of this group and any other ancillary properties owned by the gang in this area. For example, in an attempt to evade the long arm of the law, let me call it the central office of the organisation, it has been moved within the last couple of days to an establishment in the suburbs of the town. We are currently on the point of identifying its new location. When that is achieved it will be raided and closed down and any members of the group found there will be arrested and as appropriate will be charged and any goods will be impounded"

"Thank you for that very succinct yet comprehensive overview of the successes we have achieved so far and where we go from here. I think the time has now arrived for participants to be able to make comments or put questions to those, including myself, who have made presentations. Yes Sergeant Berger please go ahead."

"I know from my own experience as a beat sergeant that the development and implementation of this operation has demanded additional commitments and supplementary funding. Has central government, for example through the Home

Office, made any additional manpower or fiscal contribution to this operation?"

The Deputy Chief Constable responded politically not wishing to ruffle any feathers at higher echelons of the operation.

"As early as October 2013 the Home Office produced a Serious and Organised Crime Strategy with the aim of substantially and actively decreasing the amount of organised crime in the country and the level of serious crime that demands a national response. As you have heard already this morning, our activities here in Ayton and district are part of that national effort and are financed accordingly from both local and national funding, some of which is open for special bids."

The next question came from one of the beat constable, Ahmed Kahn.

"This must sound like awfully naïve, but there has been talk amongst us about cocaine, heroin, cannabis and crack. What exactly is crack and where does it stand in the market price-wise?"

The Chief of the CID hazarded a somewhat unsatisfactory response.

"I believe that there is no pharmacological difference between powdered cocaine and crack, this latter of which is absorbed into the body by smoking, whereas the others can be taken in various different ways. Crack is a more expensive and much more potent drug and sadly fatalities occur more frequently through its use by both young and older consumers".

Sergeant Julie Harper put the next question.

"If as has been said, drugs are the biggest earner for the gangs, why are we bothering to work to close down the brothels?"

Detective Inspector Maria Clarke, who had been trained partly in the United States, answered at the invitation of the Deputy Chief Constable.

"A very apposite question, if I may say so. I guess there are several reasons but the final decision is a humanitarian one. True the two are interactive. The one, closing the bordellos, cuts off an important supply of flexible cash readily available for whatever nefarious activities a criminal gang want to use them for including locally. But the raids on brothels have the satisfying feeling of knowing that a central benefit is the liberation of abused women and children from an unimaginable sexual or other bondage. It is true, however, that drug smuggling and peddling are the activities, which bring most financial reward to the criminal gangs, about nine billion a year in the UK, not least at a time when drugs are cheaper than ever, more potent and more accessible and public demand appears to be exponential. They are more demanded than ever with over three million people addicted to various drugs in 2020 and over a quarter of a million addicted to opiates and crack. Closing those pathways of misery has the additional advantage of keeping adults and youngsters free from addiction and in some cases serious psychosis, both of which are only remediable with lengthy and very expensive measures. There are growing numbers of fatalities from drug abuse from year to year now. The government takes the bulk of the responsibility nationally for intercepting and confiscating drugs, mostly at the ports in containers of food, sometimes at the airports and railway stations. I suppose that I ought also to mention the legislative and judicial framework of our work. I am no lawyer nor expert on the interpretation of Acts of Parliament, but my understanding is that the Misuse of Drugs Act of 1971 sets out powers for the police, including powers to stop and search persons on suspicion of drug possession. But your question raises a further issue in my mind about whether we are doing our bit at this end, locally I mean. I will leave the Deputy Chief Constable to respond to that, but thank you for a very helpful question."

"And thank you to you for a very detailed and honest answer."

The Deputy Chief Constable complimented her and continued to address the subject directed to her by the last speaker.

"Thank you for passing that thorny subject on to me. The brief and unsatisfying answer is, without doubt, that we are without doubt not doing enough. It is true that local authorities do have a remit for public health but in the main it is generally interpreted in more curative ways. It does include measures like commissioning of substance misuse treatment services, social care, education, housing etc. It does not explicitly address the issue of tackling the transportation and sale of noxious drugs and catching the vile criminals, who organise the trade. That is largely left to local police forces but as the last speaker said national initiatives under the direction of the National Crime Agency to deal with drug smuggling but not exclusively at ports, etc. mean that there is some national co-ordination and a wealth of goodwill exchanges of intelligence. The legislation that Maria referred to, the 1971 Act, which established the Advisory Council on the Misuse of Drugs, has never been evaluated or reviewed for its effectiveness and the vast amount of money dedicated to that purpose since the introduction of the legislation has also not been evaluated. Who would like to put a further question? Yes, Constable Musa"

Constable Ibrahim Musa, a fairly new recruit to the force, wanted to query the way stop and search powers were being applied.

"If I may, Chair, I should like to clarify an issue associated with something that DI Maria Clarke touched on *en passant,* namely the apparent disproportionate use of the stop and search powers against people of colour.

The Deputy Chief Constable responded to that one herself.

"Yes, you are right Sergeant Musa, in what is inherent in what you are asking, namely the apparent racial disproportionality in the application of the stop and search powers across the country. Although I have to say that such powers are used overall more sparingly here in Ayton than many other police areas. We have to admit that the statistical evidence, in particular, seems very worrying. Recent figures appear to suggest that people of colour were more than eight times as likely to be stopped and searched as some other ethnicities. But let me assure you that I strongly deprecate the use of any police powers on a prejudiced and discriminatory basis. Should such use be uncovered in this police force it would straightway be the subject of disciplinary action against any officer or officers involved in such abuse of power. Moreover, I believe that this issue is being looked urgently at this very moment."

While acknowledging the important issues, which had been covered during the meeting, the Deputy Chief Constable moved to steer the final minutes of the meeting's focus on the next action, the raid on the second of the mafia gang's brothels in the coming week.

"Thank you everyone for all those good questions and the honest and open way in which they have been both posed and responded to. This has contributed to the richness of our discussions and alerted us to some areas, which require further attention and conceivably further action too. The senior planning group for the next operation the criminal gang's second brothel will be meeting this afternoon at two. We are more or less set to go and the planning group will be meeting this afternoon to check for any final issues in our planning. We move to action late on Tuesday at a time to be determined by that group. Congratulations to all on a laudatory and very productive performance so far. Hopefully this will continue through to the next raid and the final eradication of this scourge on our community. Good luck to everyone."

She then moved quickly to terminate the meeting, thanking everyone for their participation and contribution, but with the next scheduled action high in her mind.

But would it take place as envisaged peacefully and successfully? Was what was being planned the most cost-effective way of using the available resources? Would it take place at all or be futile given the counter-measures the gang was already planning?

Chapter Seventeen: A Deadly Raid

There was an air of self-confidence, although a casual observer might have described it as overconfidence, among the police ranks as they assembled in their pre-allotted positions around the house, that evening. Memories of two previous entirely peaceful and successful raids were dominant in officers' minds. The area had been sealed off for several hours when the main body of the police raiding party had arrived at eleven o'clock sharp on that Tuesday evening. The armed police unit and first aid unit were both in reserve and deployed close by.

Social service staff and their transport were at a short distance away too. They were ready to accommodate and comfort the women and any children rescued and to take them to safe, comfortable and congenial accommodation. Two black marias were parked up front offering cover as well as waiting for any males to be taken in for questioning, frisked and cuffed and then to be transported to jail. In the continued absence of the Chief Constable, still Covid-confined, in overall charge was the Deputy Chief Constable. As had now become usual practice, an Albanian interpreter was present too.

As usual, the first loudspeaker warning to commence the raid was given in English and followed immediately by the same announcement in Albanian. There was no reaction. This first warning was followed by a second warning and this time included a deadline of three minutes, within which the occupants of the house must surrender and come out with their hands over their heads. After the elapse of the time specified in the second warning, three officers behind riot shields, one carrying a ram began to advance towards the front door of the large Victorian house.

The group moved forward and were a couple of meters from the front door, when there was a distinctive crack and one of the officers accompanying the ram-bearer fell to the ground like a sack of flour. A second officer in the advancing squad turned to assist his colleague and there was a further crack and he fell to the ground. At this point, the third officer quickly dropped the ram and retreated at full speed, unharmed, with his shield held behind him for protection. Just as the officer reached safety behind one of the police detention vans, there was a third crack and a bullet struck the extreme side of the van, from which he had retreated only a fraction of a second before.

The situation was now deemed to be critical. Staff were ordered to take appropriate cover and the armed police unit was called forward to take over the assault. Superintendent Julian Charles, the officer in charge of the armed police unit in the Ayton police Force, raised some preparatory issues about the directionality and possible source from which the armed attack had come and clarified what kind of shield the officers were carrying when they advanced. He was quickly briefed on the situation by the senior officer commanding and in turn he briefed his men on the tactics, which would be adopted. They were largely well practised, but as was true in this case, their approach was still not without its dangers.

A further advance was then undertaken towards the front door of the house by a small squad of five officers behind ballistic shields and carrying a large explosive charge. At the same time stun grenades were fired in through the downstairs windows and the glass of the front door. A further small squad advanced to retrieve the bodies of their colleagues and to take them back to the first aid vehicles, which had now been advanced nearer to the scene. As the first squad was advancing there was a repetition of the firing from the house. It was, however, ineffective against the ballistic shields being used by the firearms officers. Further pings were heard as bullets harmlessly hit the officers' shields, but although accurate they were largely ineffective apart from some minor damage to the officers' shields.

A charge was placed against the front door and the officers retreated to either side of the door holding their shields in front of them. On explosion, the front door was effectively demolished and the splintered remains fell inwards into the spacious hallway, which seemed to have been restructured as a cosy reception area or snug. From outside, the room could be seen to contain a well-stocked drinks bar, comfortable chairs and sofas with multiple small, low coffee tables, some with unfinished drinks on them. The action of opening up the view from outside by dint of the explosive demolition of the front door revealed that there were no persons still in this area. So it was quickly followed by the entry of the five officers into the house and the commencement of searches accompanied by loud shouts of 'armed police'. Two further squads of armed police entered the house at this time and began to advance on either side of the front door, while the first five-person squad took up positions on either side of the front door inside to provide safeguarding cover for their advancing colleagues from behind.

The commencement of the searches by the two squads of officers was accompanied by loud shouts of 'armed police', complemented by screams and cries of distress and fright from female voices, all apparently coming from the upstairs of the building. Downstairs, from a room on the left-hand side a middle aged man appeared with his hands held high and his clothing dishevelled and incomplete. A young girl had remained in the room half-dressed and screaming in panic as he exited. The man was passed back to a back-up squad. He was searched and handcuffed and placed in one of the police detention vans, now parked nearer the front room outside the entrance. A trained female police officer was called forward to take charge of the young girl. The girl was led outside and her further care was taken over by staff from social services.

The room from which the man had emerged slowly and fearfully was given a first cursory clearance. From the appearance of its furniture and equipment and its size, it appeared to be furnished as some kind of office. This information was transmitted back to the officers outside to note for further forensic examination later.

From the kitchen area at the rear of the house on the right-hand side of the building, two women in wrap-around pinafores appeared looking absolutely bewildered, frightened and terrified. The clothes of their liberators, seemed to invoke their vivid imaginations, which led to sheer terror, based on what they thought might be going to happen to them. One of the female police officers from the advance party called to them, trying to calm them down and reassure them.

"You are safe. Do not be afraid. You are free now. Just follow me out of the building to the front where a nice cup of tea awaits us all and you will come to no further harm."

It is debatable whether the women understood the words but they seemed to understand the gestures and facial expressions of the officer as she invited them to leave the room and accompany her. The women were escorted by one of the female officers to the Social Services Department staff, who were waiting outside at a very short distance from the house. There they were offered a temporary seat and a nice cup of nerve-settling tea with sugar and milk.

After repeated calls of 'all clear here' from both sides of the front door, the whole ground floor of the premises was given clearance and a further squad of five armed men was swiftly deployed forwards to assist with the assent to the first floor. Meanwhile, two men had been detained trying to take flight from the building through the normally barred and locked back entrance and another man was caught in the process of climbing out of a ground floor window at the side of the premises. All were unarmed and in various stages of undress. Vociferously protesting their innocence of any wrong doing, they were referred back to police colleagues at the front of the house, searched, cuffed and offered the comfort of a seat in one of the waiting police detention vans.

Inside the house, one of the squads supported by another unit was preparing to ascend the main staircase. They were fairly convinced that they were likely to be attacked and were therefore carefully carrying their shields in front of them. This suspicion was confirmed as they approached the first steps of the staircase sad three shots were fired at them in quick succession, all of which were effectively dealt with by the officers' Kevlar shields.

Thinking laterally one of the team of armed officers raised with the commander whether there might be a second set of servants' stairs, as was often the case with many of these old Victorian houses. This would enable whoever was at the top of the stairs to be trapped in a pincer movement. But consequent on radio consultation with one of the senior officers, who had a plan of the house, it was confirmed that there was no alternative ascent and the plan was discarded.

The man, who had fired the shots was not alone and, after the man's initial volley of shots he seemed to have retired behind one of the protruding corners of a bedroom upstairs. He could still be seen from time to time as he peered out to observe the movement of his police adversaries. Julian Charles requested his best prize-winning sharpshooter in the police team to take the man out as a threat to the life and limb of officers. The sharpshooter waited until the man exposed the side of his head to observe what was happening and the officer fired an expert shot to the man's head. The man fell down dead onto the floor.

Consequent on that event, the team began to ascend the stairs cautiously, systematically and slowly alternating their positions and covering each other as they progressed to the landing at the top of the stairs. The officers then took up positions to cover both wings of the corridors leading from the stairs on both sides at the top. With the death of his companion, the second gunman appeared to have retreated from his former position on the landing and was nowhere to be seen. The police rightly surmised that he had fled up into the attic for which the stairs could now be seen at the end of one of the corridors. The first squad covered the stairs to the attic, while a supporting unit began the systematic search of each of a series of small rooms, little more than cubicles, upstairs.

The corridor to the right of the stairs was chosen to be cleared first with sharpshooters covering the advance. The searches uncovered a series of heart-rending scenes in each of those small rooms. The officers were accompanied all the time by a loud sobbing, crying and wailing from the female occupants. When the officers tried to enter one of the rooms, they found the door locked and had to break in. The room was slightly larger and in it a group of some twenty children, some at a guess, not more than ten years of age was discovered cowering against the walls of the room or crouching in one of the corners. They were all in great fear and distress and mostly sobbing and moaning quietly.

Two of the specially trained female officers were left in that room in a largely vain attempt to try to pacify the children with sweets and chocolate and eventually to persuade the children to accompany them outside to be handed over to staff from social services. The officers stayed with the children until the neighbouring rooms on that wing had been cleared and clearance had been given so that they could be safely evacuated via the pathway to move downstairs. Eventually by friendly persuasion and the magic of confectionary, they managed to get the children to move downstairs and out into the safe hands of the waiting social services staff.

The sound of armed police shouting their messages in the other corridor resounded throughout the house as entry was forced to successive small rooms, revealing a similar horrific scene of terrified and traumatized women and young girls. In some of the rooms, they were being guarded by male guards. The guards were disarmed, searched, and handcuffed peacefully and passed back to colleagues in the supporting units. They were finally handed over to officers at the detention vans for loading and eventual transportation to the police station.

Finally clearance of the upstairs corridors was achieved. It was now clear that so many women and girls had been discovered, that a message had to be beamed to the Deputy Chief Constable to send up additional female officers and to alert social services of the magnitude of their future task. It would eventually be confirmed that as well as functioning as a brothel, the premises were used as some kind of holding station for freshly trafficked, mainly young and some very young women, from different southern European countries and a few from various different parts of Africa. They would be held at the house before their introduction to their new work and subsequent sale to other criminal gangs pursuing prostitution in big cities or placement in one or other of the mafia gang's other brothels further up England in one or other of the country's large metropolitan areas.

The clearance of the other corridor had proceeded at an accelerated pace. The second corridor, like the first one, comprised a series of large Victorian bedrooms, each of which had been subdivided into the same smaller cubicle-like rooms as had been discovered in the first corridor. Each was sparsely furnished with a well-worn bed and wall hooks for hanging clothing and occasionally a battered and disfigured old bedside table or chest of drawers and a rather shabby timeworn armchair. At the far end of the corridor was a Spanish balcony of former glory with the glass doors padlocked and a view out onto a large but neglected garden. The doors had not been opened for some considerable time and the balcony appeared not to have been used for a very long time. This led to the assumption that this was the reason that there was no attempt to use this route for a possible means of escape. No further occupants having been found and after a thorough inspection of all the small rooms, the wing was declared safe. Attention now turned to the attic and what was assumed to be the one remaining gunman, who was thought to have shot the two policemen.

Access to the attic was difficult at any time because of the narrow and steep steps which gave access to it. In fact, on closer examination, it appeared to be little more than a ladder. In view of this difficulty of access and the estimation that the gunman was still up in the attic, the stairs to the attic were seen as a definite threat to the life and limb of any constable below. So the officer in charge, Superintendent Julian Charles, deployed a small detachment of his best and most experienced marksmen, arranged so as to have an axial view of the attic landing at the top of the ladder-like steps. They used their ballistic shields to protect their bodies.

Shots were fired by the police to try to entice some appearance by the gunman, so that he would show even some small part of his body. An additional warning in two languages was loud-speakered up the stairs saying that there was no escape from the location of the attic and if he surrendered peacefully he would not be harmed. He had a choice between capture and survival on the one hand and death if he continued to fire on the police. The message was relayed again in Albanian. No response was received from the supposed gunman.

Superintendent Charles in charge of the operation volunteered to ascend the stairs himself, while his men were covering him from below. Almost as soon as he began to make a noise with his feet on the steps, the gunman showed himself readying to shoot the policeman. One of the police marksmen shot the gunman in the head and he tumbled down the stairs dead. Afterwards the on the spot examination of what little documentation the man had on his body, led to the surprise discovery that he was not from Albania at all. He was an Iraqi Kurd from Kurdistan.

On inspection all the small rooms in the subdivided bedrooms in the attic, no further occupants were found. The attic was consequently declared clear and safe together with the rest of the house.

At that point the armed unit handed the house over to the regular police. The members of the forensic team entered the premises paying particular attention to the office and the contents of the difficult to open strong box. After a speedy, but thorough examination, the house was locked and sealed and the police units began to retire, preceded by the buses and other vehicles of the local authority Social Services Department. Restrictions on access, pedestrian and vehicular were also lifted as the last policemen left the scene.

In the debriefing session the following week, the tally of finds from the raid almost represented a king's ransom. Over two million pounds, predominantly in five pound notes, had been discovered, a massive haul of four different kinds of drugs was uncovered too, mainly in the kitchen cupboards. Moreover, a stock of vintage stamps and precious gems was found in the safe after the code was cracked. In addition, sixty five women, many of them young girls, were liberated from cruel bondage and an early death. They had all been placed in the safe hands of social services staff. They were being rehabilitated or according to their own wishes repatriated to their home country. Some few brave women had agreed to be interviewed with a member of social services staff present. Two madams were freed while under further investigation. In addition about a dozen children had been rescued and given over to the care of the local authority.

Three members of the criminal gang had been shot and killed by the security forces and seven other men were being held under arrest on a variety of serious charges including sexual intercourse with a minor. They were continuing to be detained and subject to further interviews under caution. As well, a wealth of documentation and disorganised budgetary accounts was discovered. These were being examined further by the local police and likewise by the National Financial Fraud Squad. Some of the documentation threw light on the business association between the mafia gang in Ayton and their bosses in East London.

Finally, the reassuring news came though from the medical registrar's office at the local hospital that after an initial examination and treatment, the two officers did not suffer any life-threatening or life-changing injuries. It appeared that their body armour had saved them from more severe injury. They had been treated for severe bruising and shock and would be released after a couple of days into the care of their families. They would continue to be under observation and absent from work due to the need for an extended convalescence. Insofar as it was requested, the officers' families were similarly being provided with on-going support by specially trained officers.

All members of the force were proud of their achievements, which were celebrated over many a friendly drink for many months to come. But even more difficult challenges still awaited officers, including the netting of senior figures in the local gang, none of whom had been netted in this or the previous raids.

Moreover, the police were as yet unaware of the retaliatory measures being planned by the gang, which would mightily tax and test the resilience, human resources and resource capacity of the forces of law and order.

Chapter Eighteen: A Calculated Response

When Tristen Rexhepi, the Chief of the UK Albanian mafia, entered the office of the new Ayton headquarters building on the morning after the police raid on the gang's second brothel, his mood was one of pure venom. He was furiously angry because he believed that his considered advice to what he considered to be his two subordinates, Samir Pecic and Xhoel Gegaj, to move the business with the stock of cocaine and cash to a more secure location elsewhere, had been disregarded or acted on too tardily.

He had warned that in his view there was an imminent danger of further raids by the local constabulary on a further one of their premises or their other assets. He felt deeply that his alert had found an inadequate response or even not been taken seriously and thus ignored.

This had never happened to him before and he was furious and determined that someone would pay for this further disaster in the local business, just when he was doing his best to get it on its feet again. He proceeded to pour out a whole stream of caustic venom onto his Ayton subordinates, all the time glaring at them as they tried to avoid his gaze.

"I warned you that given the manifest successes of the first raid and the one on the beauty salon as well, this brothel would be the obvious next and most high priority target for the police. Indeed, I advised you that it needed to be moved to a more secure location, like yesterday, and I recall that my loyal assistant, Noel Shkodra, had endorsed my advice. It was as clear as if it had been written down, that this establishment was all the more important because of its size, stock of drugs and cash and massive income potential. Moreover, I emphasised to you that the fact that it was a major store house for supplies of cannabis, heroin, powder cocaine and crack would be an added attraction for the police under their current Chief Constable."

Looking like a man under pressure, he stopped for an instant to draw breath, but not for long.

"This stock has been lost. It was allocated by the bosses in Albania from their purchases through Chinese middle men in South America for sale in Ayton and for further dissemination via the county lines system to the surrounding region as well. It was worth millions. Our bosses in Tirana will not easily forgive or forget such a loss. I shall be calling on Noel to prepare a detailed account of the cost of all these losses, assuming that, given the state of your books, you have no idea. That is what made it such a highly desirable prize for the local police. But there is likewise the impact on our reputation with the other gangs in Ayton to be taken into account, especially those who trade in drugs. They will now see an organisation that is weak and they will be emboldened to move into our patch. That is a usual consequence of loss of face."

He hesitated again to draw breath and Samir saw his opportunity and interjected quickly.

"But Tristen, the former brothel with stock, staff and drugs was all moved to a new location on the very night of our meeting, as previously agreed with you and Noel."

"Here! Here!" Xhoel called out in a rare demonstration of firm support for his boss.

"I said a **secure** new location! The place you chose was clearly not that! Was it? You two must know what happens to people who fail the bosses. You do, don't you? And their families? Especially as the cost in lost product and cash is so high and two of our men have died and others have been captured and are being held on bogus charges. The legal costs for those arrested and the upkeep costs for the families of those who were killed are likely to be enormous. And you don't have any spare cash here at Ayton at the moment. In fact you are well-nigh bankrupt. But tell me is it right that you delegated the assassination of the Chief Constable to an Iraqi Kurd and that he killed two policemen before being shot to death himself? You idiots! And Noel tells me that you had even paid half the extortionate fee agreed in advance. So you have paid out from your depleted cash stock and cash supply a vast sum for a job, which will now never be done. Do you get the message that catastrophe will send to Tirana? The whole thing is a mega-disaster!"

"Samir made another forlorn effort to stall the flow of vituperation, which was being deposited on himself and Xhoel, but Tristen would have nothing of it. Quite the reverse and he continued his seemingly endless stream of spiteful rancour.

"At this moment I can tell you I am considering very seriously sending the two of you back to Tirana with a note to my bosses there to the effect that you are both useless and being in office together, you are twice as useless. Hopeless in fact! And you know what that will mean!"

"What do you suggest to rectify the situation, boss?"

Samir requested knowing full well that if he and Xhoel fell, Tristen would most likely fall as well and he must know that himself. He had come down from London to straighten things out and the situation was now infinitely worse than when he had arrived a few days ago. His bosses in Tirana would surely see him as equally culpable. Maybe even more so due to his superior position in the hierarchy and the fact that the deterioration at the Ayton office had all occurred after he had interfered. They could all only hope that it would be the other guy, who would get the chop.

But Tristen continued his apparently unending litany of vitriolic menace flavoured with a torrent of bad news.

"And it's not just the stock, the treasure and the soldiers that we are losing at an unsustainable level. It our reputation as well. Already the Kurds have established a new brothel on the other side of town. Small, it's true! But it is a sign of the times. They're very effectively vacuuming up our trade as quickly as we lose it. They are already county lining more than we are and trying to undercut our prices as well. Now powerful gangs from the big cities are moving in as well to take over what we have had as a clear patch for years and they are making it pay and pay well. They win. We lose. And once the rot starts it is irreversible. I understand from Noel that a couple of our county liners have been attacked and seriously injured in a dispute between our county liners and those from one of our competitors. One was knifed and another was shot, so both are now out of action and not earning for us. I am further informed that some of our county line youngsters have already debunked to other firms, given a bonus incentive offered by both the Kurds and Turks. These losses are unsustainable even in the short term and not least in a region that was and should be once more a bonanza in both of these products and has been in the past, before you two idiots came along."

Samir sighed at the unadorned insults by Tristen and took a deep breath as he tried to interrupt the apparently unending flow of poison and what he considered to be menacing rancour that was being showered unfairly both on him and his colleague Xhoel. But he failed miserably and the flow of vitriol was picked up once again.

"I'll tell you what you have to do, and you'll do it to the letter this time or else." Overbearing in tone of voice, Tristen dictated, livid and face red with fury.

"Sure boss. Just tell us." Samir responded meekly spreading his hands on either side of his body as a sign of submission.

"Firstly, in the case of the job on the Chief of Police, I am going to bring in my main sharpshooter from London, Bajram Krasniki. He is a Kosovar and a trained sniper with years of experience in the Kosovo Liberation Army and many Serb heads to count. You will arrange for him to have whatever support he needs to do the job and depart quickly. He does not do cheap. In fact, he will be very expensive of course. You will make arrangements to set aside what he asks for, ready for me to transfer it to him on completion. Secondly with regards to the county lining, and the recruitment of new carriers from the college, you will have to be more forceful and do whatever is necessary to gain the co-operation of this young lady from the local college. Threaten her close relatives, abduct her, do whatever is necessary to produce her co-operation. But get on with it and soon! Oh and get a message to the Kurds and Turks that we will tolerate no interference from them with our county liners and sales in the region and they are not to poach our couriers or else. Any further action on that front would mean war. Hands off! Thirdly and with regard to the brothels I want two replacements set up within the week with bonus offers to our frequent customers. Mind you, no messing about with beauty salons though. I am able to offer you some help and support with arrangements for a limited replacement stock and a few locally recruited guards trained in Barking, East London. You will find the safe accommodation for these new developments here in town like lightening. Lastly get this headquarters office moved from here today, this morning within the hour to a new and safe location on the outskirts of town. Leave this place partially furnished so that it can be used by our soldiers or those from elsewhere, who are called in to help out. You still have a number of properties here on the outskirts of Ayton. So you have a choice as to which one is the most secure. Speed is of the essence now and we must move rapidly on all fronts at the same time. Let me know how you are getting on tomorrow at the same time or before if you have progress to report. In the meantime, I shall be contacting our friends in London to get the sharpshooter here as soon as possible and to obtain the new stock and guards for the replacement brothels. Some guards you can obtain locally from the asylum seeker hotel."

"That's quite a menu. But I promise that Xhoel and I shall do our best to give satisfaction."

Samir promised and his commitment was endorsed by a vigorous nod of Xhoel's head.

"Well, that's not good enough. I have had your promises before and see what they have reaped. Chaos! Hogwash! I want action as proof of your sincerity this time or you're off to Tirana forthwith."

When they met again at Tristen's request in the late morning rather than the afternoon of the next day, the first announcement was that the sharpshooter from the London gang, Bajram Krasniki, had arrived overnight because of the urgency of his task, as portrayed by Tristen. He was placed in the hands of Xhoel and driven to his accommodation before being briefed by Tristen and Samir.

"So I've done my part and got my colleague from London here immediately. What headway on the other issues, Samir?"

"Well, we are well advanced. We have identified two of our larger and older properties on the outskirts of town that would be suitable for replacements for the two raided ones. Some of my boys are there at this very moment adapting and furnishing the accommodation to purpose and they have been given the means to purchase whatever is necessary to accommodate the women and receive our clients in an appropriate manner soonest. They will be transferring some of our holdings of powder cocaine and crack to the two houses from the office here. I am reliably informed that both premises should be ready to accommodate the women you have promised to import from our friends in Barking on arrival. By the way, how many women did you say we would be receiving and when did you say they would be arriving?"

"They should most likely be here first thing tomorrow morning and the first batch will be about fifteen, maybe a few more depending on the number of trafficked women they receive from abroad on that day. The Barking office was not quite sure how many they could spare and emphasised that they will need to be transported in small numbers. They will have travelled overnight from London. It is more discreet that way, as you know, Samir. Anyway they will probably need a rest and time to settle in, so we can expect to be using the wire to inform prospective clients when they can come to our new premises in a couple of days. No more! Did you remember to fix up mainline telephone systems for the two establishments? Although, of course, most of the clients and all of our own men will prefer mobile communication as less conspicuous and less traceable and therefore more secure."

At that moment, Xhoel came back from his tasks concerning reception, accommodation and feeding of the sharpshooter, Bajram Krasniki, and Tristen addressed him anxiously.

"Have you settled in our new colleague, Xhoel? Were there any problems? Is he happy with his accommodation and its security? Did you brief him fully on his target? Supply him with photos and whatever else he needs for the job?"

"Yes, he seems to be content with the accommodation, its security and the provisions for his meals, although he stated that he is not expecting to be here long as he has other pressing commissions in the Capital. So he needs to get back. He underlined the fact that that he is so busy at the moment that he only agreed to do this job as a favour to you. He said that he will have a rest this morning and will then scout the areas where he is likely to encounter the Chief Constable and choose the spot from which he can best and most safely carry out the job. He indicated that he expected to commence surveillance for that spot tomorrow and given a fair wind, hopes to complete in the next couple of days and return to the metropolis as quickly as possible. I have given him a few pictures of the Chief of Police. Oh and he said that you already have the details of the account into which full payment is to be made on completion. It is the same as for the jobs he has done for you before. Some foreign Bank account, I believe. He did not share the details with me."

"Thank you Xhoel for the successful completion of that crucial and important job. Did you offer to introduce him to the most likely sites for the execution of this crucial task?"

"Yes, I did. He invited me to call him Bajram and thanked me most courteously for the offer. But he said that he would rather scout prospective sites for himself. It was better if he was the only person with the knowledge of the intended site. He did add that, in case of need, it was good to have a local available but to let him do his own reconnoitre first by himself. I think he was concerned though about the possibility of my being recognised at any of the sites he might scout. Thus alerting the authorities, you know."

"Yes he was always a chivalrous but cautious man. He always did prefer discretion, and he quite correctly assumes that the fewer people who know the time and place of his action, the better and safer for him. He would say that is the reason he is still alive today."

Switching back to his review of actions planned yesterday for completion today, he reverted to posing some extremely tough questions to Samir once again in a very aggressive manner.

"What progress do we have for the immediate removal of this office to a new and safer home? We do not want to make the same error twice, do we? Like we did with the second brothel. So can you just fill me in on that issue?"

"That was a bit more difficult and time consuming, but we have found an abandoned suite of offices and flats in a small cul de sac largely hidden by trees and other greenery that would be inconspicuous and safe and contain sufficient accommodation for our immediate needs. It has good communications to our other properties. It was formerly owned by a small food company that went bust during the pandemic. "

"When can we move in? That is now urgent and, as I have explained to you several times, we cannot stay here any longer."

"Some of the boys are already there making the necessary arrangements, including a barred and bolted entrance gate to the hammerhead, with a gatekeeper's shed for a guard. I estimate that by tomorrow it will all be ready. But late in the day."

"That will have to do then. But no later and make sure all the communications are appropriately fixed up, including the internet connections and telephone services. Oh, and a fixed wall safe and a secure store for the stock of drugs. We shall need to move tomorrow night from about eleven. OK? "

"Can do." Xhoel and I will be going there this very afternoon to check on the progress and we shall brief you on our return."

"Well don't forget to leave a few little shockers for our adversaries when they come to raid the empty building, which I am sure they will do in the next couple of days. A little welcome surprise present for them, so to speak."

So the scene was set for a powerful counterattack by the criminal gang and it looked as though the tables were turning. The counter-offensive was to be orchestrated by the odious and tyrannical UK and Barking mafia boss, Tristen Rexhepi.

The forces of law and order in Ayton had no means of knowing of the threat. They were, therefore, totally unprepared. Additionally they would possibly have difficulty mustering the human resources to launch any rapid counter measures at short notice.

Chapter Nineteen: A Reassessment

After his long absence on Covid sick-leave, Chief Constable Horace Lashley was back in the chair for the emergency meeting called to assess the state of play in the operation to crush the mafia criminal gang's iniquitous drug and prostitution activities in Ayton and the surrounding region. The results of the lateral flow and PCR tests had proved negative, but he still felt somewhat at sea with some of the symptoms of what came later to be called long Covid.

Chief Constable Lashley was definitely not feeling great, with pain in his body, a feeling of tension and shortage of breath in his chest and a sensation of fuzziness in his head. In addition, although he would never admit it to his men or his family, the threat of his assassination was weighing heavily on his mind. His unease about that threat persisted, however, in spite of the fact that he had been assured by his senior colleagues, that his would-be assassin, a local member of a Kurdish criminal mafia gang, had himself been killed during a recent police raid on an Albanian cartel brothel in the town.

In spite of this welcome news, he felt out of touch with the staff and their actions during his absence and their ambitious expectations. He surmised that his subordinates would probably feel similarly towards him. He had to admit that his staff, particularly senior staff, had coped very well in his absence on sick leave, although some were beginning to express some reservations about the effectiveness of the currently planned strategy.

He was depressed about those reservations, but worried about the apparent lack of leads too in the current operation to find the headquarters of this vile organisation and finally bring down perhaps the town's dominant criminal gang. *Could they be right about our overall strategy?* He asked himself uneasily.

One major gap in the intelligence was that the Force had more recently failed to receive any feedback from their placemen in the gang, as the new leader of the gang, Tristen Rexhepi appeared to be insisting that all non-Albanians should be excluded from meetings. It was nevertheless learned by the CID that these meetings were considering his ambitious plans for a counterattack against the authorities to at least recoup what they had lost in raids in the past few weeks.

Notably, the police were perplexed by the fact that when the previously identified main base of the gang was raided, nothing had been found and there was no one there. The former gang premises were deserted, but a series of booby traps had been left and one policeman had been seriously injured and two others lightly injured in the subsequent explosions during the search of the large building. The nagging question was how that could have happened. Did the gang have a leak or was it a good guess or just fortuitous after all?

The meeting called today was attended by the usual group of officers, including Deputy Chief Constable, Heather Compton-Jones, the titular head of the recently established drugs and prostitution unit. Her assistants, Superintendent Rajiv Gundara and Detective Inspector Maria Clarke, in charge of the special force on drugs and prostitution were in attendance too. Assistant Chief Constable Mark Brownlow was also present, together with approximately twenty officers, including beat officers and members of the armed response unit. In addition, John Casey was present from the National Financial Fraud Squad and, signifying a major change in the local Force's tactics on raids, there was a new attendee in the person of Superintendent Julian Charles, the officer in charge of the local armed police unit.

There were, in addition, several representatives from the local authority, including senior officer June Browning from the Department of Social Services as well as officers in charge of women's and children's departments and some assistant staff. All in all, it was thus a very large gathering.

The Chief Constable opened the meeting somewhat formally with a reference to the officers injured in a raid, which took place a few days ago.

"I should like to begin by offering our deepest sympathy and support for the three police officers, who were shot and wounded in our most recent operation to take out the mafia gang's headquarters and interrupt their people trafficking and prostitution businesses and the officers recently injured by booby traps in our raid on the former headquarters of the criminal gang. These officers and all of their families are in our thoughts today and we wish them well and a swift and full recovery. I have sent to each officer and to their immediate family, a message that they are in our thoughts today at this meeting and that we are there for them."

"Perhaps I should begin this morning by welcoming you all most warmly to this further meeting of the expanded emergency planning group. I know that this is a disappointing time for colleagues from the ranks of the police following on from the unsuccessful raid on the mafia's headquarters building in the past few days. But that is police work. Not every operation can be crowned with success and that undoubtedly applied to the recent raid on the headquarters of this criminal gang. They estimated correctly, or were leaked information, which I very much doubt, that consequent on our other successful operations we would be seeking out their central command headquarters in our town. These gangsters were certainly present in the building some twenty four hours before the beginning of the planned raid, as reported by two of our beat officers. But when our advance party arrived to do the preliminary work of sealing off the access roads, the place was absolutely empty."

The chief officer stopped at that point as if contemplating how he could counteract the manifest disappointment amongst the group and cheer them up.

"I would urge you all to take heart from our other very successful raids lately. Together, we shall finally succeed in crushing this monstrous organisation, which is damaging to us financially but much more than that, it is noxious to the health and welfare of our community and especially the health of our young people. Of that I am certain. Superintendent Charles, officer in charge of the armed police unit, you wanted to say something. I am sorry I got rather carried away. Please the floor is yours."

"Yes, Chief Constable, with your permission, I have some news that I hope will lift the spirits of members just a little. But first I want to make a plea. Our enemy is proving himself capable of and skilled in the use of extreme violence, including the use of lethal weapons. They will do anything whatsoever to achieve their goals and when their intentions are frustrated or they themselves feel threatened or cornered, they will quickly resort to extreme violence. He seems to have changed his tactics and we must change ours too, but of course in our case within the Law. In the previous raid where arms were used by our criminal adversaries, the outcome might well have been rather different. Had the three injured constables been from the armed unit, one might surmise that the injuries would certainly have been less serious or the officers would have emerged from their experience uninjured. In future raids, we should allow the armed police unit to proceed before any other units begin entry to the premises being raided. Having said that, I have some good news about our injured colleagues. They are beginning their recovery and they are looking forward to re-joining our ranks in the future. They say that doctors are predicting that there will not be any long term ill effects, although a fairly long convalescence will probably be necessary. They send their best wishes to all their colleagues and to those present in this meeting."

At that point, the Deputy Chief Constable, the head of the drugs and prostitution unit, signalled to the chair that she too had some information to share with the meeting.

"Chief. In the early hours of this morning a small minibus packed with fifteen young women and with two foreign men in control was stopped on the motorway outside of Ayton. In short, the men were arrested for people trafficking and conveyed to the police station and fifteen young women, some very young, many distressed and no doubt deeply traumatised, were released into the care and custody of the local authority Social Services Department. My warm thanks to colleagues from that Department for responding so quickly and so early in the day and at such an ungodly hour to our request for assistance. Thanks too, for immediately on arrival at the scene, taking the young women into safe keeping and care."

Felix Brigstowe, Head of the local CID gestured to the Chair his wish to add to the Deputy Chief's statement.

"I have two things to add to what was just said. Firstly initial sensitive interviews with the young women by specially trained female PCs with a female member of Social Services present has shown that there was another similar minibus similarly travelling with a cargo of young women from Moldova like the one we captured. We are still searching for that vehicle and I believe it is only a matter of time before we find it. Secondly we have important details about the organised crime group, associated with these two transports. It would appear that it is the same organised criminal gang that is the subject of a special operation by this force and whose two brothels we have just closed. We have inside information that they have not only moved their business centre to a location somewhere in the suburbs of Ayton, but that they are in the course of establishing two replacement brothels in the same districts. These young women were intended to provide what the mobsters call 'the stock' for these two new openings. We currently have feelers out to find the exact location of these two new sites."

Sergeant David Berger was the next to speak.

"Chief, the next meeting of young Andrea with that scoundrel Joel, or Xhoel, from the same organised crime group in town is likely to take place tomorrow. With your permission, I could request that the location of the gang's new businesses be raised subtly by her as a subject of interest to us. She seems to be very good at formulating cracking good questions speculatively so that her actual knowledge is not revealed nor ours either. As promised, she will of course be shadowed for her own safety by two of our officers when she meets him after college tomorrow afternoon."

"What do **you** think, David?" The Chief Constable requested his professional colleague's opinion.

"Yes that might be a good move, if she can do it without revealing what our intention is. Fine. Go ahead. But remember that the headquarters central office of this criminal gang is the main objective.

If we can take that down, then it seems to me the other two premises will automatically fall as will probably all activities of the gang in Ayton and the surrounding areas, including the indoor cannabis farms. And if that happens, it may be that the gang will decide that the excessive costs just do not merit doing business in Ayton and move away. Then we can start on doing the same to the other such criminal gangs in this town, such as the Kurdish, Turkish and Italian ones."

"In that case, I'll brief her on what we want to know and I'll discuss with her how she might best phrase her inquiries about the subjects without raising their alarm about what we intend to do next."

The Chief Constable interrupted the discussion to turn to the issue of the next moves available to the Ayton Police Force in the operation to take down the criminal mafia gang.

"It seems to me that until we find one or other, but preferably all of the premises we have spoken about today, we are short on options for our next operation. But what do others think?"

It was unusual for the Chief Constable to be so indeterminate in his questioning and it was not clear what kind and detail of reaction he might be hoping for.

"Well quite frankly I think that Ayton is rapidly becoming a narco-city, not just for the sale of drugs but for their production as well."

This was the somewhat controversial answer to the Chief Officer, offered by Sergeant Julie Harper. She continued in the same vein.

"For all the money and manpower we are pouring into the fight against illegal drugs and the casualties, caused by those drugs, consumption and addiction are increasing alarmingly and under growing demand from the Public and seemingly ever cheaper. Prices are being held artificially low in the competition for business between the major gangs, which sometimes formerly used to explode in violence and still do but more rarely now. The reason is that there are today, plenty of drugs available to cover the need for lucrative profits of all major drug gangs. The corollary is that not only the quantity, but the strength of the drugs is on an upward trend as well to the Public detriment. Deaths from all kinds of illegal drugs are mounting annually by just less than five per cent and the UK currently has the dubious accolade of having the highest number of young drug users in Europe. Unfortunately we do not have figures for Ayton, but it is impossible to imagine this growth is not happening here in Ayton too."

Sergeant David Berger politely interrupted Sergeant Julie Harper's delivery with her permission.

"Thank you Julie for permitting me just to add as a beat Sergeant that I agree strongly with what you are arguing. It may sound incredible, but at the coalface level, that is the beat, we are feeling the impact of the new concordats between the major drug dealing gangs at all stages of the business. They are combining and working together from the production in South America mainly or more recently indoors in this country, through the transportation jointly of their products, through to sale on the town and street levels. The challenge must, therefore, arise as to whether our current approach to only one such gang, however dominant it is in this illicit market, is logical and cost effective. How can we succeed in the overall objective of radically reducing drug consumption, if we do not have an overall, combined plan to tackle all of these evil groups peddling them on our streets? Thank you Julie."

Julie picked up again on the thread of her argument.

"Thank you David for those words of support. David is right, at the ground floor level, the streets, we are sadly failing the younger generation in our community. Indeed one of the very disturbing features of the new tsunami of dependence is the emergence of intergenerational drug addiction. This is a serious health and social pandemic, which to my mind demands a comprehensive response not just an attack on one of the criminal gangs, but a strategy which covers the whole corrupt trade run by all the criminal gangs in our city. I fear that when and if we crush one criminal gang, another just takes its place and that is what is happening now in Ayton. In any case, the lieutenants of this game do not live in Ayton and often not even on the estate in Barking in East London, but they are based on the Continent or in some cases in South America, way out of our reach."

Deputy Chief Constable, Heather Compton Jones, was swift to respond to what she considered an idealistic distraction from the main purpose of the meeting. She did, however, accept the rationale behind Julie's well-presented argument.

"I agree with Julie's very interesting argument that we should broaden our focus as the drug cartels have, so to speak, broadened there's. But there are two factors that suggest that we should stay with our present plan for the moment. The biggest is whether we have the resources to match the ambition. I surmise that we currently do not. The second is that this criminal group of Albanian mafia origin is the dominant player in the supply of drugs to the other gangs involved in trafficking and selling of drugs in this area. If we can only clip their wings here, we will disrupt the supply of drugs to the other more minor actors in the field."

Assistant Chief Constable Mark Brownlow added his weight to the argument of the Deputy Chief trying to keep the focus on what it was feasible to achieve given the current strained resource context rather than what he considered to be an inflated imagination of what the force could ideally do. But he appreciated the ambition and power of Julie's argument and attributed the relative failure of the governments' expensive drug strategy in making little impact on the exponential rise in drug consumption to poor implementation, lack of evaluation at close quarters and continual monitoring and thus static policy-making and consequently improvement stasis.

"I agree with Julie's argument but correspondingly with the Deputy Chief's assessments. For the moment and given the constrained nature of the resources available to us, I personally believe that we should focus all our attention on tracing the location of this criminal organisation's properties and take them out. With that approach we have a good chance of taking out some of the top people in the group and stymieing the supply of drugs not only to that group but to all the others in Ayton and the region as well. Let's keep our eye fixed firmly on the ball and find those establishments and close them down soonest. That goal has already been successfully commenced with the closure of three previous establishments, forcing the criminal gang to move its headquarters and yielding a large collection of drugs and a huge amount of cash and captured criminals and freeing dozens of abused women, many of them young women. We are currently causing the gang grievous budgetary hardship and I believe that our objective is even now within our capacity to achieve in full."

John Casey, a participating observer from The National Financial Fraud Squad added a brief endorsement of the previous point about the commercial damage already being done to the criminal enterprise.

"Chair, I hope you will permit me as an observer to make a further comment about the grave financial losses being suffered by this criminal gang. Just to set your own operations here in Ayton in a national context for a moment, what you have achieved here, when added to similar operations in other parts of the country, means that this criminal enterprise is suffering millions of pounds overall in lost income, often on an on-going basis. Viewed in that perspective your work is not only successful but nationally important too. Thank you for your engagement. All of you."

The Chief Constable responded generously.

“Thank you very much for that statement, which puts the importance of our work very firmly in a national context. As a welcome observer at occasional meetings, we always value your contributions to those of our meetings that you can manage to attend.

Police Sergeant June Chapman, a keen aspirant for promotion and an ally of the Chief Constable, tried to revert the focus of the meeting onto the next operation. She offered her support to the management plan for the next steps, prioritising the identification of the three premises referred to already and advocating their early closure.

“Like most people here, I suppose, I think that we should concentrate on the task that we have already commenced and complete it successfully, before we embark on even more ambitious plans, for which we have neither resources of money nor staff at this moment in time. We have all heard the comments of our colleague from the National Financial Fraud Agency about the grievous monetary damage that together we are currently causing to this criminal gang and the important contribution of our work to that overall national picture. That alone, should convince us to stay the course.”

It was at this juncture in the meeting that the Chief Superintendent caught up with the need to intervene and clinch the main decision, even if rather weakly, before it all went off the rails. He tried to maintain the balance achieved by his senior staff.

"I think that with those excellent contributions our decision has been identified with great clarity. It is to intensify and accelerate our search for the three establishments of the Albanian mafia gang in Ayton and close them down. At the same time, we will be trawling in as many of the gang's top brass as possible and coincidentally severing the supply chain of drugs to the other criminal gangs involved in this pernicious trade. Just as soon as we have identified the locations we shall meet again and plan the action. Thank you all very much for your participation in this meeting."

The Chief Officer stood up and together with two or three other officers prepared to leave the conference room, where the meeting had taken place to go to the waiting staff car outside the front entrance. The junior officers gave way to permit him to exit first and get into his official car. As he left the building there was the sound of a distant crack and the Chief Constable's head jerked ever so slightly backwards, he lurched and fell to the ground with a small neat hole in the centre of his forehead.

His staff were horror-stricken and demoralised.

The contract had been fulfilled.

Bajram Krasniki was soon on his way back to Barking confidently expecting an early payment of his fee directly into his foreign account for a job successfully completed.

Chapter Twenty. A Change of Heart

Driving across town to meet Andrea in the café, as prearranged the last time they spoke at the supermarket a few days ago, Xhoel Gegaj was thinking of the young woman he was about to meet. Most women he had ever met had been in the context of a dominance-submission relationship in one or other of the mafia syndicate's brothels in Kosovo, London or Ayton. Apart of course from his own mother, whom he lost in childhood, a victim of the wicked Serb paramilitaries during the civil war in Kosovo. This was indeed a new, even life-changing experience for him and he was really looking forward to meeting her again today.

He reflected that Andrea was so different from any other woman he had ever met in his life. She had a certain élan. She was highly intelligent, well-educated and very feminine, but very single minded, independent and determined as well. He had actually enjoyed being interrogated by her and her gran at their last meeting in the supermarket café. Of course that conversation had made him suspect what her purpose in speaking with him really was. But he was not somehow offended by her intention. It didn't matter in comparison with the unique intellectual stimulation and creature satisfaction that their conversations gave him. A bright light had begun to shine in an otherwise dull and uninteresting treadmill of a life.

He had found himself learning a lot from her, not least about himself. It was not just the confident and self-assured way in which she conducted herself, physically and intellectually. She had even indirectly interested him in starting to read an English woman author called Victoria Hislop and he was enjoying the story of 'The Island' by her so far. What was exciting him today was the eager thought of what they would speak about this time and what he would learn from her. It was all a new life for him and after all, what had he done with his life so far? He mused to himself.

It is true that his original intention had been to seduce her via drugs into becoming a servant of the gang, to convert her into a county liner for the criminal gang, of which he was himself a servant, and to induce other youngsters from the college she attended to follow her into that bondage as well. Or worse still if that failed, he even thought of forcing her into drug- addiction and once hooked, thence into a short life of prostitution. In addition access to children in the school was an important part of his original plan. Unthinkable now! But oh such a short time ago it was not just thinking, it was his firm intention! He was horrified at the recollection of his own intentions.

But little by little he was beginning to realise that he respected her too much, even liked her too much to still envisage achieving those goals. He experienced an uplifting feeling about her, which he did not understand. For the short while whenever he was with her, she seemed to banish the constant loneliness of his life. He just could not enact his original plan and spoil this feeling. In any case, it would be a simple waste of his first opportunity in life to have a decent, arguably even evergreen, relationship with a woman, and a very gifted woman at that. But what perplexed him most was that feeling of affinity with her and her life. She was ambitious and committed to her peers. He enjoyed her academic capacity and her athletic ability, her lifestyle and way of arguing, polite but hard.

Indeed, when he cast his mind back to their meetings so far, all too few and brief, he realised that this was the very first time in his life that he had ever accepted with enjoyable equanimity, contradictions and opinions, and especially those which were different from his own, let alone which challenged his views, from a woman. He felt that she had introduced him to the prospect of a new life and enjoyable new learning about other human beings different from a lust for domination. Likewise, she had helped him to see a new view of himself. She had, in effect, opened up for him an insatiable appetite for an alternative and better life that he was fully capable of and which was now beginning to reveal itself to him as a real possibility for him for the very first time in his life.

After parking his car at the cafe just before the agreed time, he hurried to the counter to buy a coffee and a hot chocolate and sought their usual table, which was fortunately just becoming free. A young couple were just standing up to leave the table still in engaged conversation and his thoughts drifted this way and that, imagining to himself that those two could be him and Andrea. He sat down and thought in impatient anticipation about Andrea. He waited playing with the cruets and sometimes catching the conversations and laughter of the other customers, leading normal lives with other equally normal people. He was distracted all the time by worrying about whether she would come. After all, he had rather mischievously stonewalled her on the last occasion they met. '*Force of habit!* He excused himself, although he regretted it. As the time passed quickly to the agreed hour and she did not appear, his heart sank deeper and deeper into melancholy. Would she come or had she realised his former malevolent purpose after all and walked away. If that were so, he could not blame her.

Meanwhile Andrea walked swiftly through the school gates, pushing her bicycle and bidding her many friends a hasty but cordial farewell and promising to see them tomorrow or this evening at the athletics club. She was slightly later than usual and wondered if Joel would wait or give up and disappear after waiting for a while. She did not know why she should worry. She had a full programme for the evening and she could not spare him a long time. But somehow she was looking forward to their meeting. Somehow she seemed to enjoy his company and the challenge of a sharp-minded discussion with him. Moreover, he seemed to her to be a man in desperate need of a humanly satisfying relationship. She had to recognise that she felt growing compassion for him. Or was it something more than just compassion? She thought of him and their interchanges.

Somehow he had a very acute way of answering her many questions and seemed to appreciate suggestions that challenged and excited him. She realised, full well, his pernicious purpose and his appurtenance to the gang that killed her father all those years ago. But she was beginning to forgive him, even like him a little. After all, he cannot have been a member of the gang when the murder of her father took place. He would have been a child or and even not yet alive, depending on what age he pretended to be! She smiled to herself and mounted her bicycle.

Still pondering her own emotions, she cycled swiftly the short distance from the school cycle park to the cafe. She arrived substantially later than had been their arrangement. All the time she had an anxious feeling of anticipated disappointment, would he have left? *But why?* She asked herself. If he had already left that would be one less commitment in a very busy life. After all, he was a criminal, even though she was convinced that he genuinely wanted to reform himself and his life. Moreover, she felt that she could help him to make that conversion. She locked her bicycle to one of the stanchions on the pavement outside the café shop and entered despondently, half expecting that he would have departed. As she looked at the last table they had used and saw nobody there except strangers, her heart sank. Then she cast her mind back to the previous occasion in the café when their previously routine table had been already occupied and they had been obliged to take an alternative one. She switched her search to their habitual table by the window and there he was fiddling nervously with the cruet and looking rather down-heartedly introverted. Her heart leapt. As they regarded each other across the café their faces lit up with a certain shared happiness and warm smiles.

"I'm really sorry I'm so late Joel. I was detained by some important issues about speech day that as head girl I needed to discuss with one of the senior teachers. Sorry about that."

"No problem, Andrea. Please don't worry. I'm just glad that you were able to come. No problem at all. Anyway, here's a hot chocolate for you, but if it is a little bit too cold for you now, I can easily get you another one."

"No need. I'm sure it is fine. The hot chocolates here are usually served piping hot."

"So, tell me what you have been up to since our last meeting at the supermarket café?" He began thirsting for the endearing sound of her voice.

"Well, the nearer we get to the end of term, the busier I get. I'm tying up business at the school and trying to prepare for the summer holidays and the new challenge in the autumn as well, all at the same time! For example, I was working this afternoon with a teacher preparing for the awards ceremony at the end of term, which includes presentations of book awards to scholars, who have excelled in a variety of ways during the last year. That includes some students, even if their excellence was in the extra effort they had made, not necessarily in the shape of a brilliant performance, or if they had overcome some major life issue in their personal lives or their school activity."

He listened intently to what he considered to be the musicality of her voice and appreciated every last word as she continued.

"It might be in academic achievement, progress made, improvements in performance, service to the school, athletic or sporting achievements and many other things. It is really very complicated. But it's very interesting and rewarding to me personally too. It is even more personally near to my heart as my gran, Emily, will be the one making at least some of the presentations. She is already preparing the little speech that she is expected to give, which I am vetting for her. She receives an award as well, actually two awards, a lovely bouquet of flowers and a book of her choice. She is quite keen on female authors like Joanna Trollope, Lisa Jewell and Jojo Moyes and more recently the prize-winning Irish woman author, Sally Rooney."

"What a richly diverse, busy and inspiring life you live and your wonderful relatives too. So different from my pre-war and wartime schooling in Kosovo, which now seems to me so very impoverished in comparison. Tell me, I should like to know more about the English system of education and schooling. Would you be willing to share with me something more about it?"

"Yes, I am very privileged in the excellent teachers that I have currently and have had in the past, for the most part any way. They make a very big difference. And the Ayton College has been granted an excellence award by the schools' supervisory body, Ofsted that is the Office for Standards in Education, Children's Services and Skills."

"Tell me something about the choice of book that your mother will make. As I probably mentioned to you last time, I have started reading one of

Victoria Hislop's books called 'The Island'. I'm really enjoying it. But I know nothing about English literature in general."

"Well as a present, I can get you a brief and readable account of English literature or you can look it up on the internet. Would you prefer an e-book or a paperback? I could try to have a copy for you the next time we meet up, here … or at the supermarket!"

She smiled at him in a charmingly knowing way.

"By the way, I have some paperback copies of the other of Victoria Hislop's books at home and I could lend you another one when you have finished this one, if you would like."

"I think I would prefer a paperback so I can keep it with me and read it at a convenient time such as at night-time in bed after work."

"As you wish."

"I'm interested to know something about English music as well. There are several kinds of national instrument in my home country, Kosovo. A shargia, is a plucked, fretted long necked lute and another plucked two-stringed instrument, is called a çifteli, played predominantly by the Gheg people in the various Balkans countries. Furthermore we have a music genre in Kosovo called Tallava, which is popular too in other Albanian-speaking communities elsewhere. What about here in Britain?"

"Well again, there is such a wealth of music and musicians it's impossible to give a thumbnail sketch. We actually have a school orchestra, in which I play the clarinet. I could get you a ticket to attend if you would like. But given your present profession, you would have to promise to keep a low profile and not tell people what you really do for a living."

They both smiled knowingly at each other.

"Yes please and I would come in my best suit and tie and I promise to keep a low profile and not reveal our secret. You know, I have learnt so much in our conversations since I met you. You have changed my life forever. Thank you."

"You see, Joel, there are many ways of enjoying life without hurting, harming or injuring other people. You have a choice. You could enjoy that kind of life if you wish. It is there for you to choose. Choose it now, I entreat you."

"Well only with your assistance, have I been able to go as far as I have so far."

"Oh don't be so silly. You would probably have realised yourself sooner or later what a dead end your current life is and changed it. It's what's in the heart that counts and you have that kind of heart. My father did and you still can."

"Do you play any other musical instruments?"

"No, although I play the clarinet moderately well. I began with a soprano recorder and I believe several countries have a similar instrument. Does Kosovo?"

"Similar but not the same, I believe. Our folk music uses the clarinet and the Turkish pipe, called the gerneta, but I'm not knowledgeable in music really. Never had the time or inclination."

"Hm. Interesting. I'll look the gerneta up on the internet when I get a minute."

"Tell me a bit about school sports please."

"Well this will have to be my last response, as I have a practice of the school orchestra to attend and after that this evening an athletics study group. Additionally I have a load of homework to complete before hand-in time tomorrow. But to answer your query, once again there is a huge range of different sports available. At my school we have several hockey teams, boys' and girl's football teams, mixed hockey teams, tennis, squash and badminton teams and different skill centred athletics groups. I have probably forgotten something, but you have an impression once again of the vast range and that's just in the school. There are, in addition, many other sports including some regional or minority ones. And the same applies to literature and music. At school, we have teams in board games such as chess and drafts besides and some card games, such as bridge."

"What a rich choice of activities in addition to the normal, formal curriculum you seem to offer your students at your school. So very different from my own schooling in Kosovo."

"Yes, as I said we are very fortunate here. Our youngsters have no need of drugs here. There is plenty for them to enjoy in life without hooking themselves to drugs of one kind or another and risking ruining their lives, or even losing their lives. At the city centre health centre there are furthermore excellent and confidential counselling services for any student in the school or indeed any young person who has left school, who for one reason or another feels under any kind of pressure. It's all free to those who are registered with the National Health Service, as you could be if you so wished. Anyway, I must dash now and I'll see you again next Tuesday, same time; same place. Take good care of yourself and remember what I said about the opportunity to change your life. That new life awaits you now. I can help you. But the decision is yours and yours alone. Bye now. See you next Tuesday. Hope to have the book for you by then. But can't promise. Next week. Same time. Same place."

"Bye and cycle carefully. Make sure no one crashes into you!"

He joked with a broad smile on his face.

As she disappeared from the café, he watched her cycle away with admiration and gratitude. He thought of how much he had learnt from her in just the short period of their thoroughly enjoyable conversation today. He felt happier with himself than he had done for a long time. He could not bear to think of the long wait until next Tuesday when he could see her again and maybe even receive a gift of the promised book from her. The very first time in his life and it was not even his birthday.

A further plus was that he could now look forward with enthusiasm to the visit to the college and being able to attend, *incognito* of course, a performance by her playing clarinet in the school orchestra, hear a different selection of music and see all the other instruments. Again a first in his life! He had so much to look forward to. With great happiness he cast his mind back again over their conversation today sieving it for happy thoughts and reflections to collect in his memory.

But that mood of elation was soon clouded when he asked himself how he could obtain the freedom to do what she had suggested. He was not autonomous. He had to face the thorny issue of how to sell his conversion to a more peaceful and enjoyable life to Samir and particularly to that domineering old dog from London. That could be rather dangerous, even fatal.

Chapter Twenty-One: Back in Business

There was a general air of rejoicing in the headquarters of the mafia organised crime gang, when the news came through of the assassination of Horace Lashley, the Chief Constable of Ayton. This was considered to be a payback for all the trouble he had caused the group over the past few weeks and the loss of their properties, stock, drugs, money and so-called soldiers. But most striking of all had been the loss of face vis-à-vis the other crime gangs and that was going to take some time and effort to recoup.

All that pain, however, seemed far away now. The atmosphere of jubilation was increased by the arrival of two sets of what were described as 'stock' for the two brothels and an additional four guards from London, two for each of the now completely adapted properties for the prostitution business. The group were now in business again. Or almost!

Tristen, Noel, Samir and Xhoel were all having a great laugh at the stopping by the local police of the minibus on the nearby motorway and the story that Tristen put out about it. He romanced that this was a decoy with channel-crossed asylum seekers as passengers and volunteer helpers doing the driving. The offer of a one-off bonus to any county liners, who introduced a new courier recruit, had likewise yielded a new wave of couriers, including many youngsters. These new recruits were already involved in removing some of the mountain of drugs supplied to the gang from London and the channel ports, which had piled up because the distribution of this large stock had previously been impeded due to the insufficient number of couriers.

Tomorrow the gang's business would be fully open again for the prostitution business, which should enable them to pay off some of their debts and transfer more money abroad to the bosses in Europe and elsewhere. The offer of a bonus to existing county line youngsters if the recruited another person to join the ranks of the county line 'brigade' was already paying off in increased sales and profits. There was, thus, a general sense of euphoric triumph at difficulties overcome and at the promise of a business now on the up and up again at last.

Xhoel, however, was on edge from the beginning of the meeting. He was still brooding on his conversation with Andrea and pondering his future life options and the chances of securing them against the expected vehement opposition of his colleagues. Regardless of his preoccupation with his personal relationship, conscious of his vulnerability, however, he managed to make it look as if he was joining in the general atmosphere of celebration and enjoying it as well. But he was aware all the time that sooner or later Samir and maybe especially Tristen would be probing what headway he had made in recruiting Andrea to their ranks as a supplier of new couriers or other useful activity for the firm. He still could not work out what his response could be. To keep her free by coming clean about his wish to change his lifestyle could mean almost certain death probably for both of them or even worse for Andrea.

Yet he could not, in his wildest dreams imagine a scenario in which he could now betray her. Not that it was love. Or was it? More like admiration and gratitude for the way that she had opened his eyes to the possibility of a new more normal and satisfying life and a different kind of relationship, an evergreen one, with a free woman not one whose services were available for sale or through coercion.

For his part, Tristen was overjoyed at the success of his plans. He felt vindicated that his plans had worked so well … so far! To put this clapped out set-up in Ayton back on its feet within such a short period of time was such a colossal achievement that he should soon be able to return to his fiefdom on the estate in Barking, East London and as far away from these two idiots in Ayton as he could be. Thank goodness! Moreover, he would be able to brag about his successes to Tirana. It might even earn him a return to his homeland in the

Dukagjin highlands of Albania for honourable and lengthy retirement.

His first task today would be to make the arrangements to transfer the fee for the successful completion of the Chief Constable assassination job by Bajram Krasniki, his London pal. He needed to transfer the payment to the overseas account that his friend had given him for payment for previous such jobs. Just a few more successes after that and he really would be able to broadcast his great achievements to his colleagues in London, especially the 'Young Turks' making such a boastful and overweening noise on that estate in Barking, and to his bosses on the Continent and in Tirana as well.

For the benefit of his colleagues in the Ayton firm, he began today's meeting by identifying the next steps in his usual arrogant and self-assured manner. Hopefully there would be no need today to spoil the celebratory ambience of the group with the vitriol he had administered to his two colleagues in the previous meeting.

"Tonight we send the message round our former clients that we are back in business. Bookings are commencing for the grand opening of the two new houses tomorrow with a bonus free drink for the first men booking a slot. Are we ready for that Samir? Make sure our competitors get the message too and above all keep the Turks and the

Kurds away from our patch. You have ten women in each house and if each one services ten men a day, we should very soon accumulate enough to fulfil your obligations and pay off your debts including that owing to Noel and myself. With some twenty thousand pounds a day from the two, we should soon be in easy street and ready for further expansion."

He cast a happy smile at his colleagues. For the first time in Ayton he was beginning to enjoy himself and looking forward to his return to his patch in London. And it showed in what he said and the way he said it.

"At that point I shall need to return to my duties in East London and leave you and Noel to get busy with the transfers and local expenses. Keep the books clean this time, mind you. I shall most likely have to depart for London probably the day after tomorrow, if all goes well. See that my car is tanked up and what's more a small but generous donation would be welcome before I leave."

"Yes boss. We are ready and able to start bookings this moment. We are just waiting for the word from you. Of course we do not wish to detain you any longer than you can afford to stay with us, given your other weighty commitments in the East London. We have already made the arrangements for the small but appreciative donation to you from Xhoel and myself and the staff here."

"Don't wait, you fool. Do it now. Get on with it and let me know how it is going later today." Was the somewhat irascible response.

"OK boss." Samir stuttered obediently. "Xhoel tell our colleagues to get started with the recruitment straightaway. No ifs and buts. Do it now. Pronto!"

"OK Samir. Can do." Xhoel responded eagerly seeing a chance to get away from the present conversation and potential discussion of the young woman at the centre of his dilemma. He stood up and began to withdraw. But he rather unwisely hung back when the conversation turned to recruitment of further couriers.

Unfortunately at that very moment, seizing the opportunity afforded by the short gap in conversation, Tristen came back in again with a demand for facts and figures about the couriers and how much produce they had sent over the line, which placed Samir under pressure once more and put Xhoel even more on edge. Samir tried to react this time looking at Xhoel in a summoning way and hoping for his help.

"Well we don't know the exact figures yet, do we Xhoel? But we do know that we have increased the number of couriers substantially as well as the amounts of cannabis, powder cocaine, crack and heroin that we have sold in Ayton and across the county lines. There is a great and growing demand locally and in the surrounding region for what we are selling, enticed, may I may say by the very attractive price set by you, Tristen, and at which all varieties are available. So that reduced price, undercutting our competitors, seems to be a great incentive for sales and for reducing the attraction of our competitors' dope. It's already attracting back some of our usual customers, lost by the previous hiatus to other gangs, and bringing in new clients besides. Noel and I shall be doing an audit at the end of this week with Xhoel's assistance and we can give you the exact details after we have completed that."

Noel briefly amplified what Samir had said.

"Yes boss. We are already topping ten grand a day from county lines and we expect that to increase dramatically as we pick up momentum with two income streams from drugs and prostitution. We can then get on with the transfers."

"Well, remember to send those figures to me regularly, after I return to Barking. As I said, if the business goes well for the next few days, I shall have to return to London, where I'm sure a mountain of other work awaits me. Noel will be staying here though for the time being." And by the way, how are the bookings for the ladies' favours going?"

"Well again we do not have exact numbers but they seem to be mounting already by the hour for the opening tomorrow as the message has been rebounding from one client to another." Samir rejoindered hopefully.

On the spur of the moment, Tristen, ever unpredictable, had what he considered to be a brain wave, which would distract the authorities from the affairs of the gang's Ayton business.

"I have thought of a strategy to discourage the eventuality of further attempts on our own premises, at least temporarily. How about shopping the location of the Kurds' two brothels and/or the one that the Liverpool crowd have impudently set up in the last couple of weeks in our patch. Dealing with those targets should pre-occupy our local wreckers, the Ayton Police Force I mean. It should take them off our backs at least for a while as well as deterring our competitors from poaching and teach all those wishing to intrude on our patch a lesson. Additionally, we could spread the rumour on the street that supermarket delivery vans are currently being used to distribute drugs by our Turkish and Kurdish competitors. Keep 'em all busy."

He gave a little chuckle as he finished at the thought of the surprised reaction of the authorities and their adversaries in the other gangs, as likewise in the supermarkets.

"Yes, a brilliant idea." Samir uttered obsequiously.

"There are several other nationality groups involved in the drugs trade in Ayton, including mobs from Turkey, Italy, Iraqi Kurdistan and one just trying to come in. I believe that this latest mob is originally from Nigeria but they have concentrated on people-trafficking up to the present. Then there are all the more local mobs from the big cities like Liverpool, Manchester and London. So we have quite a number of competitors to shop. I would propose, if you are agreeable, that we start with the Kurds, smaller than us but our biggest competitor in both sectors apart possibly from the Italians, with whom we co-operate on purchase, transportation and sale of drugs. What do you think and how shall we do it?"

"Leak the info to your new police collaborator. But make sure you include the full details of the location and number of the establishments. And do it anonymously. Start with the Iraqi Kurds. Do not involve us."

"OK boss. It shall be done as you suggest. What about the grocery delivery van rumour? Should we use that one as well?"

Samir gave a response of obedient compliance and raised another issue just to show that he was on the ball. But what do **you** think?"

"Please yourself. You cannot expect me to make all the decisions for you. But act soon and speedily, mind you!" Tristen riposted petulantly.

He then turned to Xhoel. This latter knew from the look on his face that this was the turning point that he had feared since the beginning of the meeting. He had to win this part of today's meeting at all costs, otherwise …! But how could he do that? That was the challenge. At this moment it was as if he had been struck to inertia by a thunderbolt and he could find no satisfactory reaction, however hard he tried.

Tristen commenced his assault by posing his first inquiry provocatively.

"Xhoel. You're unusually quiet today. How is that girlfriend of yours doing? Andrea is her name, isn't it? When do we get to meet her? Is she now willing to join our little business and in what kind of role?" As one of our couriers perhaps? Or would she prefer to recruit them for us? Or would she like one of our houses as her future residence with no rent to pay and lots of company?"

Tristen smiled broadly at his weak pun.

The questions were clearly a threat to Andrea, and Xhoel recognised the danger straight away. He was horrified. After all, houses was one of the gangland terms for a brothel. But Tristen was obviously intent on continuing his provocation and there was nothing Xhoel could do to stop him.

"I guess she would prefer a paid job to recruit more couriers for us from the college, which she attends. That's what her school is called, isn't it? Samir and I are anxious to hear of what advance you have made with a date due of course. I must admit that this matter seems to have taken a very long time and I should tell you, in case you did not know already, that Samir and I have only a limited stock of patience. I would like to see this matter brought to a head before my expected departure for London in a couple of days' time."

Xhoel felt sick to the core with his back to the wall in a way that he had never done before. The accumulation of Tristen's requests and threats as well as the expressed wish for a conclusion of the issue before his departure in a couple of days' time really put him on the spot. Search as he would, he could find no excuse that he in his wildest dream thought would be acceptable to Tristen and Samir and that would not severely damage Andrea in one way or another. It did not bear thinking about. What could he say?

At that juncture Samir decided to stir the pot a little and at the same time to explete his wrath against Xhoel for all the times he had let him down. So he hastened to support Tristen's onslaught on his disloyal underling and at the same time to curry favour with his all-powerful boss from London.

"Yes, Xhoel my friend. How are you getting on with the little lady? As Tristen says we do not have infinite patience or time, you know. It could be that this job needs someone with a little more knowledge about women and how to handle them. What do you think, Tristen? What is the matter with our friend, Xhoel?"

Xhoel tried weakly to respond to Samir's provocation.

"Oh, just feeling a little off colour. Must be something I've eaten."

Then Tristen compounded the pressure and Xhoel really began to feel the intense heat.

"Perhaps Samir is right and this job does require someone of a little more, let's say, maturity and experience with women. No insult intended Xhoel! Possibly someone less sensitive. Samir, given your other extensive commitments at the moment, would you be able to take this little job over from Xhoel? Say like straight away?"

“Yes sure. It will not take me long to solve this little problem. I’ll have her here within a day or two. Probably tomorrow or at the very latest by the day after, Tristen.”

At his wit’s end, Xhoel foolishly decided to seek Tristen’s help in spite of Tristen’s earlier provocation and threats. So he made what he considered to be an exploratory plea to try to find out which way the wind was blowing. Sadly his intervention proved to be counterproductive and rather weak, contrary to his intentions.

“No, Tristen, that won’t be necessary. I can assure you. I can try and do it today or at the very latest tomorrow. And in any case, I’ve already arranged to meet Andrea on Tuesday after school in the small café near her college. That would be a whole lot less threatening than a new face suddenly appearing out of the blue. I can tie this up this week.”

The counter-attack came strongly from Samir. He seized on the opportunity he saw to take revenge and teach his subordinate colleague a lesson for the continual failure to loyally support him in this and previous meetings not long ago. The time for payback had arrived and he did not intend to miss it. What he said touched a raw nerve in Xhoel.

“What’s the matter? You fallen in love with this bright young woman or something? Is she giving you what you want then? I think I fancy a taste of that as well."

Xhoel knew that he needed to scuttle that insinuation swiftly or he and she were both in deep trouble and conceivably even done for. But how to do it on the spur of the moment? What could he say to avoid what was more and more becoming an inevitability? He had to have a go, whatever he said.

"Don't be silly, Samir. Sometimes your attempts at humour and being funny are just not amusing. Of course I haven't fallen in love with her. If I am lucky I might have bumped into her once a week. Such meetings have had one aim, namely to recruit her for the firm here in Ayton."

He turned again to appeal to Tristen as his only hope of countering what he recognised as Samir's wicked plan, which was beginning to seem highly likely, namely the take-over by Samir of the responsibility of dealing with Andrea. He decided to take a risk and appeal to Tristen.

"Tristen. What do **you** think? I have started already on this delicate task, which demands some sensitivity to the family's power in local politics. That has taken time, I agree. But it was essential to avoid a bust-up with powerful local forces in politics and the local constabulary, which would have done us no good whatsoever at a time when we have our own problems. Such a situation would not have helped anyone. Surely you would agree that I should be allowed to bring to a swift conclusion for all of us? What would you do if this had occurred in London?"

But the answer that Xhoel had wanted and hoped for did not come back from Tristen. On the contrary! And the reason was puzzling him. It was neither impossible nor unusual in the mafia gang that Samir and Tristen had had a word about this and already come to an agreement as to what Samir had wanted all along. A Take-over to slate his thirst for revenge against his subordinate colleague for perceived disloyalty. In any case, whatever the reason, what he heard from Tristen was quite the reverse of the response he had hoped for.

"I'm not getting involved in this matter. It's up to the local boss to make all decisions about the deployment of their staff. Samir is the boss here in Ayton and it is up to him to make a decision, which you will then be obliged to accept according to the Coda. You invited me to say what I would do and that is your answer. But just to add a brief rider, my own decision would be strengthened by the apparent lack of urgency in dealing with this matter judged by the actions taken by you so far, to resolve this matter swiftly, my colleague. All of that would convince me that I should definitely take over the job myself, if I had the time. Samir, what do you say?"

The moment of triumph had arrived and it looked like total defeat for Xhoel. Samir was pleased as punch and showed it in his response.

"Thank you for that clarification and your support my boss. Although I have many other responsibilities at this moment and other priorities, I'll take it on myself and begin by meeting this woman in the café near the college on Tuesday as arranged by my good colleague, Xhoel."

He then turned the knife by addressing Xhoel directly.

"Leave it to me from this moment onwards Xhoel. I warn you not to seek to interfere. You've had your chance and you've blown it. You were unable to bring it to a successful conclusion in a successful and timely fashion. No problem, but that's the end of it for you. Do not interfere or the consequences for you could be very serious."

Xhoel was now unbearably aware that his gamble had failed and that it would now be futile to argue further against the combined views of his two superior colleagues, especially Tristen. So the big question now was how on earth he could help Andrea avoid this catastrophe and avoid the very cruel fate that was threatening her at this very moment.

He had a remorseful feeling of profound responsibility for what had happened. He felt that he owed her his continued protection if that were possible. But what did that mean? What could he do? At this moment that was the big challenge for him and it preoccupied him throughout the sleepless night.

Chapter Twenty-Two: A Futile Attempt

Xhoel tossed and turned in bed sleepless that night after the meeting with Andrea. He obtained little rest and no relief from his painful dilemma, to which he could find no resolution. He had two options. He could either let the river flow and allow Andrea to be abducted by Samir on some pretext or other. Or he could try to warn her about what Samir's real intention was and urge her not the go to the Tuesday meeting that he and Andrea had arranged the previous week. But really he felt he didn't have a choice in the context of his new-found feelings for her. He made a swift and final decision to alert her to the danger.

But the major problem was how to do that without Samir finding out? He had been told not to interfere and that was an order under the Coda. To defy it was a breach of the strict rules of the 'besa', a pledge of honour, which he tacitly accepted when he silently consented to Samir taking over from him in the presence of a witness like Tristen Rexhepi. To break that commitment, however much it had been forced on him, was a serious breach of the 'besa' and could be a fatal move. At the very least, he would be relieved of his responsibilities in Ayton and sent back to East London or, worse still, forced to return to Tirana to whatever fate was decided for him by the bosses there.

But did he really have any choice? He asked himself again. It could be done discreetly, he promised himself. He could wait outside for her in the afternoon after college and warn her without anyone knowing about his action … hopefully! As an alternative he might be able to catch her before school. In that case, he could wait unobtrusively outside her house, perhaps in the public park opposite. Yes. That's what he would do. He had two days to achieve his purpose and hopefully get away with it. In a last resort he could contact her grandmother, whom he had met at the supermarket. But she would be sure to inform the police or her husband, Jack and he would let Samir know too. That would mean the end of the road for Samir and possibly him as well.

Somehow, though, he had to succeed, for Andrea's sake. But then why should he take the risk for a relative stranger. After all, what had she ever done for him? The answer came to him promptly, loud and clear. She had enriched his life, not in a monetary sense, but because she had introduced him to the possibility of a new life, a different more normal life, where he did not have to continually persecute and otherwise hurt other people. If he succeeded in his ambition for a new life, she would surely continue to support him. And Samir would never know why she did not turn up for the meeting as arranged on that late Tuesday afternoon after college. Or maybe he would guess! Samir might just put two and two together and ask him where he had been and what he had been doing the whole day. But then he could fabricate an alibi and deny any part in what happened. He was confident that he could manufacture a convincing excuse for himself. And even if eventually Samir contacted Andrea, she would never betray him. Or would she be forced to do so?

When he awoke on the Monday morning after another very short and disturbed night's rest, he had still found no resolution to his problems. He took no breakfast and somehow he was drawn as if by a magic compass towards the park and Andrea's home. He cycled there. In the half light of the early morning, there were still some of the night dwellers in the park, so he felt less obtrusive and, therefore, more secure. He sat on one of the benches beneath an overgrowing tree and surrounding neglected bushes as cover. Looking down a slight slope to the house, he waited and watched, watched and waited. He did not have long to wait.

Suddenly the front door opened and her grandfather, Jack, came out of the front door and approached a large and newish car parked in front of the house. After a very short wait, to his surprise and joy he saw Andrea leaving the house and bidding farewell to her mother and grandmother at the doorway. As if rocket-propelled, Xhoel jumped up. His heart seemed to miss a beat. He was immediately ready to meet her and explain all.

Then he noticed that she was carrying a heavy load presumably with her music and athletics gear together in one hand and her heavy textbooks and exercise books in in a pack-pack in the other. Jack spoke to her but Xhoel could not hear what he said. What were Xhoel's options? He could shout to her, but that would mean revealing himself to Jack, the suspected double agent, whom he and Samir had recently met and paid blood money to. He had always suspected Jack of being a double agent; in with both sides. Jack would be sure to sell the information of Xhoel's treachery to Samir or inform the police or both. In a slightly more charitable interpretation, he might even by accident, inadvertently reveal the encounter to others and eventually it might somehow seep back to Samir or one of his mobsters. Should he, could he risk it? It would be touch and go and he held back only a couple of seconds. But too late!

After Jack had opened the boot and helped Andrea to place her material in it, he slammed the boot door closed and quickly hurried to the passenger side door and opened it for her and she got in the car. Jack slammed the passenger side car door hard, as if with a sense of pique, and rushed round to the driver's side. Without delay, he got in, slammed his door and started the engine. The car departed straightaway at some speed and with screeching tyres, before Xhoel could take any further action whatsoever. He had missed the boat!

A sense of despondency mounted in the pit of Xhoel's stomach. He could have done something and he hadn't. He blamed himself. But all was not lost. Yet! Overcoming his self-pity, he realised that this lost opportunity would enable him to make his usual appearance at work and possibly to meet with Samir and plausibly even Tristen and Noel. He would make an opportunity to show himself to them even if one did not occur in the normal flow of the day's events. He could then disappear towards the end of the afternoon, without calling attention to himself. In that case, he could wait outside the college once more for her to appear, as on past occasions. And that is what he planned to do.

But the plans of mice and men ….

How slowly the day passed. Samir was not in the headquarters building when Xhoel arrived and colleagues said that he, Noel and Tristen had gone to one of the new brothels to sort out a problem there with the one of the guards from East London and his job. At headquarters, one of the guards from London that he asked said that all three of them would probably be away all day. Xhoel waited for a while pondering what to do and finally he decided to go and join the others just to show himself.

But which of the new brothels would they be at? Neither of the guards knew which brothel they had gone to. He would just have to try his luck. Without further delay he set off straightaway at some speed in his car for the first and nearest of the two brothels. But not so quick! On the way, he encountered traffic works. To his chagrin he was held up for almost a quarter of an hour at the blockage. They were just setting up the traffic lights. Waiting ever more edgily he was at last able to start again and rapidly accelerated away from the obstruction.

At the nearest of the two brothels the car park was full to overflowing. A good sign! A quick glance to see if he could identify Samir's rather flash Audi resulted it no sighting. But Samir could have parked round the back. He was always very cautious. So, Xhoel parked partly in front of each of a couple of cars in the car park and dashed to the front entrance intending to go straight inside. He was halted at the door by one of the new guards from London, who demanded suspiciously who he was and what he wanted at the building.

"I am Xhoel Gegaj, one of the managers of the Ayton office and I am looking for Samir, Samir Pecic, who is the overall chief of the Ayton set-up and he's my boss. I'm looking for Tristen Rexhepi and Noel Shkodra, his colleagues as well, who I am told are with him."

"Do you have any proof of identity?"

"No! I don't need it! Xhoel reacted irritably. I work here."

"I'm afraid you do need identification, Mr Gegaj. I have never met you before and you are here demanding to know where the Chief is. You could be a police spy."

Xhoel needed to think swiftly. He did not normally carry identification for reasons of security in case he was arrested. So he enquired impatiently.

"Is he still here this morning?"

"Sir, I can tell you that there is no one here of that name. Nor has there been at any time today."

"Do you happen to know where he is?"

"No, sir."

With that, the brief interchange ended, leaving Xhoel with the working hypothesis that Samir and the others had not been there to that brothel and, therefore, they must have gone to the other, more distant one.

Without a further word, he turned away irascibly and returned to his car. His journey to the second brothel meant that he would have had to cross the area of the road works again. For that reason he chose to follow the official diversion recommended by the contractor. The diversion led him further into the town centre and then the directions for the diversion seemed to desert him. It could be, that in his agitated state of mind he had missed a sign. In any case, he found himself having to wind and weave his way through the inner city narrow, one-way streets, traffic lights and pedestrian crossings, with his irritation mounting by the second. Eventually, he found a way out of the labyrinth and he discovered a speedy route to the second brothel building. He pulled into one of the free parking places and rushed to the door querulously telling the guard his business at the door in a somewhat imperious manner.

“I am looking for Samir Pecic. He is my boss, I am his assistant and I have an urgent message for him.”

The guard, again one of those borrowed from East London, was obviously impressed. He took him at his word, although somewhat reluctantly, it seemed. The guard responded to his inquiry in a helpful manner

“I’m sorry sir. He and his colleagues departed just a few minutes ago. You have just missed them.”

“Do you know where they have gone?”

The guard came back rather cheekily, which further irritated Xhoel.

“I’m sorry, sir, he is not accountable to me and he would never tell me where he and his colleagues were going nor what their purpose in going was. Of course, I would never ask either.”

Xhoel was now faced with another dilemma. He tried to think through where they might have gone. Had they gone back to base or to the other brothel, from which he had made an ignominious retreat a little while ago. Of course he could call Samir on the phone. But he hesitated to use his personal mobile phone. Samir would not appreciate that. A breach of security, he would say. Use a burner phone. But Xhoel did not have one with him. He turned back to the guard.

“Could I come in and use your phone, please?” He requested somewhat penitently.

“Do you have identification, sir?”

"No, I do not." He responded retrieving his previous petulant tone.

"Then I'm sorry, sir. I cannot let you in. Such are my strict instructions from Mr Tristen Rexhepi, the big boss from London."

Silently and impolitely he turned his back on the guard and returned to his car. Without a word, he regarded his car in utter despair. But more tests of his temper were about to follow.

The car park was now full and someone had parked in front of him! He dashed back to the guard at the entrance. Mustering his most courteous tone of voice, he smilingly requested the help of the guard as gently and courteously as he could.

"I am sorry to have to come back to you. But some idiot has parked in front of my car and I need to get out urgently. I should be most obliged if you could kindly find out whose car it is and invite whoever it is to move it immediately."

"Well I am sorry to hear that sir. But of course we cannot accept responsibility for our customers car-parking in our car park. You've probably seen the notices in the car park saying that. No responsibility is what it states. The usual formula you know."

Xhoel phrased his rejoinder hyper-politely.

"This is the firm's business that I am on and I need to get away to the other house as quickly as possible. I know that it is the normal practice to require men visiting to give their car number plate details when they sign in and they are required to give their credit card details as well. What's more I know that you have a phone at your side behind the door. I know too, that there are always two of you here. So could you kindly ring your colleague and politely ask him to find out whose car it is and request him politely to move it, as this is now an emergency."

To his astonishment, the guard agreed, although somewhat grumpily and he disappeared behind the door presumably to ring his colleague. When he came back he said.

"I have done as you requested, sir. My colleague will be down in a second to see which car it is and to find the owner and seek to invite him courteously to move his vehicle as soon as possible, as it is an emergency request."

"Thank you very much."

After about a quarter of an hour, when Xhoel was becoming more and more agitated and was on the point of going back to the guard, a man appeared at the front door. He said a few words to his colleague, who pointed at Xhoel, and then the second guard approached him cheerily.

“Good day, Sir. I’m sorry about this inconvenience. It does sometimes happen when the car park is full. Very inconsiderate. I’ll do my best to invite the gentleman concerned to move his vehicle pronto. But you know how difficult that is because of the business we pursue. Is this one the offending car sir?”

Xhoel confirmed impatiently that this was indeed the offending car.

The guard approached closer to the offending car and wrote the registration number on a small pad. He then returned towards the main entrance with the assurance to Xhoel of an early solution to the problem

“I’ll be back soon, sir with the gentleman concerned.”

“OK. Please hurry. This is urgent now. I have already been here over an hour. It seems like an eternity.”

“Yes sir, as soon as possible.”

The guard disappeared through the front entrance and Xhoel walked across and waited outside by the offending car with mounting irritation.

Some half an hour later, the second guard reappeared with a spruce old man dressed in a pin-striped suit, pin-striped shirt and club tie following him. Xhoel did not say anything but glared at him ferociously. The man did not speak either but rapidly and somewhat sheepishly climbed into his car and drove it away and out of the car park at breakneck speed.

The second guard expressed his regrets once again very considerately and re-entered the house with a smile on his face. Xhoel got into his car and departed in some haste, aiming for the new headquarters office building of the mob some distance away on the outskirts of town. On arrival, who should he meet in the hallway but Samir, Noel and Tristen?

Samir looked at him quizzically and in a rather surprised tone addressed him, immediately allocating a new task.

"Ah. There you are young man. Just the man that we have been looking for most of the day. In view of the lightening of your work load, I would like you to reformulate the books again with Noel here, so that they point positively and advantageously to our current performance with the new stock, staff and accommodation. Tristen would like to take them with him when he returns to London. So if you could make sure these are finished by the end of the day that would be great! I would hope to be able to review them with the two of you first thing tomorrow morning and pass them on to Tristen, so that there is no delay to his departure."

Xhoel saw any hope of going to wait outside Andrea's house first thing in the morning disappear like a flash in the night sky. In addition, waiting outside school to alert Andrea about Samir's intention was now under threat and was a crucial and a final chance. With a sigh of resignation he answered submissively.

"OK Samir. Can do, boss."

He confirmed his acceptance of stark reality half-heartedly.

The only opportunity that now remained to alert Andrea was the pre-arranged meeting in the coffee shop tomorrow afternoon after the end of school. The time and day had been agreed with Andrea for their next rendezvous in the coffee shop, the last time they met there.

But did such an opportunity still exist given the lengthy task Samir had given him? Would it be? Could it be? How could he get away if the task was still unfinished to Samir's satisfaction?

Chapter Twenty-Three: A Reassessment

"I'm pleased to be able to tell you that we have identified the location of the two replacement brothels, which inside intelligence has informed us have been set up by the criminal syndicate of gangsters in Ayton. The buildings are currently under observation and have been for the past couple of days. They appear to have started trading, if that is the right word, yesterday. It is our intention that they should be raided later, starting later this evening. Whether those raids should occur sequentially or simultaneously is one of the issues to be decided by this meeting today. Equally, we are probably within an ace of confirming the location of the building that they are using as a headquarters. Detective Inspector Maria Clarke will inform us further about this latter issue later in this meeting."

It was with a smile on her face and an obvious feeling of great satisfaction that the newly Acting Chief Constable of Ayton, Heather Compton Jones, informed her inner circle of colleagues of the imminent intention for what was being called a final blow against the mafia crime syndicate that until recently had been dominant in the illegal drugs and prostitution markets in Ayton and its contiguous administrations. It was argued that this would be a crucial blow, not just to that illicit gang itself, but similarly to the other gangs that they were selling drugs to.

The next part of the plan of attack was for the two quite large and very recently established brothels of the criminal enterprise in Ayton to be raided first in the coming days and closed forthwith while awaiting the precise intelligence about the location of the gang's headquarters building in Ayton for the next phase of the operation.

"This time it will be for keeps." The Acting Chief Constable resumed.

"They will not be permitted to re-establish such institutions and regain their previously dominant position again in Ayton or the surrounding areas."

She added with obvious resolve.

"This Police Force of Ayton under my leadership will ensure that does not and cannot happen ever again."

There were some spasmodic expressions of Here! Here! from the assembled group. But Superintendent Rajiv Gundara intervened to enter a note of caution. He pointed out the shortage of human and other resources to support their ambitious plans for the eradication of the two brothels and eventually the headquarters of the gang too. He argued the need for a more systematic and phased consideration of resource allocations.

"Ma'am it falls to me to remind us all of the constrained situation of all our human and material resources that will be required to close both these dens of iniquity, that we have identified, let alone the headquarters as well. We have only one armed police unit and insufficient officers and detention vans in general to conduct more than one raid a night, or likely as not even a week. With respect ma'am I think we need to have a serious and open talk about prioritisation of activities to match our resources before making any decisions."

"Thank you very much, Superintendent for that very trenchant statement of our straitened resource circumstances, which I have to admit already severely limit our operational capacity. Though I am doubtful about the accuracy of your comment on police detention vans, if we accept your statement on personnel shortages, then we are resignedly with the conclusion that we can only raid at the most one criminal enterprise this week. We must therefore defer the other one to next week, or conceivably even later."

The Chief of the local CID chief (Criminal Investigation Department), Superintendent Felix Brigstowe intervened to state the need of his own unit for additional resources.

"Although I do not wish to speak in a partisan way on behalf of my own department, I cannot but agree with Superintendent Gundara. We sometimes over-estimate our capacity, to the detriment of our other routine and statutory commitments, when planning such raids. What is more, we tend to forget, or at least underestimate, the amount of time and energy we use up prior to a raid and especially following a raid, when we need to spend staff time and treasure investigating premises, examining confiscated drugs, cross-examination of detainees, preparing charges, etc. Each of these tasks tends to take more time and sometimes resources, than the actual raid itself. Without a fundamental reassessment of our resource utilisation, I fear there is a serious danger of an unbalanced and unsuccessful approach. Some areas are at risk of becoming under-resourced because of the prioritisation of other sectors, such as high profile raids, unintentionally of course, without due respect to our on-going statutory obligations. I personally am not against our overall aim of taking this group of gangsters down. But I would propose that it is deferred until we can assess the demand on our resources to mount the two raids. This will enable us to determine whether the taking out of the two brothels is the best and most efficient means of achieving our goal of taking the organisation down. The work in the CID can be very stressful and demanding for officers. I honestly believe that we are in danger of overworking our officers, with consequent sickness absences rising and thus exacerbating the staffing problem even more. I must say, quite honestly, that without a massive increase in funding to the CID, I don't believe we can continue to sustain the increasing level of demand on the Department. I think I shall leave it there for the moment and let others add their comments and suggestions. But those are the facts, as far as my department is concerned."

Superintendent Julian Charles, Chief Officer in charge of the armed police unit was the next one to be invited to speak by the Chair. He likewise picked up the resource issue, which was, for the first time becoming the major unplanned focus of the discussions.

"Thank you ma'am. I have to say that I concur with the comments of my colleague about the resource issue in the Ayton police force at this moment in time. Perhaps we had all hoped to defer the discussion to happier and more financially beneficial days, which have of course never arrived. The task of my officers is stressful and dangerous, particularly when dealing with an unpredictable and inherently violent group like the Albanian mafia. With every raid, in spite of all the precautions we take, my officers risk their lives, their careers and, in some cases officers suffer debilitating injury and in some rare cases, thank god, they are even killed. It is, therefore inevitable that so many of them suffer from stress related to post traumatic stress disorder, which naturally results in sick leave and absence from the ranks, which in turn, reduces the number of officers available for duty. In every case of injury my officers have to close up the ranks and proceed with less than the required number of officers needed for the efficient and safe conclusion of the task. They have to cope and I personally admire the uncomplaining way in which they do. But at some time, that reduction becomes unsustainable. That is where we are now. The solution in those situations is to try to make certain that there is a pool of back-up officers. But there is no finance for that at this moment in time. So we do not have any back-up. In any case, it takes somewhere in the region of six months to initially train an arms officer, always depending on their previous arms experience in the army or elsewhere. If, and it seems desirable to me, the training includes external experience, that can be an unexpected and involve a heavy on-cost to the initial bill for training and thus a further pressure on staff through the absence of colleagues. Do I see a solution to this problem? Well a substantial additional vote of funding to the Unit would be one way to begin. Do I think it will happen? No! Unquestionably not in the immediate future. And in any case, what about all the other units in the force? So we are left with the one option of tailoring our ambitions to fit our constrained and reducing staffing reservoir. As they say, you need to cut your suit to fit your cloth, however distasteful that may be. We need to begin doing that today and to address it in the way we tackle this criminal gang, whose resources are infinitely greater than ours, perhaps even boundless. That should be the subject of this gathering today. How can we box clever, cleverer than ever, with the resources that we have and yet still achieve our objectives? We need to start that process today and to incorporate it into our plans of the best and most cost effective way of getting rid of this gang of criminals using the same limited resources as we have today. For me the big point at issue today is, can we plan the most cost effective way of attacking these vile felons without additional resources. I believe that in answering that question a collegial review of resources might actually find a better, quicker and more cost effective way of achieving the same goal. That is what I propose, not on the part of my department, but for the whole force. I look forward to such a discussion with my colleagues."

The Acting Chief Constable took the lead and posed a penetrating and direct question about the programme of work to eliminate the criminal mafia gang in Ayton.

"Thank you for that astute and penetrating analysis, Superintendent Charles. But are you suggesting that we cancel the planned raid on the two brothels and allocate the same resources saved, elsewhere? In that case, may I invite you to share with us all where that somewhere else might be?"

The reply was incisive and direct.

“What I am suggesting is that we look at ways of maximising the impact of the expenditure of our scarce resources by more careful selection of targets, which will yield the most result for the same amount of resources. We need to improve our aim at our adversary. In particular, we need to ask ourselves, how we can obliterate this menace to our society for the minimum expenditure of our scarce resources, giving preference to targets, which will cripple or even totally disable our opponent? Rather than using the same resources on less critical targets, which may of course be more high profile and therefore publicly attractive. In other words go for the head as we in the firearms unit would say.”

The acting Chief Constable had a query and a request.

“I’m not sure that I understand exactly what such an approach would mean in concrete terms. Could you kindly elucidate for us.”

“Well, with regards to our discussion today, we are aiming to finalise plans to take out two brothels. We have already tried that strategy before and look what happened. It just resulted in the use of lots of our expendable resources only to see the same gang setting up two replacement brothels within days. I'm not saying that the effort was a waste of resources. But, on the other hand if we had been fleet enough in raiding their central headquarters before it moved at a time when it probably contained most, if not all, of their top people including the top boss from London, just think of what the impact would have been on this noxious business for the expenditure of the same amount of funds. Moreover, to capture those top gangsters would inevitably have led to the withering on the vine of other establishments and a desertion of the criminal gangsters employed there, because they would just never get paid and their prospective clientele would be frightened off too."

At that point in the meeting Detective Inspector Maria Clarke, in charge of the major investigation into a lucrative drug and prostitution set-up in the town, which was organised and run by the dominant crime syndicate in the City, spoke in favour of a revised approach, as outlined by Superintendent Charles.

"I want to endorse the idea that the Superintendent has put forward. For example, at the beginning of this meeting you mentioned that we were within an ace of discovering the whereabouts of the headquarters of the mafia gang under discussion today. If we save our resources and concentrate them on the headquarters target, we are likely to net, not just the worker bees, but the top men in Ayton and possibly if he is still here at the moment, the big boss from Barking in East London. That would be a blow not just for Ayton but for the country as a whole and would have the immediate effect of likewise closing the two brothels and frustrating the current attempts to set up a network of indoor cannabis farms. Thus, we save resources, but have a much greater impact that in all likelihood would ring the death knell of this criminal organisation **and** the two brothels here in Ayton, as well as the finish of their further intentions to set up drug production facilities here as well. Clearly without the centre, the peripheral organisations would be starved of resources and would be directionless. There might even be an immediate defoliation of staff from these premises. Even if that did not happen quickly, it would surely happen eventually as the mobsters search for more profitable places and jobs elsewhere in the country."

"At this stage, the Acting Chief Constable tried to bring the meeting back on to focussing on the decision to be made about the proposed raids to the two brothels.

"Well in the interests of the most efficient use of our resources, I'd like to try to bring this meeting to a decision about the raid of the two brothels and equally to closure of the meeting, so we can all leave the meeting homewards. But first and finally are there any more statements or comments? Yes, Sergeant David Berger."

"Well just briefly to endorse what people have been saying about the options we face when deploying staff on new and additional commitments, which sometimes displace commitments to routine or statutory responsibilities. In my own case as beat Sergeant, I have very few staff. Some time ago we were ordered to provide a number of officers to shadow that young lady, Andrea, who is apparently being courted by one of the mobsters to see if she can unearth important information about the movements and aims of the mafia gang, which is under investigation. So far, this has not resulted in any discoveries of significance to our inquiries. Although, of course, we did this willingly to try to keep the young lady safe from those violent gangsters. But the result of that impact on resources, and I tell you this in confidence, has been to cut coverage of such things as routine street crime, including assault with a deadly weapon, pick-pocketing, shoplifting and domestic violence. So, over-commitment to one area leaves other sectors, if not neglected, then rather short of essential resources."

The Acting Chief Constable of Ayton tried to wind up the meeting by first thanking Sergeant Berger for his contribution.

"Thank you for that thoughtful and responsible contribution, Sergeant Berger. We have had a fairly lengthy and sometimes complex interchange about the issue of resources and their link to the two brothel raids that we are in the process of finalising. So I would like to turn back to the raid on the two brothels and look for a decision on action. Does someone have a resolution that they would like to make as a formal proposition?"

Superintendent Rajiv Gundara made a swift responsive comment which aimed to pull together in a sensitive way the chords of the preceding debate and to focus them on procedures, which did not restrict the actions and decisions of the Acting Chief Constable.

"Ma'am, I do not wish to formulate my suggestions in the form of a conventional proposition that might tie your hands. I think that is the last thing you need at this tense time in the work of the Force. Instead, I would invite you to consider the unease, which has been expressed by all contributors to this discussion concerning the critical staffing situation at the moment. We have heard how low staffing can lead to frequent unintended consequences which can sometimes have a detrimental impact on the quality and effectiveness of some of our other services. This includes statutory ones on occasion, examples of which have been given by other speakers in this discussion. I think you would probably like to come back to the next meeting of this group with your proposals to address the issue. Secondly and with regards to the raids imminently envisaged. My personal view is that there is nothing to be lost by deferring them for a few days. During that time, we can reinforce our efforts to find the location of the headquarters of this group of criminals. If that is successful the reward will be the rapid availability of all our resources to mount a swift raid, which could destroy this gang of criminals and their activities across the board. Those are my suggestions."

The Acting Chief Constable warmed to the helpful suggestions made in a non-formal proposal by the Superintendent.

"While not making his suggestion in the shape of a formal proposition, Superintendent Gundara has very usefully encapsulated for us the two major issues facing us where timely action is needed. I must say that I find his suggestions fully acceptable. But are there any further expressions of agreement and support for his suggestions or expressions of dissent in fact and/or proposals for changes or total eradication of one or both planned action operations?"

"Detective Inspector Maria Clarke spoke briefly in support of the proposal.

"Ma'am, I think it's clear by the silence to your invitation, that we all support Superintendent Gundara's excellent summary of our discussions and sensitive and responsible proposals for action concerning resource allocation, at all times attentive to the need to avoid restricting your decision-making freedom."

And she turned to Superintendent Charles and said.

"We are obliged to you sir. What we need now is a breakthrough on the location of the headquarters and it is conceivable that the young lady, Andrea, may yet be the key to the solution of that issue for us. Let's hope so."

With that salutary hope, the Acting Chief Constable thanked everyone for their participation in a very frank and productive session and closed the meeting.

Although she did not know it, everything now depended on the speed with which she could involve the mobsters in revealing the location of their headquarters.

Chapter Twenty-Four: Abducted

Andrea was very confused that afternoon after the end of the school day when she entered the café for her usual meeting with her new-found friend Joel. She was looking forward to their meeting, even though she was pressed for time to complete an assignment, which needed to be complete and handed in to her teacher by the end of that week. Above all and for Joel's sake, but unaware of his restraints, she wanted to see how far her persuasive language about the better life available to him had changed his views and whether he was now searching for a better life and occupation than the rather mysterious and criminal one he was currently engaged in.

She shot a glance across the café to their regular table by the window to see if he had already obtained the two drinks. There was one coffee and what looked like a hot chocolate on the table. A man, seemingly of foreign background by his clothes and the healthy bronzed complexion, was sitting at the table. But it was not Joel! True, he was similar in a manner of speaking, in several ways to Joel. He was well-dressed, well-groomed and quite attractive in appearance but much, much older than Joel, to her way of thinking. Not at all the youthful beau of her nascent affection.

She looked round the café to see if the usual table had been occupied and Joel had been obliged to choose a different table. But there was no sign of him. She glanced back to the usual table again and she was amazed to observe the man beckoning to her with a broad welcoming smile on his face. He stood up and by gesture invited her to join him. Very courteously he withdrew one of the chairs from underneath the table and again beckoned to her to take a seat. As she sat down on the opposite side of the table he returned to his seat, sat down and in a calm voice said in a subtly American accent.

"You must be Andrea, I guess."

"Yes, I am and where's Joel. And who are you anyway?"

"My name is Sam and I lodge with Joel. We are friends."

"And why is he not here as we arranged last week?"

"I'm afraid that he was given an important job by the man, who employs us both part-time, and he cannot complete it on time to come here to meet you. So he has requested me to come and meet you and to take you to him at the place where we both live. He said he had promised to show you his lodgings last time you met. I have my car here outside and he should be back, indeed he assures me that he will be there when we have completed our drinks and driven to meet him. I hope your hot chocolate is satisfactory. He gave me detailed instructions about what kind of drink to order for you and that's what I requested from the woman at the counter."

Andrea thought about the somewhat flimsy explanation for Joel's absence advanced by this man, who described himself as Joel's friend and housemate, Sam. She thought of telling him to get lost and returning home on her bicycle straightway. Then she recalled the conversation that she and her family had had with Chief Constable Lashley and some of his colleagues at police headquarters a couple of weeks previously. She recalled the names of the criminal gang, which had been mentioned and among them she recalled the name, Samir, as one of the gang. So she deduced that this was the man describing himself as Sam today.

She thought further about her intended rapid departure for home and realised that this might be an opportunity to find out where the headquarters offices of this gang were situated. She knew from the conversation with the Chief Constable that the police had been looking for them for some time now. So she decided on a subterfuge, explaining that she needed to go to the toilet.

"I'll be back shortly, Sammy. Just popping to the loo."

"Would you like me to order a fresh hot chocolate for you? I fear this one is likely as not cold by now, as I was led by Joel to expect you somewhat earlier."

"Yes please you can order a fresh drink for me." She responded jauntily and gave him a fleeting come-on smile, appearing to be encouraging him to stay.

"Can do." He responded obediently and cheerily.

She departed in the direction of the toilet block but deviated through the back entrance of the café to check whether her shadow police officer, who should have been tailing her was there. Immediately she exited, a well-dressed woman beckoned to her and Andrea approached her.

"I am Constable Lucy Wainwright, your shadow from the local police station." the woman volunteered encouragingly and she showed her official identification to Andrea.

Andrea omitted any formalities and explained very quickly that she would probably be departing soon in one of the parked cars with the stranger, called Sam, a member of the mafia gang, now seated at her table and she believed the destination to be the headquarters accommodation of the criminal gang that the police were searching for.

"I shall be departing very soon for what I believe to be the headquarters of the Albanian mobsters in Ayton, something which the Chief Constable of Ayton Constabulary has been seeking for quite some time especially after the debacle that I heard took place at the first location. Would you be able to follow me … discreetly of course? But it just occurred to me, what if we depart from the front entrance of the café, you might miss us. How can we cover that eventuality?" Andrea asked somewhat troubled.

"No problem. We have a car in this car park and my colleague, Sergeant Frank Balbinski, is outside at the front in civvies. Soon after you re-enter, I think I shall come into the café briefly to take a good but inconspicuous look at this man. Can you please try to keep the man fully occupied in conversation so that he is concentrating on what you are saying and looking at you not looking round the café? That way I can have a good look at him and his clothing for recognisable characteristics. If there's time, Frank may go in and have a look at him as well. We will correspondingly inform headquarters of the apparently important development that is unfolding here this afternoon. It could be game-changing. Be confident that we shall follow you wherever you go and send that intelligence back to headquarters immediately for action. I am hoping that we shall have time to put a tracker on this man's car. At the moment, however, we do not know which car in the car park belongs to him, although there is a very expensive state of the art Audi sports car at the other extremity of the car park from ours, but further from the exit, which may perhaps fit the bill."

"OK, must go. Thanks for your help and reassurance." With that brief salutation, Andrea turned and hurried back into the café.

"Bye and good luck." Sergeant Wainwright called after her.

When she returned to her place at the table, she was relieved to see the man, Sammy, still there with a fresh cup of coffee and what appeared to be a fresh hot chocolate.

"Sorry to take so long. There was a bit of a queue in the ladies loo."

"No problem!" He responded with an encouraging and polite smile on his face.

"So, where were we in our conversation? We can't just sit here in silence. Tell me something about yourself."

She inquired promptly but charmingly.

“Well, there’s not really very much to tell. I am a refugee from Kosovo seeking asylum, and I’ve been here in Ayton only a short while.”

Andrea realised that these two were the first of a series of lies that she would be supplied with and they seemed to be very similar with the second version Joel had given her of himself and his background. This fully convinced her that this was the gangster referred to as Samir by the Chief Constable when they had met lately.

“You’re much older than Joel. Are you married and do you have any children?”

“Yes, I am a couple of years older than Joel and no I am not married and do not have any children,”

“Where in Kosovo did you live and do you have relatives back there?”

“I lived in Pristina, the Capital, and all my family there were killed by the Serb paramilitaries.”

“So, what do you do here? Are you registered as a refugee with permission to work here?”

“No, I’m afraid, not yet. There was some difficulty about registering refugees from Kosovo, when we arrived. But I intend to try again. I hear the benefits of registration are worth having.”

“So how do you support yourself here?”

“I do odd jobs. Look I don’t want us to miss Joel, when he returns. He may think that my meeting with you failed and depart again. So could I suggest that we finish our drinks quickly and depart? We can talk further in the car and afterwards at the house with Joel.”

Andrea was a bit concerned about his suggestion. Firstly, it seemed to be an evasion strategy to prevent her from further questioning him. Secondly and more importantly, she needed to allow time for the woman PC, Lucy Wainwright to come and have a look at this man. So she responded by trying to gain a little time.

“Sure. My chocolate is a little hot. But I’ll try to cool it down a little. By the way is your name really Sam? It sounds a little too English to be coming from Kosovo.”

“No, it is Samir.” He responded curtly.

She began to blow on her drink and at that moment, out of the corner of her eye, she caught a glimpse of the well-dressed plainclothes young PC, Lucy Wainwright, walking through the café and she breathed a sigh of relief.

He picked up the theme of his name again, perhaps realising that he had responded in a rather off-hand way.

"My birth-name is Samir. But here in Ayton I am always referred to as Sam or sometimes Sammy by my friends and acquaintances."

"You mention friends and acquaintances. I know that there's quite a community of recently arrived refugees from Kosovo here in Ayton now. Do you keep in touch with them? Have you already met some of them? Do they have social gatherings from time to time?"

"No. Not really."

"I'm sorry. Does that mean that there are no such gathering or that there are, but you don't attend them?"

"I just don't have time for such things."

Andrea now perceived that the women PC was nowhere to be seen and she assumed that the police woman had now withdrawn from the café. Shortly afterwards she noticed a well-dressed young man passing by in the café and taking an unusually protracted interest in this young man calling himself Sam. She assumed it was Sergeant Frank Balbinski, whom Police Sergeant Wainwright had referred to in their conversation a short while previously.

So Andrea continued blowing her drink somewhat ostentatiously for a while. She cast a fleeting glance around the café and when she was confident that the Sergeant was no longer in the café and to avoid the contamination of her drink she made a suggestion that she thought might appeal to this man.

"I am not particularly keen on this drink, Sam. It tastes funny. Shall we depart now so that we do not miss Joel?"

"Ok, fine. If that's what you wish. Sorry about the second drink." He responded eagerly.

With that apology he stood up and took a couple of steps towards leaving.

"Shall we go?" He suggested slightly overbearingly.

Andrea stood up and followed him out of the back entrance of the cafe and into the car park, where she noted the woman PC Lucy standing by a car with what appeared to be a mobile phone at her ear. The PC gestured a faint hardly perceptible smile of recognition and nodded her head once. At the same time, Andrea noticed the bulge of a pistol in the back of Samir's trousers and underneath his jacket. Probably a Glock, she thought to herself, though she had only ever seen pictures of such weapons on the internet as a side interest after her meeting with the Chief Constable and his colleagues.

Samir led her to a very swish 2022 Audi A5 Sportback 40 TFSI Premium car and he politely opened the passenger door for her.

"Please!" He said inviting her somewhat commandingly to get into the car. Both seated and belted up, they departed from the car park at high speed. She had committed herself now and she knew that her commitment was irrevocable, although she felt that she could have confidence in the professional competence of her new friends from the Ayton police, Lucy and her colleague Frank.

She thought briefly of her father, murdered by a member of this gang, who had never faced justice. She took solace from the thought that at last she could help to bring others in this criminal enterprise to justice and help to prevent the evil and dangerous spread of noxious drugs through the community and especially among the young, some of whom were furthermore criminalised. Some would of those children would surely die as a result of their cruel addiction.

Leaving the café car park they accelerated towards the city centre at top speed. As they sped through the narrow and sometimes one-way streets of the town centre, it became obvious that Samir was manoeuvring in case anyone was trailing him. He sometimes reversed at a junction, sometimes repeated his track dangerously fast down a road already used by them, and on one occasion went the wrong way down a short one-way street. Only after a quarter of an hour of such manoeuvring, did he leave the town centre and head for the outskirts of the town, but again doubling back and arriving at a small overgrown rather neglected-looking cul-de-sac, where a rather scruffy-looking old man opened a wooden gate and saluted to acknowledge Sam's entry near a ramshackle wooden hut.

There was a small forest of young trees and lots of shrubs with plenty of greenery camouflaging and surrounding the cul-de-sac. At the far end, she observed a medium-sized brick building with a somewhat neglected even deserted look about it, similarly camouflaged by voluminous foliage. They pulled up in front of what could now be seen as a small block of apartments, which at first sight appeared abandoned with tired-looking curtains at only a few of the dirty windows. At a short glance, there were at least three entrances only one of which seemed to be serviceable, the others being boarded up.

Of the three entrances they entered the building through the central one, at the inside of which two men were currently half-seated on tall stools on either side. They appeared to be stationed as guards in a modest and rather shabby and sparsely furnished lobby. They were unashamedly armed with what appeared to her, from her brief internet search, to be ancient AK-47s. They both stood up quickly when they saw Samir and greeted him as 'boss'.

He ignored them and led Andrea in total silence across the spacious hallway and upstairs onto a corridor past a large office with desks and computers visible and into one of a number of a small side-rooms. The room he chose was furnished sparingly as sleeping accommodation with a single bed and a small amount of essential furniture for a bedroom including a wardrobe, small armchair, a bedside locker and a low coffee table with a couple of chairs beside it together with a rather moth-eaten and ragged tab rug on a bare but polished boarded floor. Samir preceded her into the somewhat frowsy room, but turned to Andrea as soon as they entered the room. He moved to her rear and thence towards the door, as he moved to position himself in front of the door he turned and commented briefly and sharply.

"This is Xhoel's room but it looks as though Xhoel is not yet back. So, you can wait here in his room in privacy for him to arrive. He should not be long. Please make yourself comfortable in the meantime. No one will disturb you." Surprisingly he continued politely. "Can I get you a drink of something?" She refused politely fearing a possible attempt to drug her, such as she had been warned about by Sergeant Berger.

"There is small toilet and washbasin there through that small door, if you need them."

With that brief invitation he left the room and closed the door quietly. She heard the sound of him locking the door from the outside. She just hoped that her police followers had not been shaken off by his frenetic manoeuvres in his flash sports car.

Samir had thoughtlessly omitted to take her mobile from her. So she thought she would try the emergency number given to her by police Sergeant Berger during the meeting with the Chief Constable some time ago. She appreciated that she needed to do that now in case she was deprived of the mobile phone later. To her great surprise, she was put straight through automatically to the female police officer, Constable Lucy Wainwright, who had spoken to her in the café car park some hours ago.

"Hello, Andrea, it's Lucy Wainwright here. I know you will be concerned but be reassured. We are here on site with you. How are you feeling?

Have they been violent or abusive towards you? Are you OK?" Lucy asked anxiously.

"Hello. Yes, thank you. I am OK and I have not been maltreated so far." Andrea replied with a hint of relief in her voice.

"What a pleasant surprise to have my call answered by you. Where are you?"

"We are hidden in the bushes and trees at the far end of the cul-de-sac. But we can see the front of the building clearly."

"Super to hear you. I was afraid that you might have lost Samir with the pace of his driving and all the diversions he took through the town. But obviously you didn't." Andrea observed greatly relieved.

"Oh, but we did. But, and it just shows the benefits of advance planning together with a little bit of guessing. When we were in the car park, we checked on all the cars and chose the most swish one as our best guess as to which car a mobster would have, and we put a police GPS tracker on it. So although he evaded us by his manoeuvres, he brought us straight here with the tracker. And here we are just for you. One thing, which is urgent, however. We need to know which room you are in for when the rescue team arrives, shortly may I say. You will not see us. But as I said, we are both outside with a view of the front of the building where you are incarcerated. Keep your phone in your hand and come close to the window of the room you are currently locked in. Do it now please, Andrea."

Andrea went to the front window with her mobile phone in her hand and looked out. There was the car she had come in with Samir, parked next to a couple of other rather expensive-looking cars. She could see the hut with the guard's head lolling to one side apparently snoozing peacefully inside it. The gate was still wide open having been opened by the guard for Samir to drive in. She relayed the details back to Lucy.

"Just to confirm that the room, in which I am, faces onto the front, where I can see the car of my abductor, Samir. I can see the snoozing guard in the shed with his head fallen to one side onto his chest. The gate appears to be still wide open."

"Please check that there is no one outside, who could see you. If you are convinced that there is no one, please come closer to the window and wave a white handkerchief or piece of tissue very briefly and then retire quickly back from the window. That action will confirm for us which room you are in."

"Roger!" Andrea agreed and she moved to the window as directed, waved her tissue for a few seconds and then pulled back swiftly from the window.

“Thank you, Andrea. We have located you and we now know, which room you are incarcerated in. If you hear shots or a commotion, please use what furniture there is in the room to barricade the door and wait to be rescued. We will get you out of there safely.”

“I shall do it as soon as we finish our telephone conversation.”

“Be assured the rescue by my colleagues will be soon and safe. Do not worry. We are with you all the time, until you are rescued. You are a very brave young women. Now we should close.”

Reassured and a little excited at the thought of an early rescue, Andrea began moving the furniture behind the door as quietly and rapidly as she could and then laid down to rest on the bed to await her expected rescue. But would all go as smoothly as Lucy had indicated and as early as she had expected? Would Samir and his colleagues move her to another room perhaps before the rescue could be mounted? And would these mobsters start getting rough with her when she could not oblige them? How could her rescue come quickly? Would it be in time? Would it be successful?

These were some of the issues that flashed like lightning through her excited mind as she waited impatiently for the promised rescue.

Chapter Twenty-Five: Final Reckonings

The face of the Acting Chief Constable of Ayton, Heather Compton-Jones, was deadly serious as she addressed the hastily reconvened planning group of fellow officers, consequent on receipt of the report about Andrea's abduction and success in finding the headquarters of the mafia gang in Ayton from Sergeant Frank Balbinski and Constable Lucy Wainwright. Yet there was a glint of satisfaction in her eyes, with a note of concern in her voice as well.

"We are all indebted to, let me call her, our informal assistant, Andrea Burnley Crowder for success at last, in our search for the precise location of the headquarters building of the criminal mafia gang in our midst in Ayton. These criminals made a big mistake when they abducted this brave young woman. They led us directly to the new premises, which they use as a kind of headquarters for all their nefarious activities in our town and the contiguous administrations.

The Acting Chief Constable halted briefly as though she had forgotten to mention something to her colleagues.

"Fellow officers, I must apologise for the haste in reconvening this meeting after our previous meeting only yesterday agreed to delay further action for a few days to await the possible identification of the location of this gang's headquarters. Well, it has now been located by the courageous initiative of a young women called Andrea. As a consequence of her brave actions, I am sure that you will all agree that this young woman is now in extreme danger. It is for that reason that, based on the advice of my senior colleagues, I have decided to initiate a raid as soon as possible today on this gang's centre of iniquity to rescue this young woman as soon as possible and before any harm can befall her."

She paused to make sure that she had the facts in mind and in the right order and that there was no dissent.

"So far, as an interim measure the building has been sealed back and front by the two beat officers, who have been following Andrea, and colleagues called in from nearby. No one is being allowed either in or out of the building. In the meantime I have urgently sent a few additional officers to assist the officers with their vigilance on the site. That squad is on its way at this very moment. The building is, I understand, in a neglected tree and bush shielded cul-de-sac, where there are no additional buildings, businesses or people to be taken into consideration, except for the mobsters themselves. At the entrance to the road there is a dilapidated old shed and it looks like there is an armed guard in there. As well, there is a newly erected gate across the entrance to the cul-de-sac, reported by Andrea as having been left wide open a short while ago. Surprisingly it was at that time still wide open and the guard was having an afternoon snooze inside his hut. As I said, there are no other buildings within the hammerhead but any houses most immediately nearby will be warned shortly of the possible need to relocate and all approaches to the premises of this criminal gang of mobsters have been or are in the process of being sealed off, as I speak. I would like Superintendent Felix Brigstowe, Head of our local CID to outline the plan for the raid later today. Felix."

"Thank you Chief. Sorry about the rush. Basically the plan is to rescue Andrea and restore her safely to her kinfolk. That is the overarching and supreme aim of the raid. Moreover, we are hoping that this time the top men will still be inside and that this action will finally close down the criminal activities of this gang here in Ayton for good. It is a sad reflection that it is Andrea's danger, which has finally confirmed for us where the mob's premises are located after such a long search. The area is now clear except for a couple of expensive-looking cars, one of which, according to Andrea, is owned by Samir. The space will be kept clear to be free for the assembly of our advance units and their vehicles, especially the armed unit. A local beat sergeant and his colleagues, who patrol that area and thus know it very well are currently occupied directing the securing of that area. The action to free Andrea will be led by armed police unit under the direction of Superintendent Julian Charles the officer in charge of the armed police unit. They will be the first to enter the road to dispose of the sole armed guard in the hut. We hope that surprise will enable us to do that job peacefully.

He broke off briefly to underscore what he was going to say next.

“I cannot over-emphasise that apart from the officers of the armed police unit, no other officers will enter the road until it has been declared ‘clear by the Superintendent or one of his authorised senior colleagues. After the declaration of the ‘clear’ status, the other units will enter the cul de sac with members of the armed unit directing their entry and location. When all units have settled in the usual invitation and warning will be given twice in the customary two languages. We hope that the occupants of the building will see sense and obey the instructions, given over a loudspeaker and leave the building unarmed and with their hands raised. We do not know, however, how many people are currently in the building and how many of those are armed and of a mind to resist. So there is a chance that they will feel strong enough to undertake armed resistance. In the case of such an event, entry to the building will be forced by officers from the armed unit, stun grenades will be used and in the first instance anyone offering such resistance will be either tasered or in extreme cases shot. All other persons will be apprehended, searched and handcuffed and taken to one of the back-up squads for loading on to one of the waiting detention vans. All officers participating in the actual raid will be wearing body armour and carrying ballistic shields, just in case. The first armed squad of the armed unit will be advancing behind ballistic shields outside and inside the house until it is effectively declared cleared. Specially trained female officers will be available to give any necessary immediate care to Andrea and any other innocent women discovered in the building. We do not expect there to be many, but it would be prudent to be prepared for everything. This building is not a brothel and there would be little apparent reason for any other women than Andrea to be present. Needless to say, after the building is declared clean, our forensic team will enter and conduct a full inventory and examination of the premises and contents. I'm going to pass you over now to Superintendent Julian Charles, the Officer in command of the armed police unit. Julian, the floor is yours."

"Thank you Felix for that very comprehensive introduction. It hardly requires saying that the armed unit has been briefed in detail about the proposed sequence of actions in the raid, the detailed lay-out of the building and its immediate environment, as well as the appearance of the criminal mobsters inside the building. The team has been shown photographs of those we expect to be there, including senor figures from London. Emphasis has been place on the fact that by the very nature of some of the occupants, the behaviour of these criminals can be unpredictable. As we know from recent experience, in some cases they do as they are bidden and surrender. That has happened in the majority of cases so far. In other cases, as in one of the brothel raids latterly, violent resistance has been offered. Given that we expect the building to contain not only the local Ayton bosses but the big supremo from the Barking, East London set-up as well, they may regard surrender as ignominy. Speed will be of the essence in this raid if we are to rescue a very brave young lady, Andrea, unharmed. We shall of course be very sparing in the use of our firearms and we know that because of her presence we shall need to be extra careful. There may be other innocent people in the building as well. If confronted by lethal force, we shall not hesitate, however, to respond without delay and effectively. We have to be prepared for all eventualities. That is why my officers will be fully armed and armoured and will all carry ballistic shields. In advance of the opening of the raid by the loudspeaker announcements, two specially training officers from my unit will take care of the armed guard in the shed at the entrance to the cul de sac. Well I think that covers everything. But just to emphasise that speed on our part is essential for the safe rescue of this young women, Andrea. If there are any questions please go ahead, but remember that delay will not be helpful to a successful raid.

The Assistant Chief Constable, Mark Brownlow asked about the sort of contents likely to be found on site.

“Given that we believe that this is the headquarters of the gang, what kind and quantity of items do we hope to discover on this site?”

The answer came from the Acting Chief Constable.

“Thank you for that question, Mark. Obviously, we cannot know exactly what we shall find until we enter and investigate the inside of the building. As we believe it has been used as the nerve centre or headquarters of all the activities of this mob in this region, we are hoping that we shall uncover a treasure chest of items, from cash to drugs and valuable intelligence, possibly even revelatory documents about the working of this mob and how they have been transferring their evil gains out of Ayton and out of the country. Previous raids have also revealed precious stones and vintage and valuable postage stamps, used as a safe transfer mechanism for their ill-gotten gains. In some cases we know that guns are being illegally trafficked too. In general we are very hopeful that we shall similarly find some material of use to the national efforts against this criminal syndicate."

She hesitated only briefly and then added

"By the way, consequent on our very fruitful discussion about the use of our scarce resources, I should like to emphasise that we shall be documenting and evaluating the process and success, or otherwise, of the raid most rigorously, so as to improve our performance and use of resources in the future. We intend to share our findings from the evaluation with the national team working on eradicating this gang of criminals, in the country as a whole."

"Well if there are no further matters to discuss let's get to it. Good luck to us all and watch your step. We do not want any officers injured."

The armed unit was the first unit to arrive near the scene and stopped unobtrusively some short distance from the shed. The old ramshackle gate was still wide open. Two masked officers approached the shed stealthily and applied a loaded pistol to the head of the guard sitting half asleep in the shed. They skilfully persuaded the armed man inside to co-operate, to vacate the shed with them in silence and to leave his weapon on the seat inside. He complied willingly.

As the two officers withdrew with their captive, now handcuffed after being searched for phones or weapons, the rest of the armed unit entered the road and deployed to commence the initial stages of the raid covering the whole of the front of the building. The rest of the police units with a detention van and an ambulance entered the road but remained at the far end of the cul-de-sac.

When he saw the police arriving at the front of the building, Samir accused Xhoel of treachery and a violent blame game erupted between the two of them with Tristen and Noel advocating remaining calm, as they argued, the police had no hard evidence against them and their lawyers would soon have them free again. Samir refused to accept the intercession and vowed early vengeance on Xhoel and correspondingly on Xhoel's 'sweetheart'. He began to storm upstairs intending to enter the room occupied by Andrea with Xhoel trying to restrain him by pulling him back and at the same time advocating a peaceful surrender as recommended by the big boss. They ended up fighting on the stairs and eventually rolling back down entwined to the ground floor again. At this point Xhoel stood up and stated emphatically.

"I'm going to surrender! The game is up Samir!"

At the very moment when Xhoel made his statement to Samir, the first warning announcement was sounded by the police immediately outside the building and Xhoel moved towards the front door.

To the surprise of the officers after a short pause and well before the time had elapsed for the second announcement, the front door opened slowly and an unarmed man began to emerge at a snail's pace and tentatively with his hands raised. With caution, the front squad with Superintendent Julian Charles, the officer in charge of the armed police unit in the lead, raised their weapons in readiness.

The Superintendent instructed the man to approach the officers moving very slowly and with his hands held high. The man, now recognised as Xhoel, came forward compliantly a little further. As he continued to move forward there were two cracks seemingly from the direction of the house and Xhoel lurched forwards and fell like a brick to the ground with two small but clear bullet entry wounds at the back of his head and at the back of his body between his shoulder blades. The unit was ordered to retain their positions behind their shields and a second armed squad was called forward with a ram, grenades and an explosive charge. They approached the front door of the house very quickly against a barrage of rather inaccurate and innocuous shots from the house. At the same time, a third squad came forward and stun grenades were fired through the downstairs windows on both side of the front door and through a small aperture of glass of the door itself.

The door had been rammed open and further grenades were thrown through the now open doorway. The second squad then entered the hallway of the house, covered from behind by the first group. They divided into two subgroups and began to advance towards the rooms on each side of the door as they fanned out. They detained the two stunned and frightened armed guards, who had been sitting on high wooden chairs immediately at either side of the door before the raid began, and were now on the floor writhing and holding their ears near the door. They were handed back to a third group now entering the house to back up colleagues searching the ground floor and were searched and handcuffed before being led to other officers at one of the detention vans.

Officers now began to systematically clear the ground floor. They encountered an old man, well-dressed and dignified-looking with his hands on both sides of his head and apparently unarmed in what appeared to be an office in the company of a likewise unarmed younger man in a similar incapacitated condition. They would later be identified as the London and UK boss of bosses, Tristen Rexhepi, and Noel Shkodra, the mob's chief financial adviser and auditor in the UK and close assistant of Rexhepi. They were both frisked, handcuffed and led back to a detention van prior to being taken in for cross-examination and later possibly charges or release on bail.

The third squad then commenced the cautious step by step ascent of the stairs to the first floor, covered by officers from the first squad. There they observed a man battering on the door and attempting to enter the bedroom that had been identified by officers as the room where Andrea was imprisoned before the commencement of the raid. He was pushing wildly against a partly open door and against some obstacles on the other side of the door. The door appeared to be in the process of yielding to the man's ferocious attack as he fired a couple of unaimed shots round the now partly open door.

The leader of the third squad called on him to cease his actions, drop his weapon and turn around with his hands in the air. He began to turn as instructed and officers assumed that he was complying with their instructions. But as he turned he raised his weapon, appearing to all intents and purposes to be about to use his weapon against the lead officer nearest to him. A police marksman from the third squad now stationed in back-up role at the top of the stairs to protect those of his colleagues who were advancing along the corridor took the man out with two expertly aimed shots to the head and he fell to the floor dead. He was later identified as Samir Pecic, the boss of the mobs Ayton office and the abductor of Andrea.

The Superintendent of the armed squad called through the still barricaded but to some small extent open door of the room to what he hoped was Andrea.

"Andrea. Are you there? Is that you? This is police Superintendent Julian Charles. Could you kindly confirm your presence?"

"Yes, this is Andrea. Who are you?" The reassuring message came back from the bedroom.

"This is Superintendent Julian Charles of the Ayton police force. You are safe now. But are you OK?"

Yes, I'm fine, thank you. A bit tense but just very, very pleased to hear your voice."

"We're coming in to release you. First, however, we need to unblock the door. There may be a bit of noise and danger of falling furniture. Please stand back from the door to avoid any risk of injury from falling or flying debris."

"Can do and can't wait!"

The ram was used to batter the remains of the door down and to enable her to exit. This involved moving the mass of furniture that Andrea had piled up behind the door. Andrea was sitting on the bed sobbing but otherwise unhurt. One of the female officers approached and sitting down beside her on the bed put her arms round her to console her. She supported a somewhat weakened Andrea to leave the room across the rubble at the doorway and to descend the stairs. At the bottom of the stairs, Lucy and Frank, the two police officers who had shadowed her over the past few weeks, and had enabled the tracing of Samir's car and facilitated her escape, were waiting downstairs to greet her.

Police Constable Lucy Wainwright moved to hug her and addressed her most cordially.

"Thank god you're safe, Andrea. You are a very brave young woman and the police and the people of this town owe you.

Sergeant Frank Balbinski also approached her and shook her hand congratulating her on what she had done, which had led to the cracking of the Ayton mafia gang and potentially more gangs besides. Lucy then suggested a rapid journey home to Andrea.

"Come with us now and we shall take you back home to your family with all due speed. Your nearest and dearest have been alerted to your rescue and your imminent return home."

The Acting Chief Superintendent came across as well to briefly congratulate and compliment Andrea on the action she had taken and the consequential benefits they had brought for all members of her community.

"I just came across to briefly thank you for your very public-spirited actions, from which I hope our community and especially the young people like yourself will benefit mightily. You are indeed a very brave woman and an example to others of your generation. Thank you again for your assistance in making this town a better place for us all to live in. Literally we could not have done it without you.

Superintendent Julian Charles descended the stairs to congratulatory acclaim from his team, praising a successful operation. He also congratulated Andrea as she was on the point of departure. Subsequently both he and his men were themselves congratulated by the Acting Chief Constable on the swift and efficient accomplishment of the operational objective.

He replied with some considerable and, for him, unusual emotion.

"Thank you very much. Thanks to the bravery of that young woman and the skill and dedication of our officers, we have captured or eliminated all the top echelons of the mafia gangster set-up here in Ayton and damaged the national structure of that illicit organisation without any injury to our own officers. We have detained for questioning the UK boss of bosses from Barking in East London and his side-kick. So that's one! It's the first one! Now for the rest of the criminal mobsters who think they can infest our town and our land with their poison, corrupting and criminalising our younger generation. Well done everyone!"

But he added a final, sobering note.

"Without any detriment to our brilliant success here today, which is a game-changer, I have to say that viewed in the context of recent significant internationalisation of cooperative multi-gang approaches to the production, distribution and sale of drugs, it is really only a first step in a very long game stretching way into the future. It is a pinprick and we still have not just a mountain to climb but a monstrously high mountain range to scale. Today, however, we have proved that we can do it!"

Acknowledgements

I should like to express my thanks and warm appreciation to the many colleagues, with whom I have had the pleasure and privilege of working over the years, from the workers in the textile mill where I started my working life to the heights of the international organisations and countries in many parts of the world, where and with whom I have worked. Above all I owe a deep debt of gratitude to the woman who inspired the character of Andrea at the centre of this story and our many fascinating conversations.

I owe a profound debt of gratitude, loving appreciation and intellectual indebtedness to all four generations of my family and particularly to my wife, Margaret, for their forbearance, understanding, support and helpful comments during the writing of this book. In particular, I wish to express my thanks and sincere appreciation to my son, Mark, for his indispensable sustenance for my inadequate IT skills and to my daughter Angela for her constant advice, guidance and proofreading with detailed comments and positive suggestions on this text over an extended period. A particular word of thanks is due as well to my youngest daughter, Colette, who accompanied me with enthusiasm on our sometimes stressful journey of discovery through the vagaries of publishing fiction.

I should also like to thank the librarians and archivists from several cities in the UK and abroad, who so freely assisted me in consulting in situ documents, publications, newspapers and international reports; an odyssey which commenced in presence mode in the Hanover archives and library shortly after the conclusion of the Second World War and continues to this day electronically at home.

Selected Books by the Author

Parents and Teachers (with John Pimlott)
Prejudice Reduction
Education for Citizenship
A Human Rights Analysis
Cultural Diversity and the Schools (four volumes edited with Celia and Sohan Modgil)
Lifelong Education
Education for Community
Change in Teacher Education (Edited with Robin J. Alexander and Maurice Craft)
Policy and Practice in Lifelong Education
Education and Development: Tradition & Innovation (four volumes edited with Celia and Sohan Modgil)
Multicultural Education in Western Societies (With James A Banks)
The Multicultural Curriculum
Teacher Education and Cultural Change (With H Dudley Plunkett)
Multicultural Education in a Global Society
Children with Special Needs in the Asia Region

Fiction

New Life in an Old Town (Available as an e-book and paperback)
The Hydra (Available as an e-book and paperback)
The Fit Country (Available as an e-book and paperback)
Back-to-Back (Available as an e-book and paperback)
The Final Mission (Available as e-book and paperback)
Turbulent Times: Growing up in the Edwardian Era (Available as an e-book and paperback)
Deception (Available as an e-book and paperback in late 2022)
Lymphoma: A Novel (In preparation for publication as an e-book early in 2023)
Poems and Games for Happy Children (Complete but unpublished)

About the Author

After teaching in technical education and in higher education at lecturer, senior lecturer, professorial and deanship levels, James went to the World Bank and worked in the Asia region, including Nepal, Bhutan, Bangla Desh and China. Additionally he worked in some countries in francophone Africa, including Burundi, Madagascar, Morocco and Rwanda. He has held Professorships in Austria, Germany, the United Kingdom and the United States and acted as a consultant to several UN agencies, including UNESCO and UNEDBAS.

He is the author, co-editor or co-author of numerous books on subjects such as cultural diversity, prejudice and discrimination, human rights and multicultural education. He has also written many journal articles and policy papers for international organisations. After retirement he worked for several years for the UK government as the first British technical assistance in post-genocide Rwanda. At all stages of his life he has devoted some of his time and energy to charitable causes, activities and the welfare of others.

James is passionate about his extended family, reading, gardening and formerly travel. He and his wife, Margaret, live in the South of England.

Printed in Great Britain
by Amazon

85643636R00234